OF GLASS AND GLAMOUR

OF GLASS AND GLAMOUR

CHANDA HAHN

Copyright © 2019 by Chanda Hahn

Neverwood Press

Editor: Virginia Cantrell Hot Tree Editing

Beta Readers: Barbara Hoover, Felicia Thorn, Corrine Doxey & Amy Ezell

Cover Design Covers by Combs

Map Illustration by Hanna Sandvig: www.bookcoverbakey.com

www.chandahahn.com

9781950440146 (Paperback)

9781950440153 (Hardcover)

Also By Chanda Hahn

The every girl who never received
an invitation to the ball.

It's time to make our own.

CHAPTER ONE

S itting in a circle in our drafty tower, my fingers struggled to loop the yarn over the crochet hook, while my mother's enchanted mirror scried the various kingdoms. Needlework was a horrid affair, and my adopted sisters and I dreaded the menial task. After my first few rows, my gaze strayed up to the mirror and the image shifting across the smooth surface. I began to daydream about living in the kingdoms beyond—anywhere except here, our forgotten town.

Mother taught us that all good sorceresses needed to know the basics of crochet and knitting because it created muscle memory. Learning a pattern and following it through repetition was not that much different than weaving a basic sleeping spell.

I glanced down at my work and frowned. What started off as a scarf, now resembled a gnarled cat toy. I had become distracted by my daydreaming and missed a few of the loops. At this rate, I'd never so much as make anyone, even our cat, Hack (who was notorious for coughing up fur balls) take a catnap. My younger sister, Maeve, was doing so much better, and I was envious of her more advanced crochet doll that she had finished—a hex doll from the looks of it. One that resembled a particular beautiful girl in our village. I blanked on the girl's name. It was something silly and of no importance, but to Maeve, she was her worst enemy.

My eyes strayed to the empty chair to the right of Mother's and couldn't help but imagine my older sister, Rosalie, sitting there. Of all of us, she looked the most like our adoptive mother. She was the first to go into the seven kingdoms at Mother's bidding. It was quite the scandal. On the day of the crown prince of Baist's wedding to a young girl in his kingdom, Mother appeared and swapped out the brides and forced the prince to marry Rosalie, sight unseen. This caused quite a rift between the newly married couple. No one trusted a daughter of Eville, and despite her attempts to help them hunt down a murderous beast, Rosalie was accused of the murders and taken to Florin.

A smile came to my lips as I reminisce on the grand adventure—sneaking into the kingdom, donning the glamour of many of the palace staff, and being the one who had broken my sister out of prison. I may have almost blown her to bits in the process, but we didn't need to tell anyone that my spells still needed work. Together we bested an evil sorcerer, Allemar, and now my sister was living incognito in the town of Celia, hiding until everything blew over and her prince could annul their marriage, leaving him free to remarry. Just thinking of my poor sister's circumstances made me almost snap my hook.

"Meri, dear, bring me your blanket. I'd like to take a look at your pattern work," Mother said from her red, high-back, upholstered chair. Her voice snapped me out of my adventurous daydream. Her chair was in the exact center of the room, directly across from the mirror. I could almost imagine our dreary tower as a noble court and my mother sitting on her throne. I watched as Meri winced when her name was called.

She quickly smoothed her brown plaid skirt and brought over her circle blanket. Being very careful not to drop or lose the ball of yarn, she handed it to Mother and buried her hands into her skirt to hide her nervousness.

Like me, she wasn't the best at weaving sleeping spells. Meri had soft red hair, and even now a stray curl was spilling forth; she quickly tried to tame it by pushing it behind her ear. What I wouldn't give to have her shade of deep red? Being a daughter of Eville, it was easier to cause fear on sight if my hair was a darker shade, but instead, my golden tresses made me resemble a fair maiden or damsel in distress.

"Meri, what happened?" Mother chastised. "You need to tie off when you change colors; otherwise you leave a weakened chain, and we can't have that, now can we? What good would our spells be if there's a weak spot?" She pulled on the string, and the whole thing came unraveled. Her tongue clicked in displeasure. "Redo it." It was a firm order.

Meri's head dropped to her chest. "Yes, Mother."

"It's a good thing you excel at water spells," Mother chastised, throwing out an underlying barb. "There may be some hope for you yet." She turned her eyes to scan over the quiet girls in the room.

My fingers trembled, and I tried to shove my mess of knots between the cushions of the settee before she noticed my failure. No one wanted to disappoint her. Especially me. I was the family letdown.

Years ago, when I was only a few weeks old, I was abandoned on Mother Eville's stoop under the light of the hunters' moon—the brightest full moon during the month of Nochtember—with only a simple silver ring with a topaz stone. She took me in and raised me as her own.

The whole town knew of the cursed woman, and word

spread of my mysterious but sudden arrival. They watched from a distance, and when I grew up into a healthy and laughing child, many of their misgivings vanished. I wasn't the first or last of her brood to come mysteriously in the night. Over the years, more baby girls made their way into our family. Instead of leaving a box of kittens at the cat lady's house, they left children, or she would leave and come back with a child. Mother Eville took them in and taught them the old ways, the ways of magic.

If it rained on the town, you can bet it was because of something brewing in the cauldron over the fire. Snow in summer—the daughters. Fog, thunder, or lighting—the daughters. Once I even made it rain frogs—on accident of course, but it made the townspeople leery of us. They didn't trust us and avoided us at all cost. That wariness and hatred spread throughout the kingdoms like a plague.

"Eden!" she called my name in a firm tone, and I blinked at her with wide, innocent eyes. She had seen me. I was going to be in deep trouble. Probably be required to wash the dishes by hand for the next week instead of spelling them clean, which was probably better. I broke more than I washed.

She leaned forward in her chair, her focus not on me but on the mirror as an image moved across the glass. Mother had spelled the enchanted mirror to focus on the fates of the kingdom.

"Yes, Mother," I answered her, but her finger came up and quickly silenced me.

"Wait!" She froze as a beautiful serene estate appeared. The kingdom's flag, a gold sunburst on a field of blue, floated across the bottom of the mirror. I knew that palace, knew who lived there and was surprised. It was the royal family of

4

Candor, and it seemed they were making a special announcement.

The king and queen of Candor stood upon the steps waving at the crowd, a fake smile plastered across their lips. Not one for social gatherings, appearances, or matters of the state, the prince was rarely seen—which made my mother's attempts at spying on him rather useless. What good was a prince who remains out of the spotlight.

"What is it?" Aura asked, looking at the mirror with a renewed interest.

Mother smiled slyly, leaning back in her chair, her fingers steepled together. "It's happening. Just like I knew it would. They couldn't avoid the prophecy forever. Their son is now at the right age."

The room went silent with nervous tension. I looked back at the mirror at the kingdom, and my stomach churned with apprehension.

Mother moved to the mirror, her hand waving as she tried to focus her spell, creating audio so we could listen in on the special announcement. But like any spell, magic was a fickle thing, and when scrying using reflections, the image and sound were easily distorted. The mirror flickered, and the sound faded. In a show of impatience, my mother smacked the side of the mirror three times until it came back into focus.

"That's better, next time you better listen to me," she warned the mirror as if it were a living, breathing thing and proceeded to sit back in her chair.

The mirror behaved, and we caught glimpses of a serious King Ferdinand as he cleared his throat. "All eligible daughters of Candor, who are fair of face and form, will hereby receive an invitation by royal dove to attend Prince Evander's designation ball. Those who meet palace approval will be asked to stay on, to be courted by Prince Evander so he may choose his future bride."

Mother Eville jumped up, knocking the high-back over. Aura, next to me, was startled and jerked. I leaned back and tried to sink deeper into my cushion, but stabbed myself on my needle.

"Ouch!" I cried, drawing Mother Eville's eyes to rest on me. I wanted to crawl under the settee and disappear.

"It's time," she said solemnly. She turned, and every girl in the room sat still, looking at her intently.

"To do what?" Rhea asked.

"Why, what we do best—revenge."

At the announcement, my sisters stopped fidgeting and looked to Mother eagerly.

My stomach dropped, and my mouth went dry. I could see the viperous smiles of five sisters. When I looked back at the smiling monarchs in the mirror, a nervous and fake smile crossed my own lips. Yes, when my mother was done with them, they wouldn't know what hit them.

CHAPTER TWO

"Are you going to curse the royal line if you get chosen, Eden?" Maeve asked as she bounced on my bed, skewing the dresses that I had laid out to press. At seventeen, she was the youngest of my adoptive siblings and was probably the most vicious and immature of us—which was never a good mix. If we didn't pay enough attention to Maeve, we'd wake up to find dead lizards in our bed, or worse, live ones. She did leave me with an interesting thought, however. I didn't know exactly what I was going to do.

"I don't know," I answered and yanked on the dark black dress that she was kneeling on. She lifted her knee, and the black silk slid out. I glanced over it to make sure there weren't any tears. "I won't be chosen, Aura will. She's the most likely choice."

"Well, suppose you did get chosen to go, what would you do then?" she asked, batting her thick eyelashes at me.

I paused my pressing, magically suspending the hot iron in midair, and thought about it. "I suppose the smart thing to do would be to get close to the family, find what they hold dearest and take that from them."

"Cursing the royal family with boils would be the fastest

solution." Maeve flipped over on her back, her dark hair fanning out across my quilt. She held up her hand and started to examine her black-painted nails.

"But what good would that do if they could get a fairy to heal them? It has to be something more miserable—more permanent," I chastised and looked out across my dresses. They were getting pretty old and a bit threadbare. There was nothing that stood out in the crowd, nothing that was considered palace worthy.

"Has the invitation come yet?" Maeve asked. "It's been three days since the announcement."

"No," I answered, unsure if I was sad or relieved at the prospect. I wasn't altogether sure that we'd even receive one, even though we were on the border of Candor. The town of Nihill, whose name means nothing, wasn't exactly claimed by any of the kingdoms. The invitations were to be delivered by the royal doves to all families with daughters living under their roof. But in all of the years of living here, we had never received a royal invitation to anything—not a single event, parade, or christening. Not even when the king's oldest son, Prince Vincent, died, God rest his soul, did we get an invitation to the funeral. It was if we resided under an impenetrable mountain and no one could get to us. We lived on the outskirts of the town in one of the tallest freestanding buildings, an old guard tower. We were forgotten and ignored—unless someone needed something from us, and then we were mysteriously visible again.

Maeve got up and moved over to my window, pulling aside the curtain to look out. It was dreary and had been raining for hours. She exhaled on the glass and traced the rivulets with her finger. "Don't worry, we will. Maybe the royal doves don't like to fly in the rain?" She unlatched the window, pushing the pane outward, waved her hand, and the rain stopped. The clouds parted, and the sun shone down, warming the glass. "There, now we will get the invitation." She turned and grinned with pride. But I could see the doubt in her eyes.

"You needn't waste your power for that." I frowned in disapproval.

"Oh, come on, Eden, this is the most exciting thing that has happened in—well, forever. I don't have the patience to wait for a royal dodo to fly through a storm to get here."

"We are waiting just like everyone else," I said.

"But most everyone else has already gotten theirs. The mirror told me so. In fact, I heard that even Fanny Mignonette received one." Maeve's lips pouted, and I hid my smile. Fanny, that was who the hex doll was supposed to resemble. Maeve and Fanny had been enemies since they were toddlers.

It seemed that Maeve had been using the mirror to eavesdrop on the neighboring families. When I was her age, I, too, would spend hours listening to the chatter through the mirror. Until we started to hear the rumors, the negative things people whispered about us behind our backs. Then listening to an enchanted mirror's gossip lost its appeal. Apparently, that wasn't so for Maeve.

"Then we continue to wait."

Her brows turned down, and I could tell my words had upset her. "No, we don't. We're not like *them*. We shouldn't have to wait for anything." She turned her back and stared out the window in anger. Her dark hair billowed as the wind caught it, making it flow from her shoulders.

"Maeve, whatever you're thinking of doing, don't," I warned.

Her eyes flashed with power, and she looked at me, a wicked smile playing on her lips. "How do you know what I'm thinking?" She raised her hands above her head, and I watched as she seamlessly shifted into a black raven and landed on the window ledge. She danced back and forth, shifting her head side to side before letting out a loud caw and flying out into the night. Her wing knocked into my glass windchime as she left, sending a tinkling sound that followed her out.

Maeve was more comfortable flying the world in her bird form than being a human girl. I couldn't blame her. If I were as good as her at shapeshifting, I'd probably choose a bird and fly far away to the kingdoms beyond.

Sighing, I looked out across my small room and waved my hand across the glamour. The extravagant four-poster bed disappeared to be replaced by a small single bed. The black lace pillow shams were replaced by a single worn-out and flattened pillow. The soft damask, patterned carpet dissolved to reveal the cold gray stone floor. Two other beds shared the top floor of the tower with mine. Rosalie's empty mattress haunted me, her quilt and pillow tucked away in a chest. Aura's bed was covered with everything pink and girly. Our room now looked less comfortable and more like a cell. Glamour was one of the first spells I learned, and I had a natural affinity for it—unlike my sisters. They thought it was torturous practice holding a glamour for hours or even days at a time, but for me I could easily fall asleep and still keep control of glamoured objects and items—unless I lost control of my emotions. Then my glamour became as scattered as my thoughts. Also, after a few days of holding the spell, I would get an uncomfortable pressure behind my eyes. To use glamour to become someone else for long periods, I needed a personal item, or something they had recently touched.

Everything in my room was a glamour, except for my beautiful colored-glass windchime. Every year around my birthday, my adoptive mother would come in and attach a new colored-glass ornament. I adored how the sun would shine through them and turn my room into a rainbow of color, and on windy or stormy days, it played a gentle song.

I watched Maeve's dark shape fly away until nothing more than a speck remained, and then I searched the skies for a dove, hoping, praying. I couldn't believe how much I wanted to get an invitation, but at the same time, the thought terrified me. What if I failed at my spells and mess everything up like I normally did and upset Mother? *Get a hold of yourself, Eden.* I mentally chastised. *You are a powerful sorceress. You don't care what anyone thinks.* Except, deep down, I did.

Dinner was silent except for the sound of spoons scraping across the bottom of our ceramic bowls filled with beef and barley soup and a side of homemade bread. Mother was extremely harsh tonight, and a tenseness hung in the air. Normally dinner would be filled with idle chatter, laughter, and delicious talks of curses and maladies. Everyone was anxiously watching the skies, windows, and doors for the invitation.

Aura accidently slurped her soup and was immediately set upon by a disapproving glare from Mother. "Ladies don't slurp."

Aura's cheeks flushed. "Yes, Mother."

My bowl sat untouched, my appetite nonexistent. I couldn't help but glance over to Rosalie's chair and wondered how she was faring. If she was in trouble, she would send word, but I couldn't understand why she chose to go away and not come back to live with us. Her empty chair was a memorial, a reminder that one by one, each of us would eventually set out on our own adventures. Maeve's chair was empty, but that wasn't anything unusual because we were used to her flighty ways, much like her aviary persona.

A crash came from the front room as the door flew open and slammed against the wall. A large raven flew into the dining room with something white in its claws. It did one swoop around the kitchen before dropping its prize on the long wooden table. A flash of light and feathers blinded us as the bird shifted back into my sister.

Maeve moved over to her empty chair and filled her bowl with soup, not even mentioning the white, feathered carcass lying in the middle of the table like an obscure centerpiece.

Mother Eville only raised her eyebrows and muttered, "You're late, dear."

Maeve's face glowed. "I had to pick up something." She reached past the dead dove and grabbed a roll. I couldn't peel my eyes away from the crooked neck of the dove and the rolled-up tube with the royal seal tied to its leg. "It seems that our royal messenger dove got a bit lost. So, I had to show him the way."

"How lost?" I asked pointedly at Maeve.

"Uh, quite lost." Her cheeks finally started to blush when confronted with what she had just done. She shoved her roll into her mouth and took a bite, refusing to meet my gaze.

I tried to control the shaking of my hand as I reached across the table and gently untied the leather strap to release the cylindrical leather tube. I opened it and slid the rolled-up parchment into my hand. I could see golden script across the invitation, and I couldn't help but feel a surge of excitement. This was a chance for all of us to leave, to go out into the world and prove our worth to our mother. But more than that, it was just exciting to be invited to the ball. My hand stopped shaking long enough for me to read the family name across the envelope.

"It's addressed to the daughters of Beauchamp," I tried to not let the disappointment show. Six heads turned to look toward Maeve for an explanation.

Maeve slammed her half-eaten roll down on her plate, scattering her silverware across the table. "Okay, fine. I flew to the palace and snuck into the secretary's office and looked at the guest list. The house of Eville wasn't on the list. So, I—" She waved her finger in the air. "—spelled our name on it, just as the secretary was finishing up the last batch of invitations. When he saw our name, he swore. I watched as he crossed our name out. They *weren't* going to send us one." She pouted.

One by one, my sisters' heads or shoulders dropped as our mother's curse followed us. Unwanted. Unloved. Forgotten. I was angry. *Shouldn't we count? Are we not good enough? Just because we're orphans doesn't mean we don't deserve the same privileges as everyone else.*

Maeve's eyes flashed, and her face took on an angry sneer. "So, I followed the royal dove and tried to force it to come to our house, and when it wouldn't, well...." She trailed off and waved her delicate hand at the dove's carcass.

She had killed a royal dove and stolen another family's invitation and didn't feel the least bit remorseful—and at the moment, I didn't either.

"Well, well, well, Maeve. You've outdone yourself." Mother pushed back her chair and came over, taking the invitation from me and reading it for herself. I was the only one close enough to see her hand tremble slightly in anger. She waved her hand over the parchment, and the Beauchamp name was replaced with a name I did not recognize. Her red lipstick shone brightly against the candlelight as she looked us over one by one. "As much as I would love to send all of you, I can send only one."

"I'll go, Mother." Rhea jumped up in excitement.

"No, let me go," Meri said, her eyes flashing green. "I'll sing them to sleep, and they'll never wake up."

I would not want to be in their shoes if they ever went up against an angry muse. I looked around, noticing I wasn't the only one not making eye contact with Mother.

Honor stared at the far wall. Her hand clenched around her butter knife. I may joke that I was the worst when it came to weaving spells, but that wasn't necessarily true. Honor, poor quiet Honor, didn't have the gift. She was the most normal of all of us. Yes, her training wasn't like ours. She would disappear with Lorn on long trips north where she would be trained by the elves. Mother and Lorn never told us what she was being trained in and for. Most of the year, Honor didn't live with us. It just happened that she was back for the next three weeks. I knew that Mother wouldn't send Honor.

My mouth went dry under Mother's scrutiny, and I reached for the glass goblet and tried to wet my throat. For a moment, I felt a bit sorry for the royal family if either Meri or Maeve was sent.

"No, it must be Eden," Mother's said sternly.

I put the cup down with more force than was necessary, and it thunked loudly on the table. "Mother?" My voice came out a squeak.

"It is time, my darling. There can be no one else but you. This is your story."

I felt my sister's heated glare from across the room, and I tried to not look at her. Literally, I could feel the heat from Maeve's anger scorch my skin, and I started to sweat. Why was

I chosen? I wasn't the strongest. My magic was unreliable. I jumped up from my chair and smoothed the wrinkles on my black dress. "Are you sure, Mother, that you wouldn't want to send someone else?"

"No, Eden. It's time. Time for you to go home."

Home? She must be mistaken. This was home. I never wished for more. I wasn't adventurous like my other sisters. I didn't want to leave.

"I'm giving you the chance to learn what happened to your parents."

"My parents? You said they died from the plague when I was little."

She shook her head. "No, Eden. I only told you that to keep you from learning the truth too soon. You were born right here in Candor. It is your right."

The air was sucked from the room, and I struggled to breathe. My lungs burned as the room began to spin. Then Aura's calming touch washed over me as she gently grasped my hand, steadying me as she did. The air came back. My lungs filled, and I breathed again.

I was confused. Distraught.

Lies. My life was a lie. My hands began to shake, and Aura weaved her fingers gently through mine and squeezed. She was reading my emotions, and I could feel her gentle warning to me.

"Breathe, Eden," she whispered. I squeezed her hand back and took a deep breath.

My mother was still talking during the shifting of my world, and I had not heard what she was saying. I turned to give her my full attention, and she slowly came back into focus.

"I'm giving you the chance to learn of your past and choose your future."

I still couldn't understand what she was asking me to do. Go to the capital and avenge my parents?

"What does this have to do with the royal ball?"

"Isn't it obvious?"

I shook my head.

"Your mother's life was cut short by the king of Candor in an attempt to stop you from ever being born. To stop you from attending this ball. To stop the prophecy from coming true."

My sisters looked up at me, and I read the shock and emotion written across their faces. Only Honor wouldn't make eye contact with me. Aura's eyes were glassy with unshed tears. Maeve's face was filled with disdain. Meri was nodding in encouragement. "Go," she mouthed to me.

"As you wish, Mother."

"Don't disappoint me, dear." She handed me the invitation, and I curtsied.

"Let the stars guide me," I whispered our prayer and hoped beyond hope that I wouldn't fail her.

CHAPTER THREE

"She's quite mad at you, you know," Meri said, and I didn't need to ask whom she was referring too. It was my younger sister Maeve. The fact that she was angry at me for no reason actually made my own temper rise.

"I didn't have a choice. I don't want to be the one sent out for this assignment. She shouldn't be mad at me; she should be mad at Mother. I'd gladly trade her places." I opened my trunk at the foot of my bed. It was going to be easy to choose what to bring, when everything I owned fit in the little carrying case. Except the windchimes. I didn't dare bring it in case it broke.

Meri lay on my bed and swung her head over the side so she was looking at me upside down, her legs pedaling in the air comically.

"True, but she can't take her anger out on Mother, only you." Meri turned her green eyes up at me and blinked innocently.

I knew deep down she was probably enjoying the drama that was unfolding because of this. So many girls locked away in a tower spelled trouble and quite a few catfights. We hardly ever left the tower and, in doing so, had caused quite a few rumors. We were seven girls who desperately wanted to explore the world and carve their own mark into it, one delicious scream at a time. I glanced back to the empty bed. No, six.

"What would you have me do?" I hissed angrily as I shoved my only good day dress into my satchel. "Not go? Refuse Mother and gain her wrath? I need to find out what happened to my parents."

Meri smiled sweetly. "Don't be silly, Eden. I'm only warning you, so you can check your clothes for a delay trap. I'm pretty sure I saw Maeve sneak in here earlier when you were in the kitchen."

I let out a disgruntled sigh and pulled everything back out of my carrying case and looked at the bag carefully, feeling along the seams with not only my fingers but sight. I almost missed it, but my fingers tingled and burned when they ran across a small loose button. I picked up the button and tossed it into a flower vase. The heat from the button instantly evaporated all of the water, and the daisy inside withered and died instantly.

"Looks like she wanted you to have a very smoky arrival," Meri chuckled.

I fished the button back out of the vase and mumbled a few words to contain the spell. Having a fire charm, even one cursed by my sister, may have its use in the future. "Thanks for the warning." I finished packing and said my goodbyes to my sisters. Aura seemed the most excited to see me off. To them, I was going on a grand adventure. It was more of a quest than an adventure.

Meri waited in the queue till last. She handed me a small object wrapped in cloth. "Open it in the transport," she whispered in my ear. I nodded, giving her hand a quick squeeze.

Mother didn't hug me, and I never expected her to. Her

face was serious, her lips pressed into a firm line. She handed me the stolen invitation. She waved one finger in the air over my heart. It wasn't a symbol that I knew, but she drew it with ease. "In case you lose your nerve," she said grimly.

My heart plummeted; there wasn't any way to go back now. I wasn't sure what she did, but I had a feeling that it spelled trouble. I nodded but kept my eyes down. "Why am I going? Why did you choose me?"

Mother Eville's face filled with displeasure. "It is about revenge, my darling, Eden. Your revenge this time. Not mine."

"I—" I began, but she cut me off.

"Yes, you came to me in the middle of the night, that part is true. But I knew both your parents, and they deserve justice for what was done to them. Justice only you can provide."

"I don't understand." I felt dizzy and sick to my stomach.

"This is your chance to set to right what has been wrong for the last twenty-one years."

"How can I do that?" I whispered.

"Get close to the prince, and the one who destroyed your family will find you."

"I can't. I'm not.... I don't even know their names."

"You just need to have bravado."

"I'm not brave."

Mother grasped my shoulders and looked into my eyes. "I know this seems confusing since your path has been foretold. All will work out in the end."

"I don't know. I just—"

"Eden, you've always struggled with confidence and doubt. So, I will spell it out for you." I winced at how obvious my shortcomings were to my mother. She grabbed my cheeks in one hand and said very slowly for effect, "Get the shoes, get the guy, and get revenge." Then she gave me a soft pat on my cheek.

"Shoes?" When did shoes come into this equation? I looked down at my brown traveling boots, then back up at Mother, who loved to be cryptic and had probably spent all night coming up with that mantra to help me, but she was gone. A trail of purple smoke was all that was left after she apparated—another sign of just how powerful of a sorceress she was. It was a taunt.

Turning my back, I headed out the front gate and crossed over the bridge, making sure to stop and toss a coin into the water to appease the beasts that slept beneath the bridge and guarded our tower from unwanted visitors. Even though our tower was in the center of the seven kingdoms, we weren't in the center of any towns or cities. Everyone gave us our much-needed space, or they feared waking up with a tail.

It was a half mile walk before I came to a main road just as a passing caravan of wagons came through. I spotted a transport, a carriage driver whose sole job was to travel between the kingdoms. His carriage was empty, and he didn't have any of the kingdom's banners on display, which meant he wasn't currently hired for transport. I waved him down, and the driver pulled out of the caravan to the side of the road.

His team of horses were not normal horses but part fae. The size of their hooves and the excess undercoat that covered their bodies bespoke their heritage. They were a hardy breed able to travel long distances without water or stops. As I passed the horses, I could see the slight shimmer along their coat. The driver tied my trunk to the back and asked where I was going.

"To the capital city of Thressia," I answered, grinning as I stepped into the carriage.

The driver closed the door and looked up at my tower in

the distance. His carefree smile dropped, and his brows creased with worry. "You didn't see anyone from that old tower, did you?"

I was shocked and a bit appalled. I leaned forward, placing my elbow on the window ledge. Lying easily, I said, "No, I didn't. Why?"

"I hear that they're witches," he whispered, as if telling me a secret. "They'll cast a spell on you and steal your children in the night." He unwrapped the banner for Thressia and hung it on my door, signaling other travelers that he was available for more fares.

"Really," I breathed out, pretending to be interested but holding back my finger from spinning a spell in anger.

"I heard they ensnare men and eat their hearts so that they stay young." He had finished and wiped his hands on his pants as he leaned close to the open window.

"Who? Who said they eat hearts?" I cried in outrage at the lies.

"To cross paths with one of them evil sisters is to cross paths with the devil himself." He made a cross motion over his heart, and I couldn't take another insult, and there was no way I was going to be stuck in this carriage the whole ride listening to his libels.

I touched my finger to his mouth, shushing him before drawing a sigil over his top lip. His mouth gaped open in surprise, and he tried to speak, but nothing came forth. His face turned red, and he started to yell but, again, nothing.

"No, you're wrong. A spurned woman is far worse than the devil. Maybe less talking for the rest of our ride? What say you? Then I'll gladly reverse the spell once I've reached my destination."

The driver nodded and quickly clambered into the upper

seat, grabbing the reins. I knocked the sideboard for his attention, and he swung back, fear in his eyes. Secretly, I drank in that fear. Fear meant power, and I loved power.

"By the way, we're not evil. We're *Eville*." My smile was slow and cruel, and it made him shiver in his boots. He bobbed his head and snapped his whip. We were off.

Leaning back against the soft cushioned bench, I watched our tower fade into the distance. I opened up the wrapped package from my sister. It was a compact mirror—silver, circular, and small enough to fit in the palm of my hand. Perfect for keeping in touch in case of an emergency. I put it into my drawstring purse for safekeeping.

I had been to many of the outlying towns in Candor, but never the capital city of Thressia. I had heard about the progressive and colorful kingdom and seen it through the mirror, but this was the first time I'd gotten to go there. After traveling to Florin and stopping a war, I was not as eager to head into the unknown. Maeve could not be contained and frequently went farther beyond the confines of our town, even though it was against our mother's wishes.

In the middle of the night, I'd hear her tapping on the window to get in. I'd open it, and she'd fly into the room in a whirl of feathers as she transformed back into her nightdress. Her eyes glassy and cheeks flushed from excitement. She never shared with us where she went or what she did during the night. After all, what was one more secret in the house of Eville?

CHAPTER FOUR

T he carriage rocked, slowing as we entered the city of Thressia. I stared out the window in awe. It was different than my small town. Where Nihill was like an old babbling brook with few newcomers coming and going, Thressia was a raging river. People of all ethnicities and races moved among the streets, some on horses and others on tamed fae creatures, a few on wagons that moved with steam-powered contraptions. When the loud churning of a steam wagon passed me, I tried to study the copper mechanism and looked for the hint of magic that must power the cart. My mouth fell open when I saw a young man balancing on a two-wheeled thing that was propelled by his scrawny legs.

Fascinating. My word, how odd and different this kingdom was from Florin and Baist.

We had been traveling almost nonstop for the last two days. Every waystation we came to, the driver would feed his fae horses, pat them down, and take only short breaks where he would sleep for a few marks, and then we would be back on the road. He never stopped to pick up any passengers, even though he had the opportunity to increase his fare. I believe he was working on fear and very little sleep.

I, on the other hand, spent most of my time worrying, and sleeping—trying to figure out how I was going to exact revenge, and praying that I wouldn't screw it up and dishonor my family.

I wanted to ask the driver if we had reached Thressia, but then I remembered the curse I placed on him. *Drat.* He couldn't tell me, unless I removed the curse, and I wasn't sure if I could duplicate it with as much success a second time. The driver came to a stop as he waited for traffic to clear.

"Excuse me," I called out the window at a young boy walking the street, carrying a load of wood far too large for his diminutive shoulders. The boy turned, his face hollow and dark circles hanging under his hungry eyes. His hair was matted, and his pants covered in dirt. "Yes, milady?" His face turned up in the hopes of earning a coin or an odd job. He put down his load.

"What city is this?" I jabbed my finger out and made a circle to encompass everything.

"You are in the Thressia," he answered, reaching to pull up his pants that had begun to sink low on his boney hips.

"Oh, how wonderful," I said, relieved that we had arrived, but now unsure of what my next step would be. I bit my lip and debated my options.

He tilted his head and studied me. "You here for the big to-do up at the palace?"

"Why, yes, I am."

"Do you have lodging?"

"No, not yet."

"All of the inns have been booked out for days. You ain't gonna find any here."

Double drat! I hadn't thought that far in advance.

He shifted his feet, and his eyes looked to the ground. "If

you haven't found a place to stay, I'd suggest Madam Pantalonne's Broken Heart tavern. She has a few rooms to let. Just make sure you lock your door at night."

At this point, I would have taken any lodging at all, even a stable, if it meant that I could stay within the city limits. He reached down to pick up his load and hefted it back onto his shoulders. His face winced under the pressure, and I could imagine his bones cracking under the weight like brittle twigs.

"Where are your parents?" I asked, now utterly confused as to why he looked like a breeze could knock him over. His spindly legs were shoved into boots that were too big for him.

"Don't got none," he said simply and began to carry his load down an alley and turned to look over at me and pointed. "It's that way. I'm making a delivery to there now. You can follow me. If you'd like."

An orphan. Like me. It struck me how similar we both were, and I felt a moment of kinship.

"Yes." I rapped on the top of the transport, and the driver leaned down, fear radiating off him in waves.

"Change of plans. Go to the Broken Heart tavern."

Another head bob and the transport dragged forward as a plan began to form in my head. Just make it to the ball, get the prince to notice me, and get chosen to stay on. Then I will have my chance for revenge. Simple, yes, but for someone who had never flirted or had a true kiss, maybe impossible.

Madam Pantalonnes looked like it was a cesspool for thieves, rakes, and ladies of the night. An enchanted street sign hung over the door and would flicker to show a heart. Then the second flicker would reveal a glowing knife stabbing the heart. I paused to take in the ingenuity of the spell. It was a form of a flickering glamour on a timer.

"Fascinating." I smiled and stepped through the door, the driver hot on my heels with my small case.

A tall, thin woman with a pink candy-colored wig, which hung low over her ears, greeted me as I walked through the doors on the heels of the boy. "Welcome to the Broken Heart, where you can unburden your heart or drown your sorrows." Madam Pantalonne grinned. "Are you here for a drink or room?"

The front sitting room was a macabre atmosphere of black and purple velvet décor. Overly stuffed chairs surrounded dark wooden gaming tables, and purple velvet curtains kept out the light and prying eyes. Strong incense wafted across my nose, and I recognized the scent of magic and a hint of frankincense. Most of the tables were occupied with men either playing tricks or blood stones, which consisted of flipping black and red stones and cornering your opponent.

The serving ladies wore bells around their hips, bright-colored lace across their face, and silk skirts. Some of the tables were nestled in dark corners with more curtains that provided the occupants privacy.

"A room," I said, watching a serving tray with a glass of dark swirling liquid and smoke billowing from the top go past me and be served to a table of one. It was similar to one of the potions we brewed, and I wondered what exactly was in the drink.

Madam looked me over and glanced at my driver behind me. "By the hour or—"

"N-No, nothing like that," I blurted out, feeling my cheeks flush red. "For a few days at least."

Her painted lips pursed, and she gave me a sly look. "Hmm, I see. Hoping to snag the prince, are you? Many have tried to capture his heart, but let me warn you." She lowered her voice to a whisper. "The prince is incapable of love."

I swallowed nervously at the way her voice dropped. What did she know that I didn't?

"Which is why I presume that the king is tired of waiting and forcing him to pick a bride by the end of the week," she added flippantly. With a finger, Madam Pantalonne beckoned me to follow her through the front room toward the back stairs. As I maneuvered around the tables, long legs suddenly barred my path, trapping me between two tables.

"Pardon me," I snapped impatiently. There was no room to go around. He had obviously stopped me on purpose as Madam had passed only seconds before.

"You are very much pardoned," the man said and crossed his legs at his ankles. Still not moving. The way the room was dimly lit and the position of his chair had him sitting in the shadows. The candles at his table had been blown out. So, I was left with addressing his silhouette.

"I wish to pass, and you are blocking my way."

"Then do so. Just lift your skirts and step over my legs." There was a teasing lilt to his voice, and it sounded like he was smiling.

"That is improper," I seethed.

"For a lady, yes." He leaned forward, his face coming into the light. "But you are not a lady. For ladies do not stay in an establishment like this, where secrets are sold and bought for a kiss."

I sucked in my breath, one at the insult and second because the candlelight accented his strong jawline and a day's worth of growth, which gave him a rakish look. Tousled dark hair hung low over his ears, as if a woman had run her hands through it instead of a comb. The color of his cold, hard eyes was indiscernible to me in the low light. There was something otherworldly and beautiful about him, and it fascinated me.

"I assure you I have no secrets," I said, spinning on my heel to find a different way around those long, alluring legs.

His hand shot out and gripped my wrist, his thumb rubbing ever so slightly across my skin. The touch was so electrifying, it sent prickles of excitement up my arm, and I shivered.

"That is a lie. Everyone has secrets. Secrets are currency in this world, and I am the trove, the guardian of all that is whispered in the night. And, therefore, by nature, I am very rich indeed." He brought my hand up, brushing his lips across the underside of my wrist, and I felt a flicker of a feathery kiss. "What would it cost to gain one of yours?"

"You will have to go elsewhere to pry for gossip. For any secrets I have are buried deep," I answered, pulling my wrist away, his lips having left a burning sensation behind. A warmth spread uncomfortably through my stomach.

"Then I shall get a shovel." He laughed, the corners of his mischievous eyes lifting.

During this exchange, the man had stood up and pulled me even closer to his side. I was entranced by the poetry that flowed from his mouth like sweet candy, and I couldn't help but be drawn to those lips. He was a seducer. No doubt and I was his prey, and I was trapped within his gaze, unwilling to pull away.

"Dorian, stop playing with my guest," Madam Pantalonne snapped impatiently, her slipper tapping on the rug. "She is of no concern to you and will be gone in a few days once the prince finds a bride."

With her words, the spell that Dorian had woven over me broke, like the sun breaking through the clouds after a storm.

Shaking my head, I stepped back, and he was reluctant to release me, but I didn't understand why.

"Then even more so that I set my eyes on you. For you would be wasting your time at the ball. Hundreds of girls will be bedecked with generations of their family's wealth flaunted around their necks. You, my dear sparrow, will be surrounded by swans. Save yourself the embarrassment and stay here with me. I can guarantee you that I am a far better dancer then the prince."

Was he insinuating that I was ugly? Yes, my looks were by far plain compared to my sister Rosalie, the stunning beauty that she was. Would I waste my time by going and for sure not pass the criteria needed to stay? I had to stay and find out what happened to my mother, and the answers were in the palace.

My eyes narrowed, and my anger rose at his insult. My lip curled in disgust. "And you are nothing more than a mongrel."

A deep, manly chuckled followed. "A bastard mongrel that steals things that belong to others to scrape by. You are correct."

"What do you want?" I said irritably.

"You." Dorian's eyes had locked onto mine, and I could see that they were a startling gray blue. Like ice.

"Never going to happen," I snarled.

He gave me a bow. "Then, until we meet again."

"We won't," I said stiffly.

"Oh, but we will. I guarantee it. You will come to me eventually for help. They all do." He gave me a slight salute before turning to the side to allow me to pass. Within seconds he turned his attention to one of the serving ladies, his hand wrapped around her waist possessively. He muttered into her dark hair, and she leaned into him. I stood there frozen as his cold eyes met mine when he looked back at me as if knowing I would still be watching him, that I would see his philandering behavior, and he was right. I couldn't pull my eyes away.

My stomach churned as the feelings that I knew too well rose up within me. Jealousy, anger, hurt—all three emotions fueled my power, but I was baffled by the one he had stirred up. The one where I couldn't pull my eyes away from his lips —desire.

I had been insulted, manhandled, told I was plain, and then easily discarded, all in the span of a few minutes. I hated Dorian for making me feel inadequate. No one, especially a stranger, should have the power to control the way I feel. A sorceress must be in control of their emotions at all times, like controlling a wild fire. We must know when to fan the flames and when to dowse them. Dorian was like fuel that, if added to my already spotty magic, was a recipe for chaos.

I must avoid him at all costs.

Abruptly turning away from his magnetic stare, I ran my shin right into an end table and swore. I had hoped that my erratic display would go unnoticed, but a hefty laugh echoed my way.

His laughter.

He had seen.

Not daring to look back, I held my head high and came to the patiently waiting Madam Pantalonne. She had witnessed the whole exchange. Shaking her head at me, she warned, "Stay away from that one. Dorian is no good."

"Then why do you allow him to come here. Why not kick him out of your establishment?" I asked.

"I would run the rascal out in a heartbeat." She looked at him fondly and sighed. "But he is good for my heart and business."

I let my mind go wild at all the hidden meanings that

suggested. Did he bring in people, steal secrets, pay for nights of passion with the ladies, spend copious amounts of gold on drinks?

I had to bring my head out of the clouds as I almost tripped going up a flight of stairs to a small landing only big enough for the two of us to stand side by side. The carriage driver stayed on the steps holding my luggage.

Madam Pantalonne paused, hitching her skirt to pull out a key on a chatelaine that was tucked away within the folds. "It ain't much," she explained, pushing the door open, "but it will do until you find out that the palace is no place for young ladies with your gifts."

Her warning held me back. "What do you mean?" I turned, giving her a curious stare.

"It's just... bad things happen at the palace. It's no place for a respectable young lady like yourself. Now, I require payment upfront. A week at a time." Her no-nonsense attitude had me digging into my purse, giving her most of the coins in my possession, with a tip for the young errand boy as well.

She stepped back, allowing my driver to pass, and I heard the stairs creak at her departure. My driver carried my trunk into the cramped attic room with a sloped ceiling. There was only about a foot of space where I could walk side to side before my head brushed against the rafters and I needed to bend my neck. At least there was a small bed, even if it was dusty and barely large enough to fit me, and an end table.

After depositing my case by the bed, the driver shifted his weight uncomfortably and waited on the landing.

Oh right!

I gave him payment for the trip and leaned up on my tiptoes to place a chaste kiss on his lips, surprising the driver. I had never kissed a man before but knew this was the easiest way to break the spell. A static shock passed between us, and I felt the power break. When I pulled away, he stumbled into the banister. His face red as a beet.

"Whoa!" he gasped, grabbing the top of his head and then touching his lips. "That was amaz—"

I smirked and closed the door, cutting off his words.

The kiss I had bestowed on the driver's lips was trivial and made me feel nothing. But the lightest touch of Dorian's lips on my wrist had me burning for more, and I secretly wanted to know what it felt like to kiss him instead.

"Oh, Eden," I grumbled to myself. "Get these thoughts out of your head. He is nothing to you. You are nothing to him. He is just toying with you." Mother warned me that men were dangerous, and Dorian was the most dangerous of them all.

CHAPTER FIVE

U nable to sleep in a strange place, in a strange bed, with strange sounds lofting up from the floor below me, I decided to take a page out of my sister Maeve's book and explore. I couldn't let *him* know that he had flustered me. Maybe secretly I wanted to get another look at the insufferable Dorian. Plus, I didn't think I could sleep knowing he was in the same building as me.

Then I had a mischievous thought and went to the mirror and quickly began to braid my hair and use pins to create the same style, a braided crown, as I saw the girls wearing below. When I was finished, I reached down and touched my chemise while firmly capturing an image in my mind of the style of dress I wanted to glamour it too. The soft silk skirt clung to my hips and hung to the floor in a deep ruby red. A short corset showed a hint of stomach and had long silk sleeves. Using one of my own lace kerchiefs, I glamoured it into a lace veil. I smiled as I tied it around my nose and lips, hiding my grin and my identity—except for the color of my hair.

Slipping out of my room, I headed downstairs and strolled among the tables. Most of the patrons had already cleared out. There were a few still gambling and playing blood stones.

Some had moved into the curtained-off tables, and the drapes were drawn. A drunk patron reached out to grasp me around the waist, but I slyly stepped out of his reach. Picking up a discarded tray, I placed empty cups on them and proceeded to clear the tables one by one, making my way over to where I had last seen Dorian.

I couldn't explain the disappointment I felt when I saw his empty table. A quick search of the room, but no one else fit his tall, lithe body type. I sighed in despair. What good was playing a game of cat and mouse when the other player wasn't there? I was about to give up and head upstairs when I heard men's voices coming from the closest curtained-off table.

"The king has become quite eccentric over the last few years," an older voice spoke out. "He has been obsessed with soothsayers and seers."

"Not eccentric, Lord Bishop. He's downright crazy. Ever since he lost his first son and has been terrified of the curse that has been looming over his head."

"I heard it wasn't a curse but a prophecy."

The tray rattled in my hands as I crept closer to peek in. Five men were sitting at a round mahogany table—one with a gold optical lens, a portly man with an accent, a younger man with a top hat, one with a pipe, and a taller man with his back to me.

"I'd say curse. Nothing good comes when one of the royals marry," the man with the pipe said. "Remember when King Ferdinand was set to marry that beautiful girl from the north, even proposed, and then walked down the aisle with Giselle instead. I lost a lot of money that day."

"I heard it was because the girl was fae, that's why he didn't marry her."

"Ach! Nothing is as bad as the loss of Prince Vincent's fiancée. Broke his heart. No wonder he disappeared."

"I heard he died," the tailored gent spoke up.

"Bad luck! I say. The whole thing is going to end in disaster. Mark my words, the betrothal will be marked with blood and death." The man waved his optical around in challenge.

The table became quiet, and no one protested.

"Now, now, gentleman. Enough with the gossip. Let's get back to the matter at hand. The odds. Let's start with the easy favorites. Five to one on the duchy of Dorcille's girl, Adelle. Ten to one on the guild merchant's daughter," a commanding voice cut through the chatter. The man with the top hat.

"I'm putting it all down on the miller's daughter. Have you seen her, Chamberlain?" A low whistle from Bishop's lips followed his endorsement.

"Yes, that's true, but the first night is always a masquerade," the one with his back to me stated.

"So? Are you saying that beauty won't win? How do you think the prince will pick his new wife if not by looks?" Bishop asked.

"I will let you in on a little secret, gentleman. The first night is always masquerade ball designed to flaunt wealth via their costumes. Don't expect any of the ladies with little money to their name to make it till morning. They will be escorted out the door before midnight," the man I couldn't see replied.

"No? Then why the masks?" Chamberlain asked.

"It's to make sure that the prince doesn't fall for a pretty face over a fat purse." Bishop chuckled.

"Ah, yes. I see now. What about the daughter of Duchovny?" the man with the pipe asked.

"Not coming. The father deemed her too young to marry at this time."

Caught up in the gossip and the betting surrounding tomorrow's masquerade ball, my mind swirled with newfound information. I quickly learned who the top favorites were to win the prince's heart, who was broke and going to try and win the crown through deception, and who were the natural beauties that had little to offer other than their looks.

But as I stood outside the curtain listening to the intrigue, I knew that without some unnatural help, I would never make it through the first night, much less the second night of the ball. My hand brushed an invisible fleck of dirt from my silk skirt, and as my confidence dropped, so did my glamour and the dress flickered.

If I lost control of my emotions, I wouldn't be able to keep a glamour over my clothes, and how could I possibly compete with the daughters of the rich nobles?

So preoccupied in my thoughts, I didn't see the curtain move until Dorian stepped right into my path, his shoulder knocking into me, causing me to stumble. He reached out to catch my elbow to steady me but immediately let go once I was set aright, not even sparing me a look.

I frowned at being put aside so easily. Dorian was looking for someone, and I followed at a distance as he caught up with Madam Pantalonne as she was heading up the stairs.

"Madam, may I so much as trouble you for the name of the young lady you had escorted up to your room earlier?"

I hid my eagerness and turned my back to begin clearing the table next to them. He was asking about me.

"Why, Dorian, were you unable to whisk her name from her with all of your charm? That would be a first," she teased.

"Yes, sadly the little sparrow has evaded my capture."

"And your claws." Her voice grew wary. "I may turn a blind eye to your charades and games, Dorian, and never do I speak up when you romance your way through my ladies, but I swear you will leave this poor girl alone."

My tray was full, but I wasn't ready to leave. Very carefully, I put the glasses back on the table and began to clear them again. Keeping my back to them, I listened eagerly.

"Madam, I—"

"No, Dorian. I will not tell you her name. I can't. I didn't ask her, or have you forgotten what kind of establishment this is? People come here to be left alone. I respect their privacy. You should too."

I wanted to clap, shout, and hug Madam Pantalonne, for she was a champion of women and underdogs.

"Besides, she will leave soon enough. She didn't have many possessions and will not make it past the first night, and you will not swoop in when she is culled. Spare her from being one of your many trophies."

I frowned.

Even the madam had little faith in me, that I would make it through the event. Painful tears burned at the corners of my eyes, and I felt like I was back home, being passed over time and time again in favor of my younger, more talented sisters.

"Go home, Dorian," Madam commanded. "Or have you forgotten about Sisa already?"

"But—"

"Go!" She pointed to the door.

Dorian seemed on the verge of arguing with the pink-haired woman, but he gathered his cloak about his shoulders and headed into the night. I watched him step out the front door.

Sisa? Who was Sisa? His wife? A lover? A dark storm cloud

gathered over my emotions as I once again realized how foolish and naive I was. Even here, far away from my family, no one believed in me. Total strangers didn't believe in me. But it only fueled my determination.

I had come to avenge my parents, but maybe, just maybe I would steal a throne while I was at it.

CHAPTER SIX

The light came streaming in the window, burning the back of my eyelids. In my tower room at home, it was dark and dismal. My windows faced west, so it was always dark and dreary in the mornings. I hated this bright wakeup call. Maybe I'd think about asking for a different room. Maybe they had one in the cellar. I sat up, and my head hurt so much that I fell back onto the pillow.

After a full mark, I dragged myself out of bed, pulled out my satchel, and dug through it, scrounging for something to eat. I found a packet of nuts and a few stale crackers wrapped in butcher paper.

I could work with that. Changing the flavor of something was easy to do. If I could just remember the right spell. I drew a sigil over the crackers, feeling triumphant that I was going to have cake for breakfast. I popped it in my mouth and chewed slowly, savoring the... burning. Holy stars above!

Pffft. The crackers flew from my mouth, scattering across the bed and onto the floor. "Ah, ah, ah." I panted as I tried to wipe the cracker from my tongue.

It was inedible.

I turned the cracker into a peddler pepper. My eyes

burned, and I began to cough. I looked back at the purse, wishing I had something to wash it down with, like a normal plain cracker. Nope. Wasn't going to try that again. My powers useless, I grabbed the nuts and slowly chewed each one of them. The more I focused on the nuts, the less my tongue burned from the pepper.

After a few minutes, I opened the small case and looked through my sparse clothes. I put on a sensible skirt with leggings, a long jacket, and boots. After braiding my hair over my shoulder, I gave myself a cursory glance in the mirror. It would do. Before I left, I drew another sigil over the door—a "do not disturb" one that made others stay clear of my room.

Walking down the stairs, I saw an unattended tray of fruit on a side table. I nabbed a few and placed them in my bag before heading out into the street. Once I had made my way around the block, I took a bite out of the apple and spit it out. What was wrong with people? Who would turn their fruit into wax? I quickly inspected the pear and saw that it was spelled the same way. Disgusted, I tossed both into the nearest trash bin and grumbled my way back to the main square as I headed toward the palace.

The whole town seemed to be built in the palace's shadow, and even though it was midmorning, there was a chill in the air. No one gave me any notice as I walked the streets. When a few gruff men tried to gain my attention, I silenced their advances with a cold, calculated stare. Maybe they could feel my desire to bespell them if given the chance?

The market was bustling and filled with vendors selling flowers, exotic spices, and food to accommodate the group that had gathered outside, waiting to get into the palace, or get a look at the prince.

I purchased a real apple from an elderly woman and

tucked it into the pocket of my skirt before falling among a group of ladies who were watching the manor with envious eyes. The guards were stopping each person entering the palace gates and checking their faces carefully and comparing it to sketches they had in their hands. What was going on?

Three of the ladies were furiously waving their fans to cool themselves off in the warm sun and spoke in hushed tones. "What are they doing?"

"I heard that they are being very cautious with the invitations this year."

"Why is that?"

"Because of what happened with the prince of Baist. That sorceress swapped out his bride for her daughter on his wedding day."

"No!" Gasps followed.

"Yes, no one knows what the crazy hag will do next."

"Don't tell tales, Lizzie."

"I'm not telling tales. My lips speak nothing but the truth."

"Sorry, ladies. If you want to enter, you must get in line." A guard stopped them as they had wandered too close to the gates and pointed to the line of people waiting to get in.

I wasn't prepared for an inspection but decided to test my ability to sneak into the palace ahead of time. I would do some snooping to see how tough it would be to get in.

I purchased a basket of flowers from a vendor and waited for the right moment. A retinue of guards were coming from the main square and heading into the palace by the main gates. I targeted a younger-looking guard and pasted a smile on my face as I plowed into his strong chest, my finger reaching for his uniform.

"I'm so sorry," I cried out, dropping my flowers and waving my hands in the air in embarrassment.

The guard bent down and picked up my basket, carefully putting each flower back into it before handing it off to me. "No need, miss. It happens. Are you all right?" He gently touched my arm, and my cheeks flushed. I looked up into his warm brown eyes filled with concern and froze.

I was stunned by the genuine emotions that poured from him. One of the things we had been taught by Mother was to read auras. His was so pure, so filled with light that it was like looking upon the sun. I blinked and shook my head, trying to let the aura fade from my vision. A second glance, I was able to see him, the square nose, brown hair with a cowlick that didn't want to stay down, and his charming smile.

It was disgusting. I reminded myself.

"I'm fine." I pulled my elbow out of his hand and lifted my chin. I was unnerved by his virtuousness and could feel it want to inch over to my own darker aura. It was hard to breathe. I stepped back and thrust out my hand, demanding my basket. Instead of handing it to me, he took a step forward. I retreated.

He frowned, those dark brows pulling together in confusion. "Hey, filly, it's okay. I'm not going to hurt you."

"Did you just call me a horse?" I rolled my eyes.

"No...? Yes, but wait."

"Forget it. Keep the flowers." I waved him off. Lifting the hem of my dress, I hurried down the street in the opposite direction. I could hear him yelling after me, his footsteps hitting the brick road. I reached into my purse and dug until I found the apple from a stall vendor I purchased earlier. Ducking into an alley, I bit the apple, being careful to not swallow and hold it in my teeth. The juices ran over my tongue. I could feel the change take over, starting with my hair and shoulders. My hips widened, my back crooked lower, and my hands began to wrinkle—taking on the appearance of the elderly apple vendor. I turned around and was almost knocked over by the soldier.

"Oh, excuse me, ma'am. Did you happen to see a young woman pass this way?"

I nodded and pointed down the street.

"Thank you so much." He gave my arm a quick squeeze before taking off running down the alley, my basket of flowers still in his hands.

I quickly chewed and swallowed the apple and felt my body began to transform. Tossing the apple into the street, I held up a gold button with an insignia on it—Candor's insignia, a gold sun—stolen from the young guard's uniform. I had pinched it when I pretended to run into him.

I held the button in my hand and focused my attention on a glamor. The reason I chose that soldier was because he was average looking, easily forgotten. He wasn't too handsome or too ugly. Taking over his identity was easy, and I quickly made my way back to the palace gates. One of the guards waved me through, and I could see where the guards had headed into the barracks.

I had made it. I was in the palace. I grinned in excitement. A loud voice boomed from behind, and I felt a slap on my bottom.

I shrieked.

Loud merriment from the men surrounded me. "Did you hear Derek? He screamed like a girl."

I turned on the nearest offender, working my fingers and getting ready to fling some errant curse his way, but then I remembered who I was pretending to be. I had seen men do this ritual before where they hit each other on the bottoms. The world was an odd place.

"So, did you find that fine filly? Give 'er something to remember you by?" The tall guard wiggled his eyebrows at me. My cheeks flamed, and I had to bite my tongue. I nodded.

"Not gonna kiss and tell, then are you?"

I shook my head and squared my shoulders as I spotted a dark head of hair coming in through the gates. It was Derek. He was back. I couldn't believe he had given up the chase already. The other guards had begun to remove their cloaks and unbutton their belts, and I realized they were undressing. Feeling trapped, I walked down the rows of bunks until I came to a side entrance. Keeping my head low, I escaped the barracks just as Derek came through the door and to the side.

Pressing my hand to my chest, I took a deep breath and listened.

"Whoa! Derek how did you do that?" a voice asked.

"Do what?" Derek was understandably confused.

"Go out that door and come in through this one?"

That was my cue to leave. My escape had not gone unnoticed.

"Are you mad, Leonard?" Derek asked. "I just got here."

My heart pounded at how close a call it was, but I kept my head down and slipped into the closest covered building, which were the stables.

As soon as I was out of sight, I started to swear up a storm, my arms flailing as I swore to the stars above, I was going to rain down boils on all of the army for slapping me. And during my rant, I lost hold of Derek's button and it fell into the straw.

No! I kneeled down and quickly ran my fingers through the straw, scattering it, trying to find the round button.

Raised voices came toward me, and I ducked into an occupied horse stall. Keeping low, I moved to the rear of the stall, gently shushing the roan and running my hand over its haunches while I eavesdropped on the conversation.

"I don't care what you want. I want you to pick a bride from the ladies coming to the ball." The voice was old, rough, and filled with authority.

"That is difficult to do when they're wearing masks. You might as well ask me to pick a bride based on the size and make of her shoe."

I smirked at the sarcastic tone of the second speaker. I carefully peeked above the stall to confirm my suspicions. It was King Ferdinand, wearing a dark pinstripe suit. The king had a mustache. His hair, speckled with gray, looked almost white. The prince's back was too me, and I couldn't see him other than the cut of his short dark hair.

"Well, if they were perhaps made of gold or diamonds, then I'd say, yes, you should," the king answered.

"So, you're saying I should base a woman's worthiness on how extravagant and expensive her footwear is?"

"No, I'm asking you to base it on her family's bank accounts," the king snapped.

My stomach rolled in disgust at the king's demands. No wonder Mother hated him.

"I can't do that," the prince argued.

"You will, or you will end up just like your brother."

"If only all of us could so easily escape the weight of a crown."

"We will not speak of him again," the king roared.

"Aren't you worried the witch will show up? I heard that she ruined Prince Xander's wedding."

I bit my lip in fury as they spoke ill of my family. I shifted my weight on my heels when I saw the button on the floor outside the stall. Just out of my reach.

Prince Evander continued. "What if she comes here? What about the pro—"

"Of course, I'm worried. One of her daughters is already in the city. She arrived by transport last night. I will take care of it. The prophecy will not come true. I'm bringing in a truth seer to monitor the entrance. No witch, wizard, or fae will get passed the gates."

This news made me worried. It meant the driver betrayed the passenger oath, of keeping fares private. He must have gone to the king.

My fingers curled into fist, my nails digging painfully into the palm of my hand. I itched to reach my hand forth and exact revenge, strike him down, burn the barn to the ground, but instead, I restrained myself. Could I murder him in cold blood?

Patience. That was key. What was a few more days?

The king groaned as if in pain. "All I ask is that you do what you're told. Take a wife. Preferably a rich one."

"Fine," the prince snapped.

"Fine." The king huffed and stormed out of the stables. I feared for my life even more, knowing that if I was caught, there would be hell to pay.

My safety lay in the button, just out of reach. Making a rash decision, I lunged for the button and rolled into the open stall across from me.

"Who's there?" the prince called out.

Sprawled on the ground, I concentrated on the button in my hand, feeling the warmth of the magic spreading across my skin. My dread intensified as a shadow fell over me. I squeezed my eyes shut and held my breath.

The last thing I needed was for him to realize that a

daughter of Eville had indeed trespassed where they were not wanted.

"What is the meaning of this?" Prince Evander's stern voice told me that my glamour must not have worked.

"I can expl—" I opened my eyes and looked into his almond-colored eyes and lost my train of thought.

"Why are you here?" he demanded.

Glancing down, I was relieved to see that I was in uniform, that the glamour had worked. I was safe—for now.

"I've come to offer my services to you," I said, keeping my voice low as I got to my feet.

He snorted. "You're already in service to my household and kingdom. What more could you offer me?"

"Friendship." I wasn't sure why it came out of my mouth. It was not appropriate to be so casual to the royal family.

The prince looked at me strangely.

I bowed. "I'm sorry, Your Highness. It was foolish of me to offer." I turned to leave, hearing the prince's deep baritone laugh follow after me. How stupid to say friendship? I couldn't possibly be friends with the prince, but for a moment, I felt sorry for the prince being forced to marry a stranger.

"No. Stay. I need to ride for a bit. You can be my escort."

I nodded and quickly put a blanket over the horse and went for the saddles. There were quite a few to choose from, all of fine leather. I grabbed one that I thought would need the least adjusting for the prince's legs and tossed it over the thoroughbred horse. If there was one thing I knew how to do, it was saddle a horse.

"You know we have stable boys to do that?" he said when I led the horse out to him. I shrugged, not wanting to answer him in my feminine voice. "Why don't you grab Chestnut over there instead of going all the way back to the soldiers' barracks. I'm in the mood to leave rather quickly."

Nodding again, I followed suit, only this time grabbing the least fancy saddle and bridle. I began to lead the horse over to a stepping block used for women to get onto the horse. I didn't even think before I stepped up onto it and mounted Chestnut sidesaddle.

A loud guffaw came from the prince, and I gave him an affronted look. He doubled over, leaning onto the stirrup, laughing uncontrollably.

"Oh, ha ha." He wiped his eyes with his sleeves before pointing at my posture, and I realized my mistake. In Derek's height, I could easily have mounted from the ground, but what was worse, I mounted and sat sidesaddle like a girl. I gave him an angry glare and flung my much longer foot over the horse's head and sat like I did when I was a kid.

"That is funny. I sorely needed that. Thank you." The prince gave me a despondent look. "Today has been extremely stressful. I'm sure you understand."

I nodded again and nudged Chestnut out of the stable. The sooner we got moving, the farther away from the stable and my horrible mistake I could get.

I let the prince lead, being careful to stay a few paces behind him but always near. My plan was going better than I expected, but there were a few problems I hadn't thought of. What happened if we were attacked? I knew nothing about being a soldier or using the sword on my belt.

Maybe being attacked would be a blessing. Maybe they would do the work for me. He could get injured or killed, and it would make the king miserable. Voilà. My job would be done, and I could go home. But it wouldn't give me answers about my parents.

I scanned the forest in anticipation, hoping for an attack or raiders, looking for boogeymen in the darkness. The prince took it another way.

"You can relax your vigil. We are still within the palace grounds. There's nothing that can hurt us here."

My shoulders fell as another plan went out the window. Prince Evander noticed. "I'd say you were actually disparaged at the prospect. Were you hoping for a little bit of excitement?"

I shrugged.

"Then follow me," he yelled. He took off galloping down the field. I had no choice but to follow his breakneck speed. At first, I was terrified, but then I realized how well the horse followed the prince's horse, and all I really needed to do was just hold on. He slowed when we came to a side gate. The prince demanded the guards open the doors. Moments later we were back to running, the wind rushing past my face. It felt different, and I missed the feel of the wind's fingers grabbing at my long curls. Instead, it brushed past the short style of the soldier Derek.

The prince slowed and dismounted when he came to a river and began to rub his horse down. I didn't want to like the prince, but I had respect for someone who took care of his animal after a run. I followed suit and was surprised when he handed me an apple for the horse.

We both stood there in silence. After a few minutes, he motioned for me to follow, leading the animals to a smaller stream. The horses eagerly rushed forward and drank. The prince was careful to monitor how much they consumed, and I couldn't help but compare him to his father. Here was someone who cared for animals deeply, and I couldn't imagine that he'd mistreat his subjects or soldiers.

I was careful to not speak out of turn; I didn't know how to speak to royalty.

He began to undress. My cheeks flushed, and I looked away. He took off running for the stream wearing nothing but his bottoms; I followed at a slower pace. Surely, he wasn't going to jump in—yes, he was and did.

Feeling at odds and not really sure what to do with a half-naked prince swimming in a stream, I decided to turn my back and face the woods—let him think of it what he may.

"What do you think I should do?" he asked. I could still hear the splashing of water.

I had to clear my throat and focus on sounding like a man. "About what?"

"The king's orders. Marry the richest lass at the ball. . . or should I marry for love?"

"Love isn't real. It's a façade like the masks the ladies will wear." My mother's cynicism dripped from my voice.

"That so? What woman scorned you then?"

"I've never been scorned by a woman," I scoffed.

"Then a man?"

"Ah, no!" I said even faster. "I've seen what it did to my mother. It cursed her and us. Nothing good comes from love. It makes you weak."

"You're right. I saw what it did to my brother. Better to marry someone who can strengthen my hold on the throne."

The waters stilled, and I heard a loud sigh from the prince. A few minutes later, he came out of the river, water dripping off his hair and running down his chest. He stood next to me and shook his head like a dog. As the water splattered my uniform, I gave him a frustrated look, slapping the drops from my coat. He smirked.

"Are you done, Your Highness?" I asked, trying not to show my extreme discomfort at being in this situation.

He sighed again and looked back toward the palace. His face was forlorn. It seemed that it was the last place he wanted to go.

A moment of pity overcame me, and I asked him out of curiosity and a way to delay his return, "What do you want to do?"

"Hmm?" he asked, walking back to retrieve his clothes.

"About your future."

"I wish to be a great ruler, the likes of which our kingdom has never seen before," he said firmly. "But I can't do that when a forest of obstacles stands in my way." He was speaking metaphorically.

"Then forge a path through."

"I'd rather burn it down," he said and began to get dressed.

I wondered if I had overstepped my bounds. Maybe I had offended him? Well, he needed to know his own mind, and he couldn't even be a good ruler if he didn't know how to make decisions.

Keeping my hands and mind busy, I prepared the horses for our departure. A few moments later, he was ready, fully dressed, his royal riding robes perfectly in place. Even his hair looked immaculate.

The ride back to the palace was uncomfortably silent. I tried to say something, but each time the words became lodged in my throat like a nasty swig of medicine that wouldn't go down. I worried on the corner of my lip. A few times, the prince turned in his saddle and gave me an odd look, and I just sat straighter in the saddle. Did he suspect that I wasn't who I pretended to be? Was the jig up? Maybe I needed to make a hasty exit.

I was so preoccupied with thinking of ways to escape or run away that I didn't notice when we came back through the gate or entered the stable. A stable boy came to greet us, taking the reins from the prince first. As I slid off the horse, my legs almost gave out and I stumbled. The prince's dark eyebrow rose up in a furious question.

Gah! I was a horrible soldier. Maybe I should pick a better disguise next time.

I must have offended the prince because he left without saying another word. The stable boy came and took the horse from me, and I felt a moment of sadness at seeing the beautiful beast leave. We only had one sorrel horse for the seven of us sisters, and she didn't quite have the personality or spirit of this one. We all learned how to be a lady and ride sidesaddle for when we had to mingle with polite society. Too bad those lessons never included how to be a soldier.

Sneaking back out of the palace turned out to be harder than sneaking in. The guards were patrolling, and I thought for sure I saw Derek by the front gate. I couldn't possibly pass him wearing his own guise. Slipping back behind the barracks, I tucked the button into my satchel and felt my body slowly changed into my younger, shorter self. A smile of satisfaction donned my face. It felt good to be me again. I pulled a scarf from my handbag and placed it over my head. I concentrated on aging myself, putting gray into my hair, wrinkles on my face. It was easier to change and alter my own image than to put on a full glamour of another person.

I was satisfied with my appearance when the watering trough's reflection showed an older Eden. It was time to leave.

The easiest way to throw off doubt was to leave slowly, not at a dead run. Walking across the courtyard, although only fifty yards or so, seemed like a mile. I turned my foot in, making sure to limp. *Keep going, Eden.* I encouraged myself. *Keep going.*

I had made it to the gate, where the guards were speaking among themselves. I looked up and saw Derek; he gave me a curious look and turned to speak to me. "Do you need assistance, ma'am?" He gave me his elbow, and I recoiled.

"No, I do not," I snapped.

"Well, it seems you do, since you can't decide which leg to limp on."

"Maybe both my hips hurt."

"Hey you!" a demanding voice carried across the courtyard, and both Derek and I turned to see Prince Evander coming down toward us, his face an unreadable mask.

My knees began to shake; he must have figured out what I had done. I couldn't help it, but I began to sway. Derek reached out and caught my arm, his other arm wrapping around my shoulders to help keep me upright and from falling over.

"You... Derek." The prince stopped in front of us. Ignoring me completely, focusing all of his attention on the guard who was holding me.

"I would like to accept your offer."

"My offer?" Derek repeated, confused.

"Yes, and to start, I would like you to be one of my personal attendants at the ball tonight. Perhaps you can keep me from making a horrible decision and not falling in love."

"I... uh, I...," Derek stammered, unsure how to respond to the request since he didn't know why it came out of the blue. "I would be delighted to, Your Highness." His hand squeezed a little too hard on my elbow.

"Good, I'll send a servant with instructions later." The

prince turned on his heel and marched back up the steps to the palace.

Still locked in Derek's strong grip, I pulled to get away from him, bringing his attention back to me.

"I don't know you, and I know most everyone in this town. I also know that you're lying about something. I'm very good at knowing when people lie. There's something *off* about you."

Great! He may be one of the few with the natural ability to tell when people are lying.

His brown eyes studied me carefully. "Where do you live?"

"I just moved here," I croaked out.

"From where?"

"Very far away. You really shouldn't harass an old lady."

"It's my job." His eyes narrowed again. "Let me warn you. I never forget a face." His fingers released one by one from my arm, and I turned, hobbling away, unsure which way to limp. Oh, forget it. I ran.

CHAPTER SEVEN

I kept the old-lady glamour going as I walked through the town, pondering what I had learned. The prince didn't seem cold or heartless at all. In fact, he seemed nice, and I was finding it hard to dislike him. His father, yes, I could understand why my mother detested him. He seemed shallow and corrupt; whereas his son wasn't. They say the apple doesn't fall far from the tree, but that wasn't true in the case of Prince Evander.

I didn't want to hurt Prince Evander; he seemed a victim. But how could I take the sails out of wretched King Ferdinand?

Just then my mirror began to hum in my drawstring pouch.

I ducked into an alley, and scrambled to open the bag, being careful to pull my hair to the side and make it look presentable before turning the mirror to face me.

Mother Eville's nose filled the mirror. "Eden!"

"Yes, Mother." I winced at the tone in her voice. She moved the mirror farther away, so that I could actually see more of her face. This time all I saw were her eyes.

"You look horrid, child. Is it a glamour?"

"Yes, it is because the king knows I'm here. He plans to stop me from coming."

"Of course he does. That's because he fears the prophecy."

"What prophecy?" I asked.

"No, not yet. All in good time. If you know too much, then you will inevitably try to alter the future."

"You said I had a choice."

"And you do. Sort of. But I already know what will happen."

I sighed in frustration. "Doesn't matter. There's no way I can get into the ball."

"Really? There's no way?" she said, leading me. "You, who are the most talented at glamour, can't find your way into the palace. If I know you, you've already snuck in and out by now."

I couldn't hide the truth. "Yes, barely, but they will have a truth seer at the gate, and they can see through all glamour." It was a weak attempt to back out.

Mother sighed. "Yes, I see. Then you will need a magic item to amplify your gifts."

"I didn't bring any."

"Well, did you get the shoes?" she asked irritably.

"What shoes?" I waited as it sounded like Mother began to speak into another mirror. She was communicating with our fae friend Lorn. After a few minutes, she came back. "That's right, I hadn't told you where they are."

"What do I need?"

Her lips turned up in an evil grin. "Do you know anyone with a shovel?"

Mother spent the next mark going over very specific instructions about a certain enchanted item that she knew was buried nearby. How she knew was highly suspicious, but I trusted her.

Right?

The mirror went black.

A shrill voice carried through the air, and I turned in disdain to see a beautiful brunette girl push a smaller servant girl down. "You stepped on my dress! I should have you whipped."

"I'm sorry, sister," the younger strawberry blonde girl whispered and immediately leaned down and began to wipe the patch of dirt from the edge of her dress.

I carefully tucked the mirror back into my drawstring purse and watched.

"Tess, don't you dare call me sister in public. You are a disgrace to our family and our name." The older girl ripped her dress from the girl's hands, giving her a rough push on the shoulder.

"Sorry, Nessa." The sister acting as a servant looked up, her eyes filled with unshed tears.

I stepped back behind a stall and watched the two sisters interact. The taller one was loud, brassy in voice and appearance. She carried herself with an air of importance. The other sister, Tess, was meek and kept her head down, being careful to stand in the shadow and out of the way.

What was their reasoning for having the other pretend to be a servant? Why was she cruel to her? I chewed on my lip and pretended to shop, all the while keeping an eye on the two of them. The sister in the fancier dress would pick up a particular ribbon or brooch and then scoff at its price before loudly disregarding the item, her obvious contempt drawing the shopkeepers' attention.

They created quite the spectacle. Studying them, it was

easy to figure out the girls' plan. Nessa moved away, walking into a store, all eyes still on her. The servant girl was nowhere to be found. And before I even glanced back at the table, I knew the brooch was gone. She swiped it—not Nessa, but the quiet one.

"Very interesting." I smiled.

They were con artists, thieves, and it looked like they were darn good ones too. No one ever paid attention to the servant. I followed the brunette, Nessa, into a dressmaker's shop, where she was getting fitted for a dress for the ball.

"I'm not sure about the dark orange. I hear that Prince Evander favors pastels. Do you have anything else?"

"Miss, I've already told you, it is too late to change your dress. We are swamped with custom orders because of the ball. Would you like to try your luck elsewhere?" the shopkeeper said.

"No." Nessa waved her hand and stuck out her lip in a pout. "It will have to do." She kept glancing out the window nervously, as if she was waiting for something.

"Would you like me to wrap it up for you?"

"No," she said hurriedly. "I think I'd like to take a look at your trimmings, if you please. I feel that this dress needs something else."

"Very well." The shopkeeper bowed his head and went into the back wall and began to pull out drawers of lace and pearls.

Tess ran in hurriedly, her hands tucked in her apron.

"Finally!" Nessa hissed. "Please tell me you got enough to pay for the dress."

She pulled out a handful of coins and bills. "This is all I was able to trade the brooch for."

Nessa snatched the money and thumbed through the bills. "It's not enough."

"Well, it's all I could get. Maybe if I was able to lay low for a few days before having to hawk a hot item, I could have gotten more, but only Red was at the booth, and this was the best I could do."

"Fine, it will have to do." Nessa's eyes were wild as she looked around the room and then back to the shopkeeper's back. She quickly reached down and tore at the trimming on her bodice. When the shopkeeper returned, she was complaining loudly. "I can't possibly go to the ball in this? It's ripped. It's shoddy workmanship on your part."

"It wasn't like that. I swear?" He reached for her bodice, but Nessa slapped his hand away. "Don't you dare touch me. I think the only thing to do now would be to offer me a discount."

The shopkeeper was obviously taken aback. He scratched the back of his neck. "I'm sure the ladies in alteration can fix it, if you want."

"There's no time. I'll take it like it is but at heavy discount for my time and for ruining my dress."

"Fine," he named a price, and I could see Nessa's smile of satisfaction that she now had enough money for the dress.

"Wrap it up."

Tess had hung back, standing in the shadows while her older sister conned the owner. But she couldn't hide from me.

"So, you're playing the long con," I whispered into Tess's ear.

She jumped, her hand coming to her breast in startlement.

"I have no idea what you're talking about. I've done no such thing."

"You're good at lying, but are you as good as your sister?"

She smiled in pride. "Better."

"She spies the items. You resell them before the vendors even know they're stolen and use the money to make your purchases, today's being an extravagant dress. Let me guess, the prize isn't a dress is it."

She looked away from me uncomfortable. Her shoulder twitched, and I knew that I was partially right. "You've both set your eyes on the prince."

"No, not both. Only one of us. We were unable to afford enough dresses for the masquerade ball and coming nights."

An idea began to form in my mind. The inner mischievous Eden wanted to dance in excitement. The plan was perfect.

"What if I could change that?" I whispered. "What if I could grant your wish and help you get to the ball?"

She dropped her head as Tess passed her in the shadows and headed into the street. "Nessa won't like that. She won't like it at all."

"Who says we have to tell her? It is a masquerade after all."

She looked up at me with such hope that I felt sorry for the thief. She was going to be a pawn in my plan.

"Yes, yes. I would do anything to go."

My stomach began to rumble, and I prayed she hadn't heard. "Then I need you to get a few items for me and meet me tonight in the churchyard."

CHAPTER EIGHT

W hen I came back to the inn at midday, I wasn't at all surprised to see most of the tables were empty and few servers were about. Dorian was also notably absent. Madam Pantalonne, wearing a lilac wig, was sitting at a table having tea.

"Do you mind if I join you?" I asked.

"Why, of course." She smiled sweetly and signaled for a serving girl to bring out another teacup for me. Madam poured me a cup and put sugar and cream in without asking me. I didn't mind and sipped on the sweet black tea. "So, tell me what is on your mind. No one ever sits down for tea with me."

"Why not?" I asked.

"Because I do not have the best reputation in town. So that means either you want something, or you don't know my reputation." She took a sip and waited for my response.

I smiled over the rim of my cup. "Then we are the same. For where I come from, my reputation is known far and wide, and no one would dare have tea with me either." I raised my cup in salute. "To bad reputations and the women who couldn't care less."

Madam cackled, her mouth opening wide, revealing

perfect white teeth. The powdered makeup and bright-colored wigs only masked her true beauty. I could see it, the slight glamour that dulled her complexion, made her eyes not as bright, and her skin more aged. I didn't understand why she would want to look dowdy.

"You have quite the wit," she said.

"Wit may be my only redeemable quality, I'm afraid."

"What's on your mind?"

"Tell me about the king."

She looked into her teacup. "Who he is now and who he was, are very different men. He once was kind and sweet." Her voice softened; her eyes became misty. "He cared about his people and their problems. He was someone who I could proudly stand behind. When it came time for him to choose a bride from among Candor's daughters, I was of the right age and background. I attended the masked ball and was asked to stay on as one of his selected chosen. Over the next week, I fell for him hard. He courted me, gave me gifts, said he loved me, promised me the world. Then on the last day of the celebrations, he walked down the aisle with another."

The teacup froze midair to my lips. "No!"

Madam Pantalonne's hands trembled, and she took a sip. She brushed at her eyes, wiping away unshed tears.

"I believe there was someone who swayed him, whispered in his ear. I can't prove it, but I swear there was dark magic involved. He wasn't the Ferdinand I knew and loved after that. He acted like he didn't even know me. Maybe he just played me for a fool."

"You are not a fool."

"Yes, for me it was true love. I couldn't go home to my family, so I took the numerous gifts he gave me and sold them to buy this tavern. Just to be close to him."

"The Broken Heart," I muttered. "It's yours."

"Yes. Twice over, for he came back and took something very dear to me, and ever since that day, he has been different. Not the man I knew, but scared and irrational. All alike, fae and humans, have been hurt by him. So be wary when you go to the palace. All is not as it seems. Don't be naive like me."

We sat for a few moments, and she asked for my teacup. I handed it to her, and she swirled it around three times counterclockwise.

I knew what the madam was trying to do. She was going to read my tea leaves.

Madam Pantalonne turned the handle toward herself and looked into the dregs of my tea. Her eyes widened in fear, and she made a cross motion over her heart. "There's a price on your head. I see death. So much death. And betrayal from someone close to you."

"Who?"

"He's coming for you, Eden. He wants freedom." Madam Pantalonne's eyes had a faraway look about them. They were no longer focused on the cup in her hands. The warning was from someone else.

Goose bumps ran up my arms. I never told her my name. No one here knew I was Eden.

She glanced back at me. "What have you done to earn the wrath of the king?"

"I was born."

"During a hunter's moon in Nochtember?" she asked.

"Yes, how did you know?" Madam Pantalonne looked around the sparse room warily. "I'm sorry. I shouldn't have done that without permission." She put my cup on her tray, but her hands were shaking, and I watched as it clattered to the ground. The dainty teacup broke, the dark tea spilling out on the rug like blood.

Madam Pantalonne breathed out, her hand going to her heart. "Now, I know I am truly cursed. You will not be safe if you stay here."

"Why?" I demanded. "What do you know that I do not?"

"Child, you mustn't ask these questions. It isn't safe." She clapped her hands to her breast.

"Fine. I will leave, but tomorrow. I have things I must do, and tonight is the ball." I excused myself and headed out the doors.

"If you live that long." Her eerie warning followed me.

Madam's warning filled me with foreboding. She said *he* is coming for me. And the only *he* I could think of was the sorcerer Allemar, who I had helped banish to another plane. I still had nightmares of watching him scream as my sister sealed him within the realm. But we both knew it wouldn't hold him for long.

I stood outside the tavern, wondering where I could acquire the item my mother requested, when a dark coach pulled up and a man stepped out. It was Dorian. Quickly, I pulled my hood over my golden hair and began to walk away from him.

"Stop, little sparrow. Where do you fly off too?"

I quickened my steps and ignored him. I didn't get far before he caught up to me and grabbed my arm.

"Did you decide to go home? Give up and leave before the ball even began?"

"No." I crossed my arms and lifted my chin. "I have every intention of going to the ball."

"Funny how you say, 'going to the ball,' and 'not winning the prince.'"

"Priorities," I grumbled.

"Why do you look so down?"

"Because I ask too many questions," I answered simply.

He laughed. "You can never ask too many questions."

"Maybe I asked the wrong questions then."

His smile dropped. "What did you do, little sparrow?"

"Nothing," I mumbled. "But I think I need your help."

Dorian grinned. "I told you that you would come to me. Everyone eventually comes to me."

"Fine, whatever. What is it going to cost me?" I asked warily.

He leaned in close and whispered seductively, "Nothing more than a kiss."

I pondered the repercussions of letting a virtual stranger kiss me versus trying to find the item my mother requested. Then I caved.

"Okay." Before he could change his mind, I leaned up on my tiptoes and pressed my lips against his, similar to how I kissed the transport driver. My forwardness startled Dorian, and before he could respond and kiss me back, I pulled away.

"Huh," I said, surprised. "That was interesting. It was nothing like I imagined."

"Wait a minute." Dorian was obviously flustered. "I wasn't prepared. I wouldn't exactly call that a kiss. My kisses have never been called interesting. I demand a rekiss."

I flashed him an angry glare. "That was a kiss," I declared. "One kiss, one request."

"Uh, but... but...."

"Don't you dare go back on your word." I placed my hands on my hips, and he laughed.

"All right. You got me this time. But next time, I get to do the kissing. And believe me, you will not forget it or call it interesting."

"I doubt that will ever happen."

"It will. I guarantee it. Would you like to place a wager?"

"No, I would not. It won't happen," I said irritably.

"Challenge accepted." He winked and gave me a little bow. "What can Dorian do for you? Do you need something stolen from someone's house? Unbury your enemies' darkest secrets. You do remember that is my specialty."

"I do need to unbury something."

"Oh?"

"I need a shovel. One made of iron."

He scratched the back of his head. "That is an unusual request. I have to admit, I was expecting something different."

"Can you do it or not?"

"I can do it. It just may take me a few candle marks. May I ask what it is for?"

"No."

"What are you going to unbury?"

"Again. No."

"You make things interesting, little sparrow."

"Look, Dorian, I don't have much time."

He held up his hands and swung back up into his coach. "Okay, where should I meet you."

I looked up at the afternoon sun and knew I was running out of time.

"The church."

The air was cold, perfect for my liking. Dorian arrived right on time with the shovel.

"Now, sparrow, are you going to knock me over the head and drag me into the church to marry me?" he teased. Dorian was dressed to impress in an all-black suit with gloves.

"You *are* dressed for the part."

He leaned close and smiled. "For you, I would run to the altar."

I batted him in the chest and took the shovel from his gloved hand. "Thank you, but not today."

He looked put off that I wasn't falling for his charm. But I knew what kind of man he was and didn't want to end up with a broken heart.

"If you don't get moving, you won't make it to the ball. Would you like me to give you a ride? Unless you've changed your mind?"

"No, thank you. I have someone I'm meeting still."

Dorian's brows furrowed. "Is it a man? It's getting dark. I don't think it would be safe for you."

"Would it matter?" I huffed. "I'm quite capable of taking care of myself. More than capable, in fact."

Dorian turned to leave but then came back and leaned down, brushing the sleeve of my arm. "I know we barely know each other, but I want you to be safe. Just the idea that you are going to go to the ball to throw your future away and marry someone you barely know unsettles me."

"Dorian, there's a very slim chance I'll make the cut. I won't be picked to stay, much less marry the prince. You said it yourself."

The muscles in his jaw ticked, and he looked at the ground before meeting my eyes. "I lied," he whispered. "He would be a fool not to choose you."

"Dorian. You don't know me," I whispered.

"I have gifts, and one of them is knowing things." He pulled out a white mask with intricate diamonds and aquamarine gems from his jacket. The mask was probably worth a fortune—more money than my family had ever seen or owned. "Wear this tonight. It will bring you luck."

He handed me the jeweled mask and raised my hand to place a gentle kiss on the back. Unlike our earlier chaste kiss, the feel of his lips brushing my skin made me shiver.

"Until I can kiss you for real."

"It will never happen."

"Remember, I know things."

"Apparently not, since you don't even know my name."

"And I will enjoy the quest to find out." He walked back to the carriage and tapped on the roof for the driver. He waved at me before he rode away.

When he was out of sight. I picked up my skirt, grabbed the shovel, and raced behind the church to the cemetery.

Once there, I moved among the headstones and monoliths, searching. There were many religious denominations in Candor, but the fae were not buried in the church yards. They were considered heathen and buried in a separate cemetery, one that could only be seen by moonlight if you followed the toadstools.

The sun was setting, and the lamplighters were taking to the street to light the lamps. In my town of Nihill, the lamps were lit with candles, but in Candor they used hobby lanterns and trapped will-o'-the-wisps within. Their green hue floated around inside, blinking in and out, giving the illusion of candlelight.

It was hard to feel sorry for the ghostly creatures, for if not captured they would very well lead a lost child into a bog to their doom.

The first moon rays passed over my hand, and I searched the ground for the elusive toadstools, walking the edges of the graveyard until I came to a break in the trees. There I found the path and followed it until I came to a mound of glittery rocks, signifying the place my mother told me to dig.

"By the stars and light, please forgive me for what I am about to do."

I held out my hand and uttered, *"Terra Fodiunturi."*

The earth shifted and groaned, moving as if a sleeping giant underneath turned over, then settled again. Disturbing the fae was not part of my plan. But if I was going to help get past the truth seer, I needed more power, and what was more powerful than an item worn by fae?

"Terra Fodiunturi." I tried a second time, and this time the earth gave forth a giant fart as if taunting me and my lack of spell ability.

"Oh, that's it," I snapped, holding the iron shovel above my head. "I'll just have to do this the old-fashioned way." With all of my might, I shoved the iron shovel into the ground and muttered the spell a third time using the iron to cut through the fae magic. Mother would be proud.

The shovel pierced through the top layer of white stone and earth, and after a few more shovelfuls, I hit something solid and felt a current run through my fingers as the magic fought against the iron weapon. Kneeling, I brushed away the dirt and saw a golden box. Not a coffin or sarcophagus, because fae became earth when they died. They had no reason to bury the dead, but sometimes they buried a prized possession.

Taking out my piece of chalk, I drew a symbol on the box. *"Resignio"*

The box began to glow, and I heard the sound of clicks. Like a puzzle box, it shifted and moved compartments, opening and unraveling until it revealed a beautiful pair of glass slippers.

"Thank you. I will return these to you when I am done."

Dirty, dripping with sweat, I stumbled out of the fairy circle and back into the cemetery. I weaved a glamour, making me into an old woman version of myself.

I was nervous and tried to keep the eagerness out of my eyes. It was time to meet with Tess. I was thrilled that I was helping her get on equal footing with her sister. My hands were shaking with excitement as I sat on a short stone wall and waited.

A shadow slipped through the cemetery gate, and I jumped down and hid behind a tall monolith.

"Hello?" Tess's scared voice carried through the night. "Miss fairy of the night? I've brought you an offering."

I used a bit of glamour to make my appearance brighter in the dark as I stepped out from behind the monolith. I put a hint of otherworldly echo into my voice.

"Hello, my child." I eyed the bag of food she had brought and tried to keep my stomach under control. I hadn't asked for an offering but was now rethinking any future deals I made to include it in the contract. She laid out a fresh loaf of bread, cheese, and hard salami. Ugh, I hated salami, but it would have to do. I tried to keep the disappointment from my voice. "Er, yes, that is good." I spun in a circle and tried to show off the sparkly dress I wore. "What is it that you wish this night?"

"I wish to attend the masked ball."

"Is that it?" Disappointment leaked from my voice. She didn't ask for a dress, for shoes, or even for the prince to fall in love with her. She just wanted to attend. How boring was that?

"Well, small wishes only gain small rewards," I snapped, my hands on my hips. I was tapping my foot in displeasure. "Come back when you dream bigger."

"No, wait, please I'm sorry." She flung herself onto the ground, her knees digging into the mud. "I want to outdo my sister. I want to ruin her big night by stealing her thunder. I wish... I wish to make it past the first night selection." Her blue eyes looked up, and I saw all of the anger and hurt hidden inside. The years of mistreatment by an older, more calculating sister. I knew that feeling all too well as I thought of my own more beautiful sisters.

"Now that is a true wish."

Tess dug her fingers into the ground. "It's all I've ever dreamed of, showing her that I can be more than the dumb servant and thief. I can play the part of the lady as well. She thinks we can continue the con until she entraps a gentleman in marriage. But then she wants me to still attend her in the house. I can't. I can't play the part of a servant anymore."

"Yes," I whispered excitedly. "Yes. You will have your revenge. I will help you."

"Tell me what must I do."

"Did you bring me the items I asked for? Items that have special meaning to you."

Tess nodded and took the satchel off her shoulder and handed me the bag.

I tried to hide the frustration from my face. How was I supposed to get this girl to the masquerade ball with this junk? I dug around in the items she had brought and noticed how worn but loved they were. A book, braided string, a gold-and-purple-striped ribbon, a worn pair of silk slippers, flower seeds, and a squash. What was I going to do with a squash?

"I hope you're not expecting me to turn that into a coach?" I said, turning my nose up at the yellow vegetable.

"I don't know what you're capable of. I had heard tales of godmothers."

"No!" I cut her off right there. "There are no such things as godmothers. Just get over here and stand still," I huffed and took a look at what she was wearing. I asked her to come in her nicest dress, and she was wearing the same outfit that I met her in—a ratty dress that had seen better days. "Is this really the best you have?"

"It is." She shrugged. "Anything of value, my sister takes."

I stared long and hard at the items she was currently wearing and the pieces that she had brought me in her bag.

"Okay, what I'm about to do is give you an enchanted dress. But it only works if I tie it to a physical object that you are wearing or holding."

The striped ribbon would do well. I drew another sigil over the piece and held it out to her. "Put it on."

Tess took the ribbon and tied it around her neck. When she did, her clothes began to change. An A-line ball gown of shimmering purple silk fell around her waist. She gasped and did a little dance of excitement.

I untied the ribbon and pulled it from around her neck, and the glamour dropped. I felt the pressure lesson. This was going to be tricky. To hold a glamour over a poor girl for a few days would physically drain me. But if it meant getting revenge on the older sister, then it was worth it.

I enchanted the braided string next. This time when she tied it around her neck, a lovely string of pearls appeared and her dress became a soft baby blue. I spent the most time creating the perfect glamour to connect to her satin slippers. They produced a white tulle ball gown. I took the flower seed and blew them over her dress. Where each one landed, it turned into a delicate diamond. That should get the prince's attention. It screamed heiress.

"This is the loveliest dress I have ever seen. It even feels real. How do you do it? Can you teach me this magic? If you did, I wouldn't have to steal anymore. I could just create what I want," Tess begged.

"You're too old to be trained," I said stiffly. It took years, twelve to be exact, to learn the level of magic it took to be good at glamour.

"Too bad it's not real."

"It will hold up to touch and smell and will be real. But should anything happen to me or you betray me, it is gone."

I turned my back on her so she couldn't see what I was doing and pulled out my invitation and studied it carefully. I tore a page from the very back of the book she brought, cringing while doing it. It was painful to destroy a book. I glamoured the page to be the mirror image of my own invitation.

"Full name?" I asked.

She blinked and glanced down.

"Tesselyn, daughter of...." She trailed off and fidgeted with her hands. "See, I wasn't born in Candor. I traveled all my life with a show. I don't have a family other than the members of my troupe."

I chewed on my inner cheek in thought. "You will be the daughter of Duchovny for tonight," I said remembering the name of the daughter that was too young to attend. I added the name on her invitation, and she brightened. "Here is your own invitation. Don't lose it."

Tess took the invitation with trembling hands. "Oh, thank you. How can I ever repay you?"

"Just shine. For you are not meant to live in the shadows of others."

Tess's eyes filled with tears. She blinked, and they ran down her cheek. "Oh, thank you, godmother." She gave me a hug, and I had to remember to not roll my eyes at being called godmother. I patted her back awkwardly.

A bat flew by, and I waved my hand. The animal squeaked in protest before landing on the ground in front of me. It was white, an albino bat.

"Lend me your wings, dear friend," I whispered, waving my hand over it. The bat grew in size, its arms flapping as it shifted until it was the size of the mountain bears of Hillock.

A button served as a seat that was large enough for two people upon it.

"C'mon, Tess." I gestured to the bat. "We mustn't be late."

"Is it safe to be near?" She was now hiding behind a tombstone.

"Of course, it's safe. He wouldn't dare harm us. I'm in complete control of him." To show her that he was indeed gentle, I lifted my skirt and stepped up to sit on the button bench seat. I opened the bag and broke off a piece of the bread and began to eat while I waited for her. My stomach's rumbling subsided.

Tess stepped from behind her hiding place, but she still wouldn't approach the bat. My patience was wearing thin; I had little time for her dalliance and fears.

"We haven't got all night," I snapped, waving my hand that held the chunk of cheese. Using magic, I lifted her into the air and plopped her down on the seat next to me.

It was showy and a bit reckless of me to try and control so much. But I knew that as long as I wasn't distracted, I could hold this charade for a long time.

"Let's go," I commanded the albino bat. I waved my hand to give it a gust of air under his wings to help lift him into the night. Air whipped past our faces, and I gripped the side of the bench, leaving nail impressions as we bobbed up and down with each wing beat.

Tess's face was clenched in terror as she hung on to my arm for dear life. Next time, I would remember to place a rope across our laps so we wouldn't fall out of the seat. I was too focused on creating a memorable entrance to the palace that I may have let the thought of safety slide. Up and down. Up and down we bobbed, and my stomach began to feel queasy.

I released my hold on the loaf of bread and wedge of cheese, letting them fall to the ground. Tess had gone green and was no longer hanging onto my arm but hanging her head over the side.

Thankfully, I could see the palace as we circled above and came around to the front. The palace was lit from below by spot lanterns, and colored lights danced across the stone walls. The king had really gone all out to impress the women of the city.

"Where's it going?" Tess asked as the bat veered away from the entrance and head toward the large towering tree.

"Oh no," I gasped as the bat began to reach out with its legs to grasp onto the branch. "He's landing. Hold on!" The bat flapped its wings, and we fell backward toward the ground as he landed upside down.

"Aaah!" Tess screamed as she lost her grip on the bench and slid out of the seat. I flung my arm across Tess and slowed our descent till our feet touched the ground, landing completely unharmed.

"Did you know it was going to do that?" She pointed up at

the now dozing bat as it hung upside down, its large arms wrapped around his body.

I tried to lift my head and pretend that nothing out of the ordinary had happened and that I was still in control, but that last burst of power really took its toll on me.

"I suspected as much." I wiped my palms over my dress and motioned for her to follow me. "Carry on, we can't dally."

Approaching the palace at night was a completely different experience than during the day. The steps were covered with a runner. Enchanted lights and lanterns spun, creating a rainbow of colors, and even the outdoor fountain's water was turned to gold.

"Oh, and one more thing." I stopped and gave her the mask that Dorian had given me. I did not need luck. If anyone needed luck, it would be Tess.

She squealed and put on the mask. It only added to her beauty, and since we were similar in height and size, I could see how it would have looked on me. The mask really was the most beautiful mask I had ever seen. I watched from the tree line as Tess lifted her skirts and headed toward the entrance.

It was now my turn. I waved my hand over my dress and turned it into a stunning deep blue. But it needed something else. I mirrored the night sky by bringing the light of the constellations into my dress. When I moved, the stars on my dress shimmered like magic. My hair was curled and pinned up with a few loose curls that fell over my shoulder. My mask was blue with gold lines that represented the constellation Cinder; an elf queen of old. I slid the fae glass shoes on my feet and grimaced. They were cold and a half size too big. I would be lucky if I could keep them on. But I needed extra protection tonight, and my mother said I needed to get the shoes. Now that I had them on, what were the rest of her instructions? Get the guy, get revenge.

I heard the sound of a lone beetle chirping in the night, and I had a deliciously devious idea. I found him on a hosta and charmed him into a sapphire hairpin and tucked him into my hair and smiled. He would come in handy later. One of the very first charms we learned was how to bug the other sisters' room by enchanting insects to spy for us.

Holding my head high and with purpose, I walked down the path to the palace, through the gates, and lined up to enter the manor.

Each guard wore the same white mask with a long nose. I couldn't help but feel pride in my appearance as quite a few heads turned to watch me ascend the steps. Any male escorts were turned away at the door as each of the ladies passed through a security checkpoint that consisted of the guards and a blind faun. A fae with the torso and head of a man and lower legs of a goat.

A woman in pale pink tulle stepped passed, and the faun leaned forward, his blind eyes unseeing, and he took a sniff.

"Human," he said.

The faun was the truth seer. They could see through glamour, but if he was blind then that meant he was smelling for the magic in our blood.

The next girl in line stepped forward, her hands trembled as she waited to pass through the doors. I stepped out of line and watched as girl after girl went through the security. I could see Tess's dress farther down and already into the hall, and I let out a sigh of relief. Glamour magic affected the eyes of the beholder, so the blind faun wouldn't have known. He may have smelled a hint of glamour, which had different smells depending on the caster. According to my sisters, my glamour smelled like spun sugar. So nothing to raise alarm with the faun. Plus, he would only see her dress had changed. Nothing to worry the palace guard over. But if he is relying on smell alone, he may be able to smell the magic in my blood. That would be hard to hide and I had to pray that the shoes would mask my scent.

An elegant woman in a dark plum dress with pale skin slowed before the truth seer. I could see her aura from where I stood. Darkness clouded her thoughts, and black and purple magic emanated from her. A sorceress like me.

"Invitation," the guard demanded, and I looked up at the tall man who was studying each of the women very carefully.

The woman in the purple dress handed him the invitation, and he read the name aloud. "Miss Bellamy Borstein."

"Witch!" The faun's nose crinkled, and the guards rushed forward and grabbed the woman by the upper arms.

"No! I'm not," Bellamy cried out and began to struggle.

"The king has made his wishes clear. No sorcerer or fae shall enter the palace or be punished," the guard ordered.

"Someone, help me!" Bellamy cried out as the guards began to drag her away.

None of the ladies moved. I looked away, unable to make eye contact.

When no aid came, Bellamy's attitude changed. "Very well," she snarled. "I will just help myself." Her eyes turned dark, and she began to glow. I felt the static electricity build, and my skin prickled as her magic amassed and her darkness spilled forth.

I heard the crack of thunder as two bolts of lightning struck the guards holding Bellamy. They fell down, their bodies burned, the woman unharmed. Bellamy raised her hands above her head and bellowed, "The king and his vile offspring must be killed. Only then can the fae be free from his tyranny."

More guards came rushing forward, and I knew they would end up like the others if I didn't do something. But what could I do? Bellamy was powerful, more powerful than me, and if I challenged her to a duel, I would most definitely lose and end up imprisoned or dead.

My mouth fumbled as I tried to remember the spells to bind her hands, but I couldn't remember the right words. *Capistro? Capistero?*

Bellamy was making a huge spectacle. Calling down the wind, storms, and lightning with a finger and wreaking havoc. She sent a bolt of lightning to the north window, and the beautiful stained-glass window shattered. She sent a wayward bolt of lightning toward a coach, and it erupted into flames. The driver jumped from the seat and frantically began to untie the horses.

It was chaos. The women waiting outside ran for cover, and I just stood there and watched.

Bellamy cackled.

Oh, I hated when witches cackled. It always gave the wrong impression. That we were maniacal and unhinged. I took a few steps forward, standing right next to the faun and his guard. The faun's nose twitched, and his knobby knees shook in fear.

An errant bolt of lightning shot out toward them. With a wave of my hand, I blocked it and sent it flying above us into the balustrade. The stone began to crack, and I looked up and frowned as it began to topple over.

"Uh-oh!" Why didn't I pay more attention to my surroundings? "Watch out!" I cried and pushed the guard and the faun back just as the balcony came crashing down. The faun fell to the ground and the guard went through the open doorway. I knelt by the faun and saw that he hadn't escaped completely unscathed. There was a cut on his forehead. "You are okay. I got you," I soothed.

His soft fur-covered hand grabbed mine. "Stop her," he whispered to me.

"I can't," I whispered back. His guard reappeared with more troops, and I saw that they had chains with symbols etched into them. I had seen ones like those before. They had been used on my sister to bind her powers.

"I know who you are. You must. You're the only one who can." The faun squeezed my hands.

"I told you. I can't. I'll just mess up like I always do."

Bellamy's cackling became louder, and my jaw clenched in annoyance.

"Your greatest weakness is that you don't believe in yourself," he said.

"That's because I *am* weak."

"She would never have chosen you if you were weak."

"Who?" I said, but knew he had referred to my mother.

"Will no one challenge me?" Bellamy cackled. "Oh, King Ferdinand. Come out, come out. I have come to fulfill the prophecy."

I groaned and bunched my fingers in my dress while simultaneously trying to think of a way out of this. I reached into my drawstring pouch through my glamour and felt the button I stole from Derek. I ducked behind a column, clenched the button between my teeth and felt the change take over. Running passed the guards, I grabbed the chains from one of them. They looked perplexed as I stumbled into the road to confront Bellamy.

"You, a lonely palace guard? What will you do?"

Closing my eyes, I concentrated on weaving a glamour of a large army around her. Over and over, I created a guard and another, most of their faces blurred by magic because I couldn't concentrate on getting hundreds of face details right. The only thing that mattered was confusing her. The glamour was for her eyes only. No one else saw the show I put on. Screaming, she used lighting to strike at each of my glamours. I could only imagine what everyone else saw. One lone soldier, walking around the witch as she struck out blindly. Hitting nothing.

I kept my head low as a streak of lightning brushed past my cheek. The air crackled and the hair on my skin rose, so I knew it was a close shot. She turned toward someone who caught her eye.

A young girl ran for cover behind an angel statue, just a few feet to my right, making her a target of Bellamy's rage. I ran to the girl and knocked her out of the way as Bellamy blew the statue to smithereens.

"Run!" I yelled, pushing the girl into action.

Waving my hands in front of me, I crowded Bellamy with more guards, but not pressing down on her, leaving just enough distance to keep her on her toes.

I blurred my own image, making myself fade into the background. Sneaking up on her, I tapped her on the shoulder. I pictured the spell clearly in my mind and held on to it. I was not afraid. I couldn't be afraid.

She turned in surprise, and I touched her forehead. "*Somnus,*" I whispered. She fell to her knees and then plopped to the ground in a deep sleep. "I did it!" I whispered as I tried to contain my excitement over the successful completion of a sleeping spell. Reappearing amongst a group of bystanders, I rushed forward and leaned down with the manacles.

Cheers erupted as I clamped the manacles on Bellamy and waved over one of the guards to help. They came reluctantly to my aid. As more guards surrounded Bellamy, I noticed a familiar face come as well. Derek! Using more glamour, I created a mystifying haze, making it impossible to look straight at me, as I spit the button out of my mouth and joined the frightened ladies that had gathered together in a huddle for protection.

"Did you see that guard?" the woman with copper hair in a yellow silk dress asked. "He saved my life!"

It took over a candle mark for the chaos to calm back down, and they began to let the women back into the ball. I secretly hoped that they would cancel the whole ordeal after what happened. Then I could go home and try again later. But that wasn't about to happen. More guards came and surrounded the entrance, and I shifted my weight from foot to foot in my glass slippers nervously.

The faun knew who I was, knew what had happened. There was no way he was going to let me through.

It was time. I was next. I stepped in front of the faun, closed my eyes, and waited for the word witch to come from his mouth. This was it. I wouldn't get farther than the front door, but at least I could tell my mother I tried.

"Invitation," a familiar voice declared.

I looked up and almost fainted. Derek had replaced the first guard. He was staring at me carefully, his brow furrowed in thought.

Grateful that I still had my handbag, I retrieved my invitation and held it out to Derek who looked it over carefully, probably trying to determine if it was forged.

"Eden De Ella."

"Hmm, yes?" I looked up as he said my name—a name I

was unfamiliar with. When I asked my mother, she had said, "It's an old family acquaintance."

After a few seconds, when Derek didn't wave me through, my stomach dropped in trepidation. He knew.

"This might be her," a voice spoke from the shadows.

My head snapped up in surprise when I saw the transport driver in an ill-fitting suit. He looked uncomfortable. Sweat dripped from his greasy hair that had been hastily combed over.

I held still as he leaned over and gave me a cursory glance. He blinked a few times and squinted but then shook his head. "Hard to tell with the mask on."

"Would you remove your mask?" Derek asked.

My fingers trembled slightly as I slowly untied the mask and focused putting the slightest glamour over my face. There was nothing I could do for the color of my hair, but I could adjust everything under my mask. I widened my pert nose, and added a distinct beauty mark under my left eye. I gave the transport driver a confused and blank look when the mask came down.

"Naw, that's not her." He shuffled back into the shadows and waited.

The guard looked me over carefully, then turned to the faun. The faun's face looked confused. He had probably sensed my magic. "Verik? What is your opinion?"

Verik, the faun struggled, his hands waving before me as he reached out to grasp my hands. I couldn't help but see that nasty cut on his forehead. It needed to be bandaged and not to be left open and bleeding while he worked. Seconds ago, I was afraid, but now I was angry at his mistreatment. I wanted to ease his pain.

I reached out for him, touching the soft downy fur that

lined his hands. "Here, I am right here." Warmth spread through my body into his. He gasped and took a step backward, but he did not release my grip. His eyes were closed, and I could see tears pool in the corner. The wound stopped bleeding, and the cut healed before my eyes, but the blood still lingered, masking to the world that I had healed him.

"Ah!" he whispered. "It's you." When he opened his eyes, I could see they were no longer covered with a milky white film but were a startling hazel. Those eyes met mine, and he knew—knew I wasn't just a human girl, that I was the one who had fought the witch and healed him from being blind.

I sucked in my breath and waited. Waited for him to call the guards and have me taken away and imprisoned.

His lips pulled back. My knees trembled beneath the gown as I waited for judgement to pass. He smiled softly, a twinkle in his eyes.

"Human," he whispered.

"What?" Derek and I muttered at the same time.

"Human," Verik said again. This time as an order, he commanded, "Let her pass."

I didn't understand what had happened, other than I had earned the respect of the truth seer. His head gave the slightest bow and tilted toward the doors. I replaced my mask and removed the glamour over my face.

Picking up my gown so I wouldn't step on it, I strolled through the doors to the main foyer and paused in awe. Two staircases wound up either side of the room to the floors above, and below the staircases was another set of gold double doors leading down into a ballroom. From the main hall I could hear the symphony of musicians and their instruments—a harpsichord, flute, viola. The floor, a white-and-black-checkered marble, had an intricate blue runner down the steps, and it was there I almost lost my nerve, but I put one foot in front of the other and followed the crowd into the ballroom.

My breath caught as I surveyed the hundreds of beautiful gowns of taffeta, silk, and organza that paraded in front of me, swirling in a kaleidoscope of color.

The servants, dressed in white with matching domino masks, were walking around with silver trays, offering refreshments. The prince's guards stood on the outer walls in their pressed black uniforms and white long-nosed masks called zannis. Scanning the crowd of sequins and pearls, I didn't see the prince, and by the murmur of the women in front of me, I dare say he hadn't yet made an appearance.

The queen was sitting on the throne alone, King Ferdinand absent and probably dealing with the witch they had taken captive. The queen seemed bored and was whispering to a servant, gesturing using her fan to single out and point at ladies in the ballroom.

I was surprised to recognize Nessa in a pale orange with a monarch butterfly mask, laughing shrilly and running her fingers over her own necklace, drawing attention to the stolen wealth. She picked up and pocketed a gilded fan a lady put down when she took a drink.

Keeping Nessa in my line of sight, I took a lap around the ballroom, being careful to watch the servants and guards.

I reached up to pull out the enchanted beetle. Whispering a word, I lifted it up into the air, and my spy took flight, looking for important gossip. I could hear the buzzing of the beetle's wings until it landed on the shoulder of a young woman wearing a zebra mask.

"Why would he stand us up?" the zebra woman argued irritably. "You would think, if he called a ball, that he would at least attend it."

"They're taking extra precautions because of the witch that was captured outside. I'm surprised that the queen is in the room still," her companion in a gold tiger mask spoke up.

"No, I bet he's just waiting until we are all here so he can make a grand entrance."

They were useless. Servants continued to offer drinks to the ladies, and I could pick up scattered bits of conversation, but under it all, there was still a bit of fear.

"Do you think the prince will actually choose a bride?"

"My feet hurt," one whined.

"I can't breathe in this dress," another muttered.

"There's no one here on the same level as us."

Shallow. All of the conversations I picked up were self-centered and shallow, very befitting to the age and caste of the women who were here. It was easy to see a group of girls gather together in a corner seeking shelter. Their dresses were not as fine, their jewelry not as polished. They were probably the farmers' and milliners' daughters, those belonging to the lower caste. It was easier for them to group together. If they milled among the dresses way finer than theirs, they would look like a drab flower. They had better hope of outshining each other.

Thinking back to what the king had said about money, I slowly walked over to the ladies and brushed my hand gently across their dresses. The cheap fabric turned into silk. Tulle skirts filled out, and hundreds of gems and pearls appeared across their fabric. The homemade paper masks glittered with diamonds, and the girls shone with an inward beauty that demanded attention.

They wouldn't notice the glamour, but others would. I smiled as my devious plot thwarted the king's plan. Who knew, maybe one of them would win over the prince.

A page came forward and stood near the throne. The music ceased, and he loudly cleared his throat. "Ladies, Prince Evander has been delayed but will arrive shortly. So that you do not stand by idly, he has provided you with dance partners and music. The page clapped his hands, and the guards who were standing at attention on the sides stepped from their posts and entered the dance floor, each bowing before a woman. I was thrilled to see that the girls in dresses I glamoured were some of the first to hit the floor.

Astonishingly enough, there were the exact number of guards as there were ladies waiting for a partner. One made his way toward me, and I ducked behind a stone column. I had no interest in having any man's hands on me, no matter how chaste a dance may be.

Thankfully, the guard took the hint and left me alone as I listened to more gossip.

"And then he pushed me out of the way of the witch and saved my life. It was so dramatic." The copper-haired girl was relaying her adventure to one of the guards. "You don't happen to know his name, do you?"

I held back my grin at her lack of subtlety.

When the waltz came to a halt, the guards switched partners, each of them rotating to the next available lady.

There were a few more dances, and it seemed that with each dance there were more and more guards standing on the sidelines. Where had they come from?

A guard with dark hair made his way to me, and I moved away, stepping closer to the thrones, hoping that I would hear some gossip. But my stupid beetle landed by an open window where a group of ladies were using their fans to cool themselves.

"I find this unacceptable," a woman snarled irritably. "If I get chosen as his queen, I will make sure that this will never happen at a ball in the future."

Her voice was low, and it hadn't carried far, but a guard heard it and came forward and gently took her by the elbow, whispering softly into her ear. Her face paled and her hand went to her mouth. The two of them left the room, and a few moments later, the same guard returned without the woman.

Another guard guided a lady in an elaborate orchid-colored dress off the dance floor and into a side room, only to return a few minutes later alone.

They were thinning the crowd. They must be under certain orders to immediately reject a woman based on a certain criterion. My pulse started to race, and I became angry when I knew what that criteria was—money and probably personality.

By now I didn't know if I necessarily hid my true intentions, for I was glowering behind my mask.

"I take it you're not one for dancing." A tall guard appeared near my elbow. He was leaning with his arms crossed against the same column that I had ducked behind earlier. "I haven't seen you dance all night."

"You've been watching me?" I asked, surprised. Turning, I studied the guard, seeing his blue-gray eyes peeking at me through the long-nosed mask. I saw the stubble along his chin and instantly recognized him beneath the mask

Dorian.

"Did you not like the mask I gave you?" he asked. "I have to say, it caused quite a bit of confusion when I approached the woman wearing it to find out it wasn't you."

I pinched my lips to keep from laughing as I imagined him going up and teasing Tess. Did he pull her onto the dance floor, try and seduce her with words? We were similar in height, and our hair close in color. How long was he with her before he realized it wasn't me?

"Can you believe it, when I asked her where she got such a beautiful mask, she told me her fairy godmother."

I rolled my eyes. "I told her there are no such things."

"So, you did give it away. I'm a bit hurt, sparrow."

"Now that I know it was your way of keeping tabs on me, I'm glad I parted with it. For I don't want you following me around, and for that matter, why are you here?"

"I'm here because I have orders to be," he said softly as he rocked back and forth on his heels.

"I bet," I snapped.

"It's true. I'm invaluable to the king. I provide him information."

"You mean secrets."

"Yes, I keep tabs on certain people for him, and he pays me very well."

"You're a spy?"

"Of sorts."

"And tonight you are spying for the king?" I became uncomfortable. What if he figured out who I was and told the king? Dorian seemed extremely persistent, and I had no doubt he would eventually find out who I am.

"Yes."

I fell silent. We stayed like that for a whole dance. Then Dorian gestured to the dance floor. "Would you like to dance?"

"No."

"Let me guess. You can't dance?"

"I'll have you know that I dance just fine. It's the company I reject," I said irritably and moved away from him as I focused on more hints of conversation from the servant closest to me.

"The prince is not in his room," a servant whispered to another. "I checked on my way down."

"I wonder where he has gone to?" a male attendant muttered.

Dorian did not give up easily, and he came up behind me again. "By the way, I'm glad you're okay," he whispered over my shoulder.

"Why wouldn't I be?"

"I heard about the skirmish outside. It could have been a lot worse."

"You did?" My voice cracked, and I tucked my fidgeting hands into the folds of my skirt as I wondered *how much* he heard.

"I was worried that you were one of the ladies caught in the crossfire. A few were injured by flying debris; others left, too scared to even enter the palace. As I told you before, sparrow, this is a dangerous place and you don't belong here."

"My name is not 'sparrow,' and that is not for you to decide."

"Actually, it is. I can snap my fingers and have you escorted out." Dorian gripped my elbow and began to pull me toward the hall.

"Why do you dislike me so?"

"Dislike?" His lips turned down, and his grip tightened painfully. "I don't dislike you."

"Well, I dislike you," I snapped, letting my anger get the best of me. I dug my fingernails into his arm. "Release me."

Dorian grunted in pain and let go of my arm.

I turned to run away but almost bowled over another guard who was standing behind me.

"Sorry," I muttered as he caught me, saving me from taking a hard tumble to the floor.

"One as beautiful as yourself, I would be a fool not to catch you." The masked guard flashed me a charming smile.

Dorian glowered at me. Now that I was here, I wanted to stay—if only to annoy Dorian, who wanted me gone.

"Dance with me," I begged, hoping to find safety within this new guard's arms. I was happy as long as I was nowhere near Dorian.

The masked guard obliged. He grabbed me around the waist and spun me into the middle of the dance floor. I was unprepared for the spinning, and I let out a surprised sound that sounded like a bark, which set the man into full-throated laughter. At first, I clung to his shoulder and arm, scared that the spinning would continue until I passed out, but he expertly maneuvered us into the middle of the floor.

"What do you think of this?" He gestured with our hands to the room full of people.

"I find it exhausting," I answered truthfully.

"Really? Of all answers I expected tonight, that wasn't one of them."

"Then I will ask you the same question. What do you think of all this?"

I waited as he pondered the question. "You're right. It *is* exhausting."

"Yes, many women dressed in their very best to try and impress a prince they've never met, hoping to fall in love within seconds and live happily ever after. It's ridiculous."

My partner missed a step and spun me around. A mixture of swirling colors filled my vision, and then I was brought back and crushed against his uniform, and the long, white nose was back in my face.

"Then why come?" His voice was harsh, firm. I had upset him. "Why waste your time here if you don't believe in any of this? Or is there a different reason for you to be here?"

I was proud when the word "revenge" wasn't the first thing to leave my lips. I took a breath. "Because I don't want to let my mother down."

His mouth turned down in an unsightly sneer. "Let me guess, she's a gold digger, forcing you to come in hopes of you marrying the prince."

I gestured to the room full of prospective brides. "One man, hundreds of ladies, and whoever isn't chosen will leave brokenhearted. The odds are not in my favor. So why is it, if I chose to protect my fragile heart and come to a ball. I am a gold digger? Have you ever done anything that your heart wasn't in, just because you didn't want to disappoint a parent? A mother maybe?"

He took a deep breath, his mask dipping toward the floor. "Yes."

"Well, I'm adopted. I'm wearing shoes that don't even belong to me and truthfully give me blisters." I shifted my weight on my feet to prove how uncomfortable I was. He snorted. "I'm the least talented of my sisters and can't for the life of me figure out why my mother would send me here when there isn't anything special about me."

"I can." Was that a smile that formed under the white mask? I wasn't going to believe it. "Forgive me, for I may have misjudged you."

I waved my hand at him dismissively. "Everyone does. I'm used to it."

He grabbed my hand out of the air and held it. "It shouldn't be that way."

"No, it shouldn't. But it is. Even now we are being judged." I nodded to the king who had finally joined his wife on the dais and sat on his throne. I remembered what he had said about picking women based on their wealth. "I bet they are already selecting their future daughter-in-law, based on—" I paused for effect. "—the size of her family fortune."

The man laughed. "And how extravagant their dresses."

"Or shoes," I added.

The man choked and began to cough as I tossed back Prince Evander's joke to his face. I lost sight of Dorian for a second, but saw his tall form leading a woman out of the room. Seconds later, he returned, and I could feel the heat of his gaze on me. He was just waiting for his chance to kick me out.

I ground my teeth together in anger.

The prince didn't need to be here, because Dorian and the guards, were already doing the work of selecting his next wife. It was sickening. My stomach dropped, and I wanted to yell, stomp my feet, and scream. This was wrong!

I remembered Mother Eville telling us she had once been engaged to the prince of Sion, but that when her family lost her money, he broke off the engagement. Her father had approached the other princes to see if they would marry her, and they laughed because she had no dowry. It was only when they saw her and her beauty did they realize they were a fool. Even King Ferdinand had proposed to her, but she turned him down. The choices the kingdoms made over the years were not good—or kind. She watched as they fell into greed and darkness and fought against each other, making deals to claw their way to the top.

Brokenhearted, Lorelai perfected her craft and raised us to be the tools of justice. I watched as the king shook his head and pointed to a girl, and one of the guards escorted her out of the room. Queen Giselle, sitting next to him, pointed to a particularly beautiful gown and nodded in affirmation.

It was a glorified beauty pageant, and I knew I was no great beauty, if not for my glamour. What was I supposed to do here? How was I going to get revenge for my family? Rosalie probably would have cursed them with the pox. Maeve would have probably set fire to the whole palace and burned it to the ground. Meri would have sung and flooded the whole room with water.

I was here and not sure what to do. I could make people's dresses sparkle. I was left with an empty feeling and a question that I didn't have the answer to.

As soon as the dance was over, the guard stepped back. I saw Dorian move briskly toward me. He was going to escort me out in front of this kind guard and embarrass me.

"I need to leave," I said abruptly, depression creeping up on me like a hungry beast, which meant I was about to lose control of my emotions and, therefore, the glamour. In a few minutes, I would be standing in the middle of the room wearing my simple brown dress and glass shoes.

"But you haven't met the prince yet," the guard stated.

"It doesn't matter. I... don't matter." My self-confidence lowered with each step I took toward the open doors that led outside.

CHAPTER NINE

As soon as I stepped out onto the patio and the night air brushed against my skin, I felt calm and could breathe easier. I descended the stairs and stepped into the lower gardens, finding myself surrounded by tall hedgerows. When I followed the footpath further, I discovered a wooden bridge that crossed over a stream. The stream was filled with colorful paper lanterns. I stopped on the bridge and watched as the lit lanterns floated under me. Every twenty paces or so was a stone gazebo with benches. The one closest to me had a string quartet that played music as other guests, like me, sought solace among the gardens.

Once I was able to calm down and get my emotions regulated, I felt my control on my glamour strengthen. I could feel a slight strain on the back of my mind from controlling Tess's glamour from a distance, but I wasn't worried.

One of the paper lanterns became ensnared in some rushes by the edge of the bridge, but I couldn't reach it from the grassy edge. I found a dried reed from the riverbed and went back up on the bridge and leaned over, trying to knock it loose. It was the challenge of doing it that kept me leaning forward on my tiptoes. Then I felt myself falling over the railing.

"Whoa!" I yelped, but strong hands grasped my waist from behind and kept me from falling.

"Careful now!" the voice warned, as he pulled me backward, my stocking feet touching the wood bridge.

"Thank you, I—" I turned around and looked into the amused eyes of the masked guard from ballroom. His hands were still on my waist, and he was looking at me closely.

"Look what I fished out of the stream," he said.

I blushed and looked down as my dress was in a bit of disarray. I tried to smooth out the wrinkles.

"Well, are you going to throw me back or keep me?" I challenged.

He looked at me silently and didn't move.

My face burned with embarrassment at my forwardness. I tucked a stray curl behind my ear and tried to move away, but he stopped me. "Wait." Very carefully, he reached up to untie his mask.

I didn't want to believe it, but I knew. Sometime during our dance, during our conversation, I figured it out. But it was still surprising to know I was right. That it wasn't a guard at all but Prince Evander pretending to be the guard.

"I'd like to keep you," he said. His amber eyes searched my face, and I felt my breath catch in my throat.

My hand reached up to cover my mouth in surprise.

"Why are you hiding out here," Prince Evander asked, "when the ball is inside?"

"Why, isn't it obvious?" I teased, thinking back to when the prince had gone swimming in the same stream farther downhill. "I decided to go for a swim." Keeping my face serious, I turned and beckoned to the stream.

He looked at me like I was a fae that had sprouted three heads, and I desperately wanted to take back the words I had spoken. I shouldn't have been so informal with him. I closed my eyes, and then heard it.

A deep chuckle. "What an odd girl you are." Evander couldn't contain his amusement.

The simple statement crushed me, for I had heard it many times before.

Odd.

Weird.

Different.

None of them were said in a positive tone, much less by royalty, and this time it hurt even worse. The smile fell from my lips, and he saw.

"No, wait. I followed you out here for a reason."

"What reason is that?" I asked.

"To tell you, you were right. Most of the women in there will go home tonight, sight unseen. And of those remaining, one of them will be my future wife."

"Why the charade?" I asked. "Why pretend to be a guard?"

"Why not? Tonight, everyone is pretending to be someone else. I thought it would be fun to get to know a few of the ladies without letting them know I'm—"

"A prince," I finished.

He grinned, and I couldn't help but smile back. "It was quite eye-opening, hearing what they said about me or to my guards when I was just an ordinary man behind a mask. It made it quite easy to send most of them home."

Our conversation came back at me like a whirlwind, and I quickly replayed all of my snarking comments and words. I was not polite, quite blunt, and not at all charming. He came to send me home.

"I have made up my mind, and I would like to—"

"I understand," I interrupted him before he could ask me to go. "You don't have time for someone that isn't here for the right reasons." I sighed. It was foolish of me to tell him I was only here to appease my mother.

"What?" Evander said. "No, I want you to stay."

Never in my wildest imagination would he have asked me to stay. "Stay? Why?"

He looked completely perplexed by my confusion. "I just asked to keep you. You were listening to our earlier conversations, right? This ball is to help me select my future wife."

"I understand. I just.... I'm just.... Are you mad?" I thought to myself. But by the surprised look on the prince's face, I realized I had said it out loud.

My hands shot to my mouth again, and I mumbled through my fingers, "I'm sorry, Your Highness." Terrified that I had insulted the future king, I did the only thing I could think of. I bowed. No! Wrong. I grimaced and curtsied. But then felt so confused, I did a mix of both and looked up at Evander's face.

His lips were pinched in a firm line, and my shoulders dropped. He looked angry.

Then his shoulders began to shake, and he bent over and laughed at me. Straight up, belly-aching laughed.

My mother would not be proud if she were here to see this. "I should go."

"N-no. Sto-o-p. P-please don't g-go!" Prince Evander couldn't stop laughing, and he reached out to grab my hand. When his laughing had died down, he wiped at his eyes and gave me a serious look. "Yes, I must be mad. Because I would like you to stay. Here at the palace. Each of the chosen will be given a room here so that I can properly court them."

This was what every girl dreamed of. Except me. I never wanted to marry a prince. I couldn't rule a country. I wasn't strong or courageous like my other sisters. I was sent here for revenge and answers, and yet I found myself wanting to have a normal dream, like a normal young woman. Dancing at a ball with a handsome stranger.

"Why? I already told you that I'm no heiress, and I have no great family lineage. I would bring nothing to you or the crown. We would make a very bad match."

"See what I mean? You're talking me out of courting you, and I don't even know your name. The reason I want you to stay is because you were honest. No, you were brutally honest. You told me to my face that you were here for the ball and nothing else. You didn't even mention coming for me."

"I *didn't* come for you," I said, leaving out that I only came to find out who killed my mother.

"Ouch, even now your words cut like a sword."

Again, with my mouth. All night my own words had been bitter, contrite, and hurtful. There was no class or decency. I was forward, direct, and a few times outright silly.

"But, yes, you are nothing like the others, and quite frankly, having you here would irritate my parents."

"If they only knew." I inwardly chuckled.

"Will you stay?" he asked. "You will be given a room here and you have the freedom to come and go as you please."

"I...." I couldn't speak, so I nodded.

Maybe I imagined his look of relief. "So now you know my secret." He flipped the mask in his hands and looked up at me, a smile at the corner of his mouth. "But I'm afraid I don't know yours? Who are you?"

My hands trembled as I reached up to untie the ribbon to my mask. They froze on the ribbon, my eyes glued to my glass slippers that were peeking out from beneath my glamoured gown.

"Evander!" a man came storming across the grass toward us, his mask in his hand.

"Ah, Dorian!" Evander turned. My head snapped up at hearing his name. I stepped behind Prince Evander, letting his much larger frame hide mine. "What have you discovered so far?'

"The witch seems to have come alone and had no other agenda than to cause a ruckus. She is safely locked away and won't be able to bother anyone. As to your future prospects, there are around twenty that have been selected based on the king and queen's criteria, including the ones you personally chose. The others have already been sent home," Dorian stated.

Evander shook his head. "And to think, I haven't even met them."

"Don't worry, Your Highness. The ones being sent home are all being compensated. We carefully vetted them, and I can honestly say that if you asked tonight, all would marry you sight unseen."

Evander sighed. "That's the problem, I haven't seen any of them. This is stupid."

"Evander, it's tradition. It's how it is always done. Now, it's time to formally greet them. You're already late."

Evander gave him an exasperated look.

"Your duty cannot be cast aside," Dorian chastised.

"That's funny you should be the one lecturing me," Evander said, "when you're the one who's late for everything."

"I'm never late. I just make an entrance."

"But there's one more I want to invite," Evander said and waved at me to come stand by his side.

"Really, Evander. I don't think you need any more. There

are quite a few beauties that would make excellent princesses. I could even give you their names right now."

"Uh, Dorian, she's right here," Evander whispered, and I could feel the awkwardness in the air.

I gathered my courage and stepped around him into the moonlight and revealed myself.

Dorian's face turned down, and I saw his displeasure. "No."

"You don't have any say," Evander said.

"Well, I should, and I say no. That one will bring you nothing but trouble." He pointed at me.

"Dorian," Evander warned, his voice dipping low. "You don't have the authority to undermine me."

Dorian's jaw clenched, and he gave a cursory bow, his hand waving in a dramatic flair. "As you wish." As Dorian bowed, his eyes bore into mine, and I could see his anger burning within. He spoke between a clenched jaw. "I will add this *flower* to your collection."

Something about the way he said it made me uncomfortable.

Evander turned toward me. "I will see you soon. Maybe then you can tell me your name." He gave me a wink and Dorian a pat on the shoulder before heading into the ballroom, leaving me alone with a quietly seething Dorian.

Dorian turned and offered me his arm but didn't say anything. I ignored it, picked up the hem of my dress so I wouldn't trip, and headed back toward the ballroom. Dorian gave a frustrated grunt. His long legs caught up to me in two strides.

"So, you got what you wanted," he said sourly. "You have been invited to stay on at the palace."

"It's not really what I wanted," I said, stopping on the steps outside of the ballroom.

Dorian spun on me. "Then what do you want? Because a few moments ago, you didn't want to leave, and now you don't want to stay."

I placed my hands on my hips and raised my chin. "I want to spite you because you seem to despise me."

"I... I don't. It's not that—"

"The more you deter me from coming, the harder I will fight to stay. You're not treating anyone else with as much contempt as you are showing me."

"It's because I'm trying to help you. He's not who you think he is," Dorian snapped.

I waited for further explanation, but he clamped his mouth shut and looked down in remorse. He reached into his inner jacket pocket. "Here."

"What is it?" I asked as he put it in my hand.

"A token. To prove that you're one of his chosen."

"It's beautiful." I held it up and admired the gold coin with a moon stamped on it. I had never owned anything as beautiful or as expensive as this and probably never would again.

"Yeah, well, all of them will get one like it." He pointed into the ballroom. Evander stood among the final twenty women, giving them instructions.

"The token you receive will match an assigned room. This will be yours for the remainder of your stay here at the palace. For instance, if you received a rose, then our servants will escort you to the rose room. But each day there will be fewer of you as I begin the search to find my future queen."

Squeals of delight came from the twenty women. I stood outside looking in and was pleased to see that Tess was among the few selected as well. I felt a hint of pride that I had helped her get this far. Now it would be up to her. The others I didn't recognize because of their masks.

"See, you are not so special," Dorian said, gesturing for me to join them. His words hurt. They cut like a dagger on my already fragile heart. "You are going to miss the introductions to the king and queen." He came up and whispered in my ear. "Or have you taken my advice and decided that this is no place for you? Because now the claws come out, and it is about to get ruthless between the women. And the prize is not a prince but a throne."

I gripped the coin in my hand and felt a renewed sense of will. "Then let the games begin."

My answer surprised Dorian. I headed toward the exit.

"Where are you going?"

"Back to the Broken Heart tavern to retrieve my belongings."

"Prince Evander will be suspicious if you don't stay on," he said.

"I will be back tomorrow morning," I said as I detoured through an open door and headed outside. I was heading down the stone steps when he grabbed my wrist.

"You shouldn't go back there," he warned.

I sighed and spun on my glass slippers and almost fell on the stairs. "First you say stay. Then you say go home, don't come. Now that I'm here, you are saying to not leave. You are a difficult person to understand."

"That's because I have ears everywhere. The king is looking for a daughter of Eville, Sparrow, and I happen to know that your transport driver picked you up in Nihill, and if I know that, then so does the king."

"If he knows it, it is because you told him," I snapped.

"No, he didn't hear this from me."

"Why is he scared of me?"

"He's not scared of you. He's scared of the prophecy."

"And yet, I know nothing of this prophecy," I snapped at him.

Dorian became quiet. He whistled, and his black coach pulled up. I began to associate the black coach with Dorian's black heart. He opened the door and ushered me inside, his hand on my elbow. Once inside, I shook off his touch, and he sat on the padded bench seat across from me.

I gathered my skirts to one side and pressed against the far wall, refusing to make eye contact or even acknowledge his existence. The ride back was filled with silent tension. He had no qualms about staring at me the whole ride, while I pretended to not notice.

When I became nervous, I had a tendency to fidget, and I found that the only way to overcome my anxiety was to tuck my hands under my thighs. When the coach pulled down the familiar alley, I stood up and moved to the door before it had come to a full stop. The coach jerked, and I tumbled into Dorian's lap, his hand going around my waist to steady me. The heat of his hand burned through my dress, and I could feel it as if it was on my own skin.

He held me cradled in his lap, and those gray-blue eyes met mine. I could feel his desire. A heat burned in my stomach, and when I struggled, his grip tightened around my waist.

"Not yet," he whispered, his eyes dropping to my lips. His head lowered, and I closed my eyes, waiting for his lips to claim mine. Instead, his forehead touched mine and his breath brushed across my lips as tender and soft as a kiss. His mouth stopped an inch from mine. So close and yet miles apart, neither one of us going to take the leap. He groaned and thrust me from his lap and toward the door.

"Leave before you make me do something I regret," he grumbled.

His threat had me fumbling with the latch in my hurry to escape him and the thoughts that were creeping up on me. I missed the last step out of the carriage and tripped. "You, dear sparrow, are a mess."

"Yes, and someday someone will love the mess that I am."

"No doubt," Dorian said as he stepped out of the carriage after me. "I will wait for you to gather your items."

"No need," I said, nervous that he would follow me further. I gathered my skirt and rushed inside, passed a laughing Madam Pantalonne and her room full of patrons. I dashed passed a mysterious stranger, who followed me with his gaze, his hand resting on his belt and dagger. I pushed him out of my mind.

I hurried up to my room and locked the door behind me. I packed most of my items in my small case and put my drawstring purse on my nightstand, ready in a quarter of a mark. It would be nothing for me to go back out with my case, get back in the carriage, and return to the palace tonight to take my place among the chosen. But that would mean another awkward carriage ride with Dorian.

No, I couldn't subject myself to that torture. I would stay the night. Let him wait in the carriage for me until morning. It would serve him right. I tucked my glass slippers in my drawstring purse, which was spelled to hold larger items in its small interior, and removed a piece of chalk. Very carefully, I drew a protection spell over the door to keep out intruders and Dorian —or at least I hoped it was a protection spell; with my luck, it was a recipe for cookies.

CHAPTER TEN

I was standing alone in a cemetery. My feet sank into the wet grass as I moved through the darkness. A lone wailing came from further in, and I felt compelled to answer, the cry so desperate and forlorn. One wail became two; then there were more that rose up into a symphony of sorrow. Will-o'-the-wisps fluttered along the top of the tombstones, and where they alit, their fae glow would light up the names on the tombstone. Each of the names etched into the marble was a name of a young girl. My mouth felt dry, I couldn't swallow as the date on the tombstones all happened within a few weeks of each other.

A plague. I concluded.

A weeping came again, and I followed the path until I saw a woman in black veils, sobbing over a newly dug grave—three feet deep and quite a few inches over five feet.

Not a man then.

A woman.

The woman continued to wail, her black veil dragging through the upheaved dirt.

"Why? Why couldn't you have done as you were told?"

"I'm sorry for your loss," I tried to say to the woman, but the wind whisked my voice away.

"Why weren't you strong like your sisters?" The woman moaned.

Perplexed and unsure how to help the woman in black, I stepped closer to the grave and the will-o'-the-wisp fluttered by the tombstone, making the name legible.

Eden Eville.

"No!" I gasped and looked down into the empty grave. Where seconds ago it was filled with nothing but packed dirt, now I could see myself. Dressed in a white dress with lace cuffs, my golden hair hung loosely over my shoulders, my eyes closed in death.

It wasn't me. It couldn't be me. If I was there, then the woman was my adoptive mother.

"Mother." I leaned down to touch her shoulder. She spun, the veil falling from her face, and the face wasn't my mother's at all. It was the wicked and hideous Allemar.

His lips pulled back into a snarl, and he lunged for me, his hands going around my throat. I screamed and fell backward into the grave.

My grave.

I slammed onto the wood floor, the air knocked from my lungs, and I couldn't gasp as Allemar's fingers dug painfully into my throat.

Allemar's face changed as I woke from my dream.

A stranger with a mask over his face was trying to strangle me. The door was still closed, but the window's shutters were open.

He had come through the window and attacked me, and I had fallen to the floor.

He sat on my chest, making it impossible for me to take a breath and pull his fingers from around my throat.

I kicked my heels violently against the floorboards, hoping to alert someone, anyone of my plight, but what good would it do if they couldn't get through my spelled door?

In desperation, I reached out and tried to claw at his eyes, and he released my throat long enough for me to take a breath and try to scramble away.

I lunged for my purse that had fallen to the floor, grabbing it as strong hands tangled in my hair and drug me back across the floor. This time I had enough air to scream.

Seconds later, someone was pounding on my door, but I couldn't answer. My attacker flipped me back over and had his hands back around my throat.

"If you can't speak, you can't cast a spell on me, can you?" the killer hissed. His breath smelled of death and ale. Fresh blood dripped on my face from where I had scratched his eyes.

What he said was almost true. Except not all spells needed words to cast or conjure. But trying to do one and fight for my life was proving difficult. I kept one hand on his palm, trying to pull it away from my throat. My vision became blurry as my left hand dug through the purse, searching.

The pounding on the door became louder. A key turned in the lock, but the door wouldn't budge. I heard Madam Pantalonne's distressed voice outside. "I knew it would be bad if she returned. Why couldn't you have kept her away?" she yelled at someone. She knew something bad was happening, and she was right.

My finger felt the heat the button gave off. Gripping it in my hand, I slammed it against my attacker's cheek, and it activated. The charm began to sear into the man's face and my palm.

Both of us screamed in unison from the pain, but I dare not let go. For if I did, I would surely die.

His fist connected with my jaw, and the charm slipped from my fingers. I cried out in despair. My vision swam as a dark figure covered the window, blocking out the moonlight.

Two shadows danced; one sailed through the air, and my nightstand broke. I tried to crawl my way across the floor, my burned hand held close to my breasts as I searched for the piece of chalk that had also escaped from my purse and rolled near me. Locating it, I tried to draw a symbol of protection, but I couldn't remember the right emblem. My tears made my vision blurry, and I tried to wipe away the wrong spell, but I was spent, my hands shook and the chalk broke in my blood-coated fingers. I wasn't even sure whose blood it was.

I had failed.

I heard the footsteps draw near my prone form. I closed my eyes and waited, waited for the end, for the assassin to finish what he had started.

The chalk was pulled from my grip, and I let out a sob of despair.

"Shhh, sparrow," a deep voice whispered. "I have you." Dorian gathered me close and lifted me into the air. My face pressed into his warm chest.

I heard the scratching of chalk, the door opened, and light spilled forth from the hallway.

"Is she alive, Dorian?" I could hear the worry in Madam Pantalonne's voice.

"Yes," he whispered.

"And the other?"

"No."

"Good. Now, go. I will take care of the mess."

CHAPTER ELEVEN

I awoke in an unfamiliar room. Barren except for a stand with a pitcher of water, fireplace, small mirror on the wall, chair, and a trunk. Where was I? What happened? I rubbed my sore throat and knew that it was bruised. My palm had already been tended to. A clean bandage was wrapped around my burn.

A knock came at my door. Sitting up, I pulled the soft quilt up to my chin and waited, hesitantly. Dorian entered, followed by a house elf in a tattered green dress, carrying a silver tray filled with food and tea. The house elf set the tray on the stand next to the pitcher of water and tended the fire while Dorian pulled a chair over to sit next to me.

"Well, that was an exciting evening!" He flashed me a reassuring grin. He had a day's growth of stubble on his cheek. When he reached for my neck, I flinched.

"It's okay. I just want to see how it's healing." I released the blanket, and he leaned in close and frowned. "You're going to have some nasty bruises, and your throat may be raw for a few days, but other than that, you're fine."

Dorian handed me a warm cup of tea, and I took a sip; the warm liquid felt like gold as it soothed my throat. As I continued to sip the tea, he looked at me quizzically before unwrapping my palm to reveal the burn imprint of a button.

"A fire charm. Interesting. Where did you learn that?"

"It's my sister's," I tried to say, but the pain had me hissing.

Dorian applied a burn ointment to my palm and wrapped it in a bandage that he had brought in. It wasn't a big burn, barely noticeable compared to the one my attacker had received, but he was careful when he tied the knot so that it wasn't too tight. "It's a good thing you had it. I was almost too late because *someone* had barred the door with a spell." My cheeks burned in embarrassment at being caught using magic, but Dorian didn't seem to care. He just looked intrigued, not scared of my use of power.

"Did you do it?" I asked. "Send someone to try and murder me?"

Those icy blue eyes studied me carefully. "No, but I know who did."

"And?" I waited for him to tell me, but he didn't. I leaned back in disbelief. "You're not going to tell me?"

He clenched his jaw and looked away, refusing to meet my gaze. "It's not your problem. I have dealt with the situation, and he will no longer be able to harm you."

"You mean you killed him."

His eyes narrowed, and his voice was grim. "Yes."

I saw the sun come in through a high window, and I began to panic. It was late midmorning. "Thank you for your hospitality." I looked around at the sparse room and couldn't hide the discontent on my face. "But I really must be leaving."

His lips pressed into a thin line, and his knuckles turned white as he tried to rein in his anger. "Where are you going to go? I forbid you from going back to the tavern, where only a few marks ago, someone tried to kill you. They could still be after you. You aren't safe. The only safe place for you is home."

"Why would I go home? I came here for a reason, and after last night's events, I am more determined than ever to go back to the palace, and no one is going to stop me."

"Not even if I asked you to?" he said, his hand gently grasping mine. "What if I said it was someone at the palace that tried to kill you? You're not safe." His fingers brushed across mine gently, and my breath caught. He was playing with my emotions, manipulating me to do his will.

I pulled my hand from his and spoke coldly, even doing my best to throw as much power into my voice as I could. "You're right. The palace may not be a safe place, but I'm not worried about them. It is *they* who should be worried about me."

"Please, don't go."

"You don't know me," I snapped. "You know absolutely nothing about me. You have no right to ask anything of me."

Dorian stood up, his back stiff, anger radiating off him in waves. I had upset him. "So be it." His voice dropped in tone. "You're right. I know nothing about you, and be warned you also know nothing about me."

I threw back the quilt and saw my bare feet that poked from my chemise and looked around. My clothes. "Where are my belongings?"

Dorian looked grim. "All of your things are back at the tavern. But you can wear any of the dresses from the trunk I brought for you."

I gingerly stepped out of the bed and opened the trunk. Inside were simple day dresses. "Who do these belong to?" I asked.

"Sisa," Dorian said.

"Who's Sisa," I asked curiously, remembering Madam Pantalonne's comment.

"My fiancée," Dorian said without any inflection.

All of a sudden, I felt hollow, despondent and very stupid. For a minute, I thought I was here because he cared about me. But that wasn't so. He was to be married, and it was improper of me to be here.

"I would prefer my own clothes, please."

He glared at me, and I felt it like a stab to the heart. "I'm sorry, sparrow."

"What?" I asked, confused at the change in his tone.

"It's for your own good." He moved to the door and stepped outside, one hand on the door handle one on the key in the lock. "At least until Evander is married."

"I don't understand." I moved to take a step toward the door. Dorian swung it closed. "No!" I rushed to the door, but the key turned in the lock.

CHAPTER TWELVE

"**D**orian! Let me out!" I grabbed the knob and twisted, then pressed my ear to the wood but only heard his retreating footsteps. I pounded and screamed in frustration when it didn't budge. I was furious at being imprisoned.

How dare he! Did Dorian not understand that I was a daughter of Eville and should not be treated like this? I was a powerful sorceress. Okay, not all-powerful like Rosalie, and maybe more of a mediocre sorceress that messed up more often than not, but I couldn't—wouldn't let this stop me.

Backing up, I tried to remember the spell to unlock the door. It was a basic one. "Not Lochni," I muttered as I tried to visualize the spell in my head, not wanting to blow the whole house up. "*Lochen,*" I uttered triumphantly and waited for the click as the door unlocked.

Nothing happened.

"What the...?" I grumbled and raised my hand and tried again. "*Lochen!*" I said as loud as my still raw voice would let me. I saw a glow around the lock, and then it faded.

A counterspell! The door had an anti-lockpicking counterspell!

Drat! Turning around, I took a closer stock of my

surroundings. The room was small with a high window that was barred from the outside. It would be impossible to even get to the window. I wanted my revenge on the one who tried to assassinate me; how dare Dorian try to take my vengeance from me?

Not to be deterred, I pulled a corset and a simple blue dress out of the trunk and laid them across the bed.

It took a few moments of struggling to get into it by myself, and I tried to use my magic to lace up the corset. My first attempt had me gagging and gasping for air as the corset wound too tight. My second had the corset falling on the ground.

I cursed and stomped around at my lack of focus and control at the simplest skills, but I wouldn't give up. Holding onto the bedpost, I closed my eyes, preparing myself for the pain, and tried again.

"Cinchio."

The ribbon laced up. I felt the tug and opened my eyes to see that it had indeed laced correctly and ended with a bow. My sister Rosalie would not have approved of my waste of magic, but I was just relieved that I hadn't strangled myself with the spell. I put on the blue dress; it was one for around the house, not for attending the king or queen.

In the trunk was a spare comb and pins, which I put to good use in doing my hair. I pulled up my dress and looked at my bare-stocking feet. There was nothing in the trunk for footwear, and why would there be when he didn't expect me to leave?

Luckily, he had grabbed my spelled drawstring purse. I opened it, searched into the deep pocket, and was excited when I pulled them out one by one. They weren't damaged, but still beautiful and very uncomfortable.

It was the king who sent the assassin for me. He wanted to stop me from coming, and I wanted to know why.

I slipped the shoes on and looked in the mirror, seeing a young woman a few years older than me with dark blonde hair and blue-green eyes. She looked familiar, but I wasn't sure how it could be possible. I had unintendedly taken on the glamour of the previous shoe's owner.

The mirror shimmered, and I stared back at myself—my eyes a watery blue, my hair golden and warm. I looked scared, unsure, and even now was biting my lip with trepidation. I was weak, powerless, and hid behind my glamour. But I used my magic to turn my simple blue day dress into a dress fit for a princess—an off-the-shoulder blue gown with layers of blue skirts that billowed out from a jeweled belt with matching gloves.

I laughed and almost began to cry. The only magic that came naturally to me was glamour—a magic for hiding, covering up, and deceiving others. Too bad I couldn't deceive myself into thinking I was better at magic, because it was my sister's delayed trap that saved my life, and then it was Dorian. I desperately didn't want to mess up again.

With a wave of my hand, I was able to disguise my bruises on my throat, made them fade into the background, same with my burn. Glamour would hide all of my injuries.

No one would suspect the nightmare I survived only a few hours earlier.

I now understood what my mother had known all along. That the king of Candor was not a kind man. He was evil and cruel, and with a snap of his fingers, he was willing to have me killed. Me, someone who he had never met and had done him no harm. Dorian wouldn't tell me who sent the assassin, but he didn't need to. I already knew.

At first, I didn't understand why Mother had sent me. Now I knew. It was to put a stop to the evil that was King Ferdinand. I had to be sure, but I thought the only way to do that would be to kill him.

Walking to the fireplace, I leaned down and found an old piece of cinder that had burned down to ash. Using it the same way I used chalk, I drew out the spell for transportation, being careful not to miss a sigil. I must be crazy, because I wasn't even sure it would work, but I needed to try.

Using the flint box I found on the mantle, I stacked the wood and quickly lit a fire. When it was fully ablaze, I stacked a few more logs, trying to estimate how long the fire would go for, because the spell would only hold until the last cinder burned out. When it blew out, I would be pulled back into the locked room.

Looking down, I groaned at the ash now coating my dress.. As soon as my glass slippers touched the ash line, the ground began to glow, the fire turned white, and sparks that looked like fireflies flew out of the fireplace.

It was now or never. I either stepped into the fire and transported or burned to death.

"Stars, please guide me," I muttered as I closed my eyes and jumped into the blazing fire.

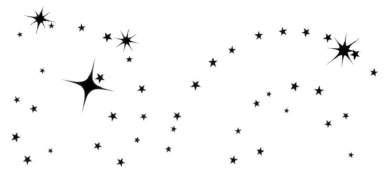

CHAPTER THIRTEEN

Blinding white pain shot through every limb, and white flames wrapped around my body. I held back a silent scream as I was pulled into a fiery vortex. One second, I was standing on the edge of a fireplace in Dorian's house, and the next I was stepping out of a pillar of black smoke into a full and busy kitchen, for the spell would only transport to another fire that was already burning.

Screaming and hysterics followed. Rolling pins rolled off the tables and trays of food were abandoned as the kitchen staff scattered, calling for the guards.

"Witch!"

"Demon!"

"Lord, have mercy on my soul!"

I could only imagine how I must look—a woman stepping from the flames in a billow of mysterious black smoke. I would be terrified as well.

One would have thought an invading army was coming by the screams of the palace staff. I had only begun to dust off my hands and dress when I saw golden eyes blinking at me from within the fire.

"Oh, hello," I said softly to whatever creature was living

within the hearth. There were any number of fae that lived within a fireplace, and not all of them were friendly. This could be a kobold or any form of fire fairy, and their job was to protect hearth and home. I could have disturbed this being.

The golden eyes blinked once, and I fumbled at what to do next. Grabbing the edges of my dress, I decided that it was best to ask for forgiveness.

"So very sorry for disturbing your slumber. But I thank you for the use of your hearth. Would you like me to stoke it again for you?" I saw that the fire had died down and that the creature was lying within the black embers.

The eyes blinked twice, and I took it for affirmation. I grabbed the poker and very carefully moved the coals around and then added another piece of wood from the fire. As I did, the fire picked up again. The golden eyes belonged to a salamander, a fire elemental that was black, and he glowed with an inner fire like a coal. He jumped out of the fire and ran up and down my body and over the floor, gold and red flames trailing behind him before he rushed back into the fire. A great gust of fire exploded from the hearth, causing me to step back and cover my eyes.

The elemental must be attracted to the magic left behind by my spells. He was burying himself right into the coals. I was about to lean down and stir the coals again for him when I heard the sound of the guards. Their heavy boots echoed on the floor, creating a more ominous sound than the lighter leather footwear of the servants.

"Oh, no!" I looked around the kitchen in a frenzied and rushed forth to an abandoned apron. Quickly, I donned the apron and glamour to become the matron who owned the garment. With only seconds to spare, I buried my hands in the thick soapy dishwater and began to hum loudly to myself.

Ten soldiers filed into the room one by one and looked around.

"Hey, you!" one called out to me.

I continued washing.

"You, ma'am, turn around."

I did and feigned a surprised expression. "Well, my heart. Where did everyone go?"

"Did you see anything, like a witch come from there?" He pointed to the fireplace.

"Stitch?" I mumbled. "Did you say stitch?"

"Witch!" The guard spoke louder.

"Witch? Why didn't you say so?" I cackled, having a little too much fun at their expense. "Of course, I believe in witches."

"Have you seen something strange?"

The other guards had spread out and began poking around the kitchen and looking into the fireplace.

"Didn't I speak to you outside in the hall?" One of the guards stared at me, confusion all over his face. "And I could have sworn you had an Islayan accent?"

"Nope. That wasn't me. Oh my, look there! In the fireplace. Do you see it?" I called loudly, and my salamander friend decided to help me out. He grew to the size of a small dog and began to dig into the logs, kicking the charred and burning wood onto the stone floor. Burning logs rolled into the table, and the guards were rushed for tongs to try and put out the fire.

I mouthed the words "Thank you" as I slowly backed up toward the door. One of the guards set his gloves on the table, and I snatched them, sliding them on my hands. I glamoured myself to look like the guard and marched out of the kitchen. A crowd had gathered at the end of the hall, everyone looking toward the kitchen with terror, while I heard the commotion of the guards.

"Where did she go?"

"I don't know. She was just here."

"Search the palace and alert the king! The witch is here."

"Carry on!" I ordered, marching passed the servants. "There's nothing to worry about. Just a pesky elemental in the fire."

"Not again!"

"I thought we got rid of it?"

"No, I don't believe it. I saw a girl. A woman. That was no elemental."

I picked up my pace and ran down a hallway, tossing the gloves in a nearby planter. I felt the glamour shift and change, and now I was back to myself, except for the active glamour around my injuries.

Two servants were speaking amongst themselves as they passed, and I eavesdropped on their conversation. "I heard the ladies were dancing and celebrating till almost dawn once they found out they were selected."

"You haven't been here long, have you?" the second servant answered. "Don't expect to get much sleep yourself for the next few days. Every night they will stay up till near dawn and sleep till late afternoon. Then spend hours primping before they emerge from their rooms. We call it royal candor time."

"You surely jest."

"I don't. But right now, they are gathering in the women's parlor where they're to meet with the queen."

I stepped from the alcove into their path too, and they both stopped and gave me a curtsy. "May we help you, miss?

"I seem to be a bit lost."

The second servant with her hair in a bun giggled. "The palace is a bit of a maze. Were you heading to the women's parlor?

"Yes."

"Follow me, miss."

The two servants, adorned in blue dresses with white collars, led me to a brightly lit sitting room. This was where most of the women would spend their days sewing, playing music, or walking in the garden. I wasn't the first to arrive and had to hold back my surprise when I saw that Nessa, in another pale orange dress, was sitting near Queen Giselle and doing her best to impress her. I couldn't fathom how she had made it past the guards, but who was I to judge the prince's taste.

A high-pitched laugh sprinkled the air, and I turned to see more girls file in the room. I took a cushioned chair near the window and picked up a book. While pretending to read, I listened in and picked up a few of the girls' names.

Adelle already looked like royalty with perfectly coiffed, dark black hair. Her family was third or fourth cousins to the queen. Harmony, the guild merchant's daughter, was bubbly and beautiful, her hair a gorgeous copper and her eyes blue like the summer sky. She was the one I had saved from Bellamy. Her personality sparkled and drew people in; she made people feel welcome and safe.

The closest girls near me were Ariah, Helia, Mellisande, and Sela—all from wealthy backgrounds and felt that they were a shoo-in for the crown. Tess was sitting on a padded stool on the opposite end of the room away from her sister. I could see there was tension between the two sisters. I hadn't expected for both sisters to be chosen. I was ignored, which was how I liked it. Even at home I was the quiet one, the one who watched from the outskirts, studying my other sisters.

"Isn't it just lovely?" a bubbly voice broke me out of my daydream.

"What is?" I asked, blinking up at Harmony, who decided to befriend me by sitting on a padded bench near me.

"Why, the book you're reading. It happens to be one of my favorites. Who is your favorite character?"

I was caught. I opened the book straight to the middle and hadn't even been reading or turned a page in close to a candle mark.

"Oh, uh...." I quickly looked down and picked a name from the page. "Beryl."

Harmony frowned. "Really, the villain? The witch who curses the kingdom and poisons the princess."

Oops. "Yes, but you have to wonder why. What drove her to such extremes?"

Harmony gave me a thoughtful look before breaking out into a grin. "That is true. Everyone always believes it is because the villain has nothing better to do than to wreck the hero's happily ever after. But we never do hear the witch's side of it, do we?"

"No," I said, bluffing.

Harmony reached over to grasp my hands. "I think we are going to be the best of friends. Don't you?"

I started to shake my head but quickly nodded. "Yes." My smile was forced, pinched. She was too sweet, too kind, and I had been taught to never trust an offer from a stranger that was too good to be true. Harmony was too good, and standing next to her, all of my faults were brought to light.

"May I have your attention, please," Queen Giselle spoke up.

The chatter in the room died down. "We held the royal ball to bring all of the eligible ladies to the palace in the hopes of Prince Evander finding a suitable bride. But it is not just the prince you have to impress. It is also me. I can and will send ladies home that do not fit our criteria of being a future monarch."

Smiles, all of the women were smiling supremely, and I was frowning. The book I had been holding onto slid off my lap and fell with a thud to the floor.

The queen's clear green eyes looked right at me disapprovingly.

"Sorry." I picked up the book and put it on the side table, but I was so busy watching her, that I missed the table and dropped the book right back on the floor.

Snickers followed, and my cheeks burned in embarrassment. I scrambled for the book and decided to avoid the table and tucked it under my thigh and beneath the folds on my skirt.

Harmony let out a chuckle and then winked at me knowingly. We spent the next few candle marks listening to the queen drone on and on about protocol, dining etiquette, and so forth that I found myself frequently staring out the window daydreaming, waiting for something interesting to happen.

A knock at the door interrupted Queen Giselle, and Prince Evander stepped in. He looked quite debonair in a soft blue suit, and I stilled. His eyes wandered all of the strange faces, as if he were searching for someone. I heard Harmony hold her breath, and I waited as he slowly made eye contact with all of the woman. When he looked at me, our eyes met for a few seconds, and then he moved on. My heart dropped in disappointment, but then I remembered he had never seen any of us without our masks. If he was searching for me, he wouldn't even know what I looked like or my name.

"Ah, yes, Evander. It is time for you to meet the young women without the masks."

"I'm quite looking forward to the opportunity. It is such a beautiful day, that I thought we could go for a stroll in the garden."

Squeals of delight came from the girls and most stood up excitedly.

"As you wish, my son." She cleared her throat, signifying the break in etiquette for some of the ladies. I was too shocked to move, and therefore hadn't broken custom. When Queen Giselle stood, Harmony and I did too, and she gave us small approving smiles. I knew how rare and valuable those smiles were.

Harmony latched onto my arm as we left the parlor in groups of two and three. Adelle, Nessa, and Sela were flanking the prince, vying for his attention. Tess had dropped behind, trying to stay out of Nessa's line of sight.

"Isn't this so romantic?" Harmony murmured into my ear and sighed.

"I fail to see how one man courting dozens of women is in the least romantic."

"But that is how it's always done and has been for generations. Giselle was selected at King Ferdinand's ball. Although, there is just as much tragedy as romance. You remember Vincent?"

I did but hadn't given the dead prince much thought. After all, his death had been five years ago.

Harmony's green eyes filled with tears. "Prince Vincent had fallen so deeply in love during his courtship, that when his fiancée was murdered the day of his wedding, he couldn't live without her and took his own life." She sighed and dabbed at the corner of her eyes.

I rolled my eyes. "What a waste of a prince."

"No, it's not. There are tales written about their undying love." Harmony sniffed.

"What kind of example is that? If he loved her, he should have gone on living."

"Hush!" Helia had turned around and gave me an ugly glare. "You shouldn't talk of the royal family so." When Helia had turned back around, I stuck my tongue out at the back of her head, which sent Harmony into a fit of giggles.

When we reached the gardens, we all took seats in groups of four or five in the gazebos while Evander called each of the women up one by one to talk to them. Helia, Harmony, and Tess sat in the same gazebo with me.

Tess was fingering the ribbon in her hair and had a worried look on her face. She was probably wondering how long the glamour would last, or what would happen when she made it through the three glamoured dresses her fairy godmother had given her. So far, my glamoured items were still in effect, their strength had not waned. I was proud of that.

Tess let out a long, sad sigh before looking at the four of us. She paused when she looked at me. Her eyes narrowed in suspicion. "Do I know you?"

"I don't think so." I subconsciously rubbed my throat. It still felt raw and made my voice sound lower, rougher, older.

"I could have sworn we've met." She went back to touching the ribbon.

"Do you know the girl in orange?" I asked, trying to change the subject. "You two seem familiar with each other."

"Never met her before in my life," Tess said snippily.

"That's not what it sounds like to me," Harmony jumped in. "What family are you from?"

Tess looked around worriedly and then added, "Duchovny."

"Never heard of them," Harmony said.

"Yeah, well, my family travels a lot," Tess added but became distracted. We all followed her gaze, and I frowned when Evander walked toward us.

I heard four quick intakes of breaths and then their release as Prince Evander passed us and went to the next gazebo, holding his hand out to Adelle. All eyes followed them as she sashayed, her arm on his, as they walked over to the bridge.

"What are they talking about?" Helia wondered aloud.

"The weather, favorite color, family lineage—all of those would be appropriate topics to discuss," Harmony said.

My lips pinched, and I watched their body language. Prince Evander pointed to the paper lanterns. She nodded and laughed as Evander pretended to almost slip in and fall. My frown grew deeper as I remembered his hands on my waist.

Helia, Mellisande, and Sela were next, and every single girl he walked back over to the bridge. I didn't like that he was sharing our spot with the others. Tess was beaming when she returned; she couldn't stop smiling after their encounter. Harmony was teary eyed, and her nose was red from crying.

"Are you okay?" I asked worriedly.

She dabbed at her eyes with an expensive embroidered kerchief, and knew it was Prince Evander's. "Yes," she sniffed. "He's so kind. He had known my older sister and gave me his condolences. She passed away a few years ago." Harmony smoothed out the kerchief and lovingly folded it in her lap.

Harmony, perfect Harmony with her magical tears that seemed to only make her more beautiful when she cried. They were a weapon when used right, and it seemed that she knew how to use them. I, on the other hand, knew better. If I cried, my face turned as blotchy and red as a tomato. It was better if I kept all tears hidden away.

Finally, it was my turn, and it seemed he was getting short-tempered, for he didn't come himself but had a servant lead me over. Evander was frowning and looking down at a broken reed he was smacking against his hand. It was the same one I had dropped on the bridge. He was trying to figure out who the mystery girl from last night was since he never saw my face or exchanged names. From his body language, I could tell he was frustrated.

My inner voice, the self-conscious part of my brain began to whisper that it was because he changed his mind about asking me to stay. He only wanted to find the odd girl and send her home. But because he didn't know which girl it was, he was testing all of them. My thoughts became dark, and I stopped ten paces from the stream and the rushes.

Evander looked up from the reed, and his face lit up. It became hopeful. "Come join me." He waited for me to come to his side, but I couldn't. I was rooted to the spot. "What's the matter?"

My brain screamed at me to say something, anything, but I was afraid if I spoke he would recognize my voice.

"Oh, are you afraid of water?" he asked in disbelief.

I nodded. I didn't imagine that his smile faltered. His shoulders dropped an inch, but he kept up a good front.

"Well, then let's head over to the bench by the willow trees."

My feet were dead weight as I plodded along. Even sitting down, I kept my back ramrod straight.

"What is your name?" Prince Evander was being pleasant.

"Eden," I answered.

"Eden...?" he prompted for more.

"Just Eden."

"No last name?"

"Does it matter?" I challenged. "It is something else by which I am judged."

"Not at all. You could be adopted and wearing shoes that weren't your own, and it wouldn't matter to me."

There he goes throwing out cues from our earlier conversations. He was baiting me.

"That's good," I said softly and winced. I rubbed my throat. I didn't sound like myself either.

"What did you think of the ball?" He gave me a long look, and I didn't want to repeat the silliness I said last night.

"It was wonderful," I said, giving him a bright smile. "I have never danced so much in my life." I may have thrown a simper in there and watched as Evander cringed.

What am I doing? This was going badly. I was purposely sabotaging myself. I was uncomfortable, and Evander was distracted. He was still fingering the reed in his hand and looking back at the stream. I was becoming irritated. Here I was trying to get a second chance and get to know him, and he wouldn't even look me in the eye. Without thinking, I pulled the reed from his hands, and he tried to snatch it back.

"Not so fast, Your Highness." I gestured to the ornamental dagger on his hip. "Is it practical or purely for decoration?"

"Depends, are you going to stab me with it?" he asked warily, his hand going to pull out the dagger.

"Only if you say something that annoys me," I added.

Prince Evander handed me the dagger, but I watched as he adjusted his stance. He faced me but leaned slightly away, his hands loose at his side so as to protect himself or disarm me.

I ignored his body language and began to run my fingers over the dried-out reed, measuring it out and doing some quick calculations in my head. Taking the sharp edge of the knife, I began to carve out a mouth piece, and then, using my knuckle, I measured spaces for six finger holes. My sisters and I had made plenty of reed flutes growing up because they were easy to come by and cheap to make.

When I had roughly dug out the first finger hole, I offered him the handle of the dagger and reed, and he gladly took it from me and began to dig out the rest. He was stronger and more familiar with the weapon, making much faster work of the holes than I did.

And all the while, we didn't say anything, just sat in each other's presence. When he had finished, he held up the flute like a child having whittled his first horse.

He handed me the rough reed flute, and I placed it to my lips and gave it a cursory blow.

Pffffitttt!

It made a horrible high-pitched noise like a dying cat. Twenty-one pairs of eyes looked at us, and I didn't like being the center of attention.

I laughed, and so did Evander. "Maybe we messed up," he said.

"No, we didn't. It's just been a very long time, and I'm not as good as my sister, Meri. It may take me a minute," I wheezed, wiping the tears from my eyes. I took a calming breath and centered myself, this time focusing on control and the notes.

The second try was far better than the first. It was a low, soft note, and then I began to play an old ancient song of the fae, one that my teacher, Lorn, had taught me.

It was a song of longing and lust and loss—or it would be if one actually translated the fae lyrics that accompanied the melody, but I knew no one here would know it.

It wasn't played by talented hands, only competent, and I may have missed a note or two. But when I was done, I shrugged my shoulders and handed him the flute. "You try," I encouraged.

He placed his lips on the reed, and I couldn't help but watch them as they touched the same spot mine had moments ago. He blew the reed flute, and his first attempts were worse than mine, but he didn't give up until a long whistle came forth. His look was filled with triumph and joy, and I wanted to bottle this feeling that we shared.

Evander handed me the flute, but I wouldn't take it. Instead, I stood up and moved away. "You keep it. So that you can get better."

"I was that bad?" He smiled.

"Well, you couldn't possibly get any worse," I teased.

"Thank you," he said. "This was very enjoyable. I didn't expect this."

My smile faltered. What did he mean? Did I do something that was out of the ordinary again? Odd? Wrong? I began to self-evaluate everything I said.

Evander saw my worry and read into it. "We didn't talk. You didn't grill me with a thousand questions or flaunt your many talents and credentials. You never spoke of how you'd make a good wife and queen." He sighed warily and ran his hands through his dark hair.

He must have had the same conversation, or variation, with the last nineteen girls.

"That's easy," I said, "because I wouldn't."

"What?" His head snapped up. "Are you saying that you wouldn't make a good wife or queen?"

"Yes, I mean, no." I looked down at the grass and bit my lip. How could I explain to him that, if he knew who I really was, he would turn his back on me? And if his father knew who I was, he would have me thrown in the dungeon at the first opportunity.

"What is it?" he asked, I could hear the frustration in his voice. He thought I was playing games.

We stood facing each other, and my nerves began to get the better of me. I tucked a stray hair behind my ear. Evander watched my moves like a hawk, and he was about to say something when we were interrupted.

"Your Highness." Adelle had joined us. Her rouge on her lips made her all the more seductive. Her hands ran down his arm, resting gently on the reed flute. "Let me play for you. I am highly trained and will play you a song that will be easy on the ears."

I was shocked, appalled at the nerve, and watched as he released the instrument. Anger churned inside me when I saw her fake red lips press against the flute, and rage burned when a note so pure flowed seamlessly from the instrument we created.

She put my flute playing to shame, and I instantly became the third wheel. Evander had his hands clasped in front of him, and he listened patiently. He gave all of his attention to Adelle. And why wouldn't he? She was beautiful, exotic, and poised—already a queen in stature.

My stomach rolled, and I felt ill. Lowering my head, I silently excused myself and headed back to the group. Tears threatened to spill forth, but I held them back. I refused to show my emotions to anyone, but they wavered, and I saw my dress flicker into the simple blue day dress.

I gasped and looked up. All of the ladies were watching the exchange between Adelle and Evander. If mine flickered, then so did Tess's. I glanced at Tess, who seemed a bit panicked, her hands running over the ribbon to make sure her glamour was still intact.

No one seemed to have seen the flicker except for.... I felt the glare, the power of a stare that prickled the back of my neck.

Queen Giselle was watching me. Her eyes narrowed, mouth pursed in thought.

Had she seen?

Did she know?

The simple reed flute I had haphazardly made was being played to a height I didn't even know was possible, and Evander was now fully enraptured.

My emotions were building, and I tried to ground myself, by tapping into the ley lines of magic when my feelings were so raw was dangerous. I reached deep into the earth so I wouldn't lose hold of my glamour.

I didn't care. I just wanted it to stop. I was tired of being second string and constantly shown up. At home it was by my sisters. And even now, moments that were supposed to be mine, Evander shared it with every girl here, and now I was being shown up by my own musical instrument.

A storm cloud rolled in with no warning. The wind picked up, and it started to rain, where minutes ago it was a cloudless sky. Fast and furious, the rain came. The girls ran for the gazebos, seeking shelter from the torrential downpour. Evander pulled Adelle farther into the shelter of the willow tree, and now the long, willowy branches hid them from my view.

Servants appeared with parasols and ran to give cover to the queen, but she didn't seem to be upset by her dress being soaked, for now the rain and wind was blowing sideways. I stood in the middle of the path, the rain soaking my hair and dress, not moving. Not caring.

The willow branches moved in the wind, and I saw Adelle with her arms wrapped around the prince in what looked like a loving and tender embrace.

I was going to be sick.

"Come, my child." Queen Giselle stood by my side, her hand resting on my shoulder. Three servants with parasols were sheltering her from the onslaught. "We have much to discuss."

More servants were rushing from the palace with parasols and blankets to shelter the ladies from the rain and usher them inside. Prince Evander and Adelle were running hand in hand toward a different set of doors farther from us.

Silently, I followed the queen into the palace and into her private parlor, while the other girls were taken back to their rooms. I was shivering from the cold but doing my best to keep my teeth from chattering.

"You're not like the others," Queen Giselle stated and moved to sit in a chair by the fire. "You're different." She poured me tea in a cup with gold suns around the rim.

"D-Different isn't bad," I said, my teeth chattering. I took a sip of the tea. It warmed my mouth as it passed and soothed my still sore throat.

"It can be," Queen Giselle said. "But I want to know more about you."

"W-What do you want to know?"

"Where are you from? Not from Thressia. I know most of the girls from affluent families, and you are not one of them, despite your elegant gown."

"I'm from a small town on the edge of Candor," I answered. "It's barely a blip on the map."

"You worry me," the queen stated.

"I don't understand."

"Precisely. I know nothing about you or your family, and that can be a problem."

"I won't be a problem," I assured her.

A rap at the door stilled anymore questions from the queen. "That will be all. You can retire to your rooms, and I will see you tonight at dinner."

I curtsied and backed out the door.

One of the servant girls from earlier was waiting for me. "Miss."

"Yes," I said, shivering.

"I will take you to your room now and bring you fresh clothes, although, when I went to your room earlier, I didn't see any trunks. Have you not had your servants sent to the palace?"

"No, I will have them send my things over later."

"Right this way."

My rooms were in the east wing, and I was the last room on the end of the hall. My assigned servant, Cristin, was quite a chatterbox. Adelle had the room on my left, and Harmony was right across from me. Seeing a speck of ash appear on my gloved hand, I picked up my pace and was partially running. It wasn't that my glamour was wearing off, but that the spell was dying out and, any second, I would be transported back into the locked room. If I didn't move, Cristin would see me disappear right before her eyes.

She opened the door, and I rushed in, barely giving a glance to the room or the decor.

"Anything you need, miss?" Cristin asked right outside my door.

"No." I closed the door in her face and disappeared.

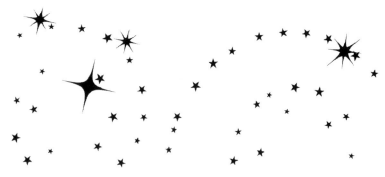

CHAPTER FOURTEEN

Freezing. I was freezing cold. My fire had gone out, and I was out of wood. I kicked off my shoes, which released the glamour on my dress. I wrapped a blanket around my shoulders and curled up on the bed. I was too exhausted from causing the thunderstorm to work a spell.

Moments later, the door opened and Dorian entered with a house elf carrying another tray of food. I didn't move or open my eyes. I couldn't. I had a dull ache over all my limbs and heart. The elf placed the tray on the nightstand, and Dorian reached over to touch my forehead then my sleeve.

"You're freezing cold!" he exclaimed. "And you let the fire go out."

"I'll be fine," I snapped and rolled over, pulling the blanket over my dress as I shivered, praying that he didn't notice my dress and hair were damp from the rain.

"I'll have one of the house elves bring you warmer clothes."

"I don't need more clothes. I would like *my* clothes."

"I'll go and get them later tonight," he said.

"Thank you," I whispered, too tired to fight. The door opened and closed, and a few moments later it opened again.

Through lowered lashes, I could see Dorian as he covered

me with a wool blanket. He stacked wood by the fireplace and rebuilt the fire until my room was toasty warm. "Let me go," I begged, still huddled under the blanket.

"I can't. Not yet."

"Then leave," I demanded.

"I could stay if you want. Keep you company."

"I already told you. Let me go or leave. I don't want to be anywhere near you."

I heard his footsteps move away and door closed, followed by the click of the lock.

I sat up and looked over at the newly rebuilt fire and stack of wood.

I debated going back, when every part of me wanted to crawl into my bed and wallow. But that wasn't what my mother taught me. Strong girls didn't hide, they showed their pride. It wouldn't matter if Evander picked Adelle to be his bride. It wasn't the least concern of mine who he picked.

I was here to find answers to my past. To find out why the king had my real mother killed.

After giving myself a pep talk, I glamoured my dress, added more logs to the grate and redrew the traveling circle. When the fire was blazing hot, I stepped into it.

The plume of smoke announcing my arrival was not as obvious as before. My maid had stocked the fire to my room and kept it lit, and by the stars of luck, I appeared in my own room. Now I had more time to look over my surroundings. The room was extravagant, with a polished oak four-poster bed, walls covered in a blue and gold fleur-de-lis pattern. Cherubs decorated each of the candelabras and chandeliers. Even the fireplace had angels holding up the mantlepiece. A pianoforte overlooked open double windows that led onto a verandah.

What had happened since I had left? I was about to go out and explore, when Cristin appeared at my door with instructions to bring me down to dinner. So maybe no one had noticed my absence.

The dining room was exquisite. Floor-to-ceiling paneled windows overlooked the garden, and, down the middle of the room, a long mahogany table had been set up with the finest china of blue with a gold sunburst. Lovely gold-rimmed glass goblets filled with mulled cider set at each place setting. I was scared to touch anything for fear of breaking a plate or glass.

Intricate name cards were placed on each plate with our name penned in gold ink. I found the one with my name and glanced at the names on either side of me. Harmony was on one side and Melisandre on the other. Across from me were place cards for Nessa, Adelle, and Sela. But more importantly, the table was only set for ten girls.

Our group had been cut in half just since this afternoon.

When I saw Adelle walk into the room, I immediately regretted my choice of dress. I was wearing a pale pink dress that accented my golden hair. Adelle had worn a deep purple that made her dark locks look black. Her lips were painted a deeper red, her hair braided and wrapped to look like a crown was already perched upon her perfect head.

Prince Evander entered the room, and we all stood, my chair scraping the floor with a loud screech. Adelle snickered, while Harmony gave me a comforting look.

"Good evening, ladies," Prince Evander said, gesturing for us to be seated. "I would like to apologize for the interruption to our earlier outdoor excursion, but we all know one cannot control Mother Nature."

My lips pinched as I tried to hold back my mischievous smile. No, not everyone can, but I could. Sometimes.

I placed my cloth napkin in my lap and glanced at Evander, trying to not be obvious in my perusal of him. In fact, all ten of us were trying to not look at him. He had showered and changed. His tailored jacket had the blue ribbons and the gold family crest of the sun upon the lapel.

Dinner was an awkward affair. The prince would try and direct a question to one of the ladies, but it was frequently interrupted as another would chime in with her own opinion.

"Harmony, what are your hobbies? Do you sing, perhaps? Is that why your family chose your name?" he asked.

Harmony beamed at Evander. She was enchanting in a lavender dress. I found myself watching her. Her enthusiasm and passion was contagious.

"No, my prince. I believe it was my parents wish that I would have the voice of a songbird, but the heavens had their own joke. For when I sing, it is more of a dying crow." Her comment made everyone laugh, even Evander.

I laughed as well, for it reminded me of my sister Maeve. I looked along the table at all of the preening faces, the glittering dresses, and the food. Oh my, was the food delicious. I was happy to not answer any questions if it meant I could shove more of the bite-sized hors d'oeuvre in my mouth.

"Why, I can sing, Your Highness," Adelle added. "I've been trained by some of the best tutors in Rya."

I popped a stuffed fig in my mouth and struggled to chew as jealousy filled me at Adelle's comment.

"I can as well," Sela chimed in.

"I can play the pianoforte," Melisandre spoke up.

I kept my head low and tried to not let guilt eat away at me, while I tried to conjure enough spit in my mouth to swallow my own pride and the fig.

When I cast a glance up toward Evander, I was startled to meet his gaze. Was he watching me?

A light soup course was brought out, and I turned to thank the server who handed me my soup.

"Tha—" My thanks died on my lips as Dorian brushed against my shoulder. Was he still vetting girls by being a servant now? He paused and looked at me with confusion when I stopped midword and waited for him to recognize me and yell at me for being out of my room. His only reaction was a widening of his eyes, and he pressed his lips together in displeasure for a split second before a stony mask slid over his features.

"Do you need something, miss?" he asked, speaking between clenched teeth. He was angry.

"Nope. No. Uh-uh," I said quickly, waving him off and picking up my spoon to dig in and take a sip.

He tried to warn me. "Careful, it's ho—"

"Hot!" I said over a mouthful of burning liquid that was scalding my tongue.

Dorian was already ahead of me and handed me my glass. I quickly took a sip to ease the molten-hot lava that was burning my mouth. Unfortunately, my burning mouth escapade did not go unnoticed by the masses. Adelle looked smug, Melisandre shook her head in disapproval, Nessa snickered, and only Harmony looked upon me with sympathy and took a huge spoonful as well.

Waving her hands, she grasped for a drink. "You're right. It is hot!"

Harmony, miss perfect Harmony, had done something just

as stupid to help keep the pressure off of me. She gave me a wink as she guzzled down her drink.

Dorian reappeared with a jar of honey and two spoons. "Here, if you suck on a spoonful of honey, it will ease the burn in your mouth, but not your other burns," he tossed out.

"Why, thank you. I will." Harmony took a large spoonful and then followed it by closing her eyes and making a moaning sound.

My hands were shaking, and I was scared of dripping honey across my dress.

Dorian leaned down and whispered into my ear, "Would you like me to put a spoonful in your mouth?" His husky voice suggested so much more. It seemed he had gotten over his anger and decided instead to punish me in a different way.

Terrified, I snatched the spoon out of the jar and jammed it into my mouth. I made no noise and instead turned to glare at Dorian, while the spoon was still hanging between my lips.

Hopefully, no one else heard the deep husky laugh or his parting whisper of "Too bad." But he didn't leave. Dorian stood along the back wall—watching, waiting to refill drinks, and taking away plates as servants brought out each course.

Somehow, of the five servants in attendance that were rotating around the table, Dorian always made sure he was at my elbow, carefully, taking longer than necessary to remove my dish or fill my glass. He would cast me a look, and I would quickly look away. I hated this new form of punishment he was doling out for me escaping. He shouldn't be surprised.

Others began to notice how much attention the male servant gave me, or maybe they just noticed how truly attractive he was. His uniform was tight across his shoulders, his body tall and lithe, and he stood a good six inches over the other servants. I had to deal with his nearness, his light touch, and his scent. The mix of spices and earth played havoc on my senses.

When dinner came, I kept my hands in my lap and refused to look his way as he placed the plate in front of me. "Just for you. It is wild pheasant in mushroom and wine sauce."

"Thank you," I said stiffly, frustrated that he was endeavoring to tell me exactly what each course was. Yes, all of the servants were doing it, but for some reason, Dorian doing it irritated me.

Everyone began to eat, yet I couldn't. My hands were shaking from nervousness and frustration at his closeness.

When I didn't eat, he stepped forward and leaned down over my shoulder, his mouth inches from my ear. "Is the pheasant not to your liking? Would you perhaps like something else? Perhaps something sweeter? I would be more than happy to accommodate you in any way you ask." His lips touched my earlobe, and my body jerked, my knee banging into the table. My pulse raced, and my cheeks were flushed from heat or embarrassment. I wasn't sure.

But I didn't enjoy what he was doing to me—the teasing, the hinting, the playing with my emotions. He leaned back down and whispered again. "Is something wrong?"

"Go away," I snapped. "Leave me alone. Go pester someone else."

"Is something wrong?" Prince Evander asked me, and I looked up at Dorian as my answer.

The two men exchanged a long look, and I could see Evander's displeasure. I was surprised when Dorian quickly backed away from me. "No, there's nothing wrong, Your Highness," he answered, keeping his head down.

He switched positions with another servant on the other side of the room and was now in my direct line of sight, which was even worse, for he was serving Adelle and Sela. Both seemed pleased by his attentiveness. I watched as Dorian, a true master of seduction, met his match in Adelle. When Dorian would whisper in her ear, she would ever so carefully lean in to him, so her shoulder would brush against him, and his lips brush her cheek. She didn't jump or shy away. Her hand would reach up and lay gently across his sleeve a little longer than necessary.

Dorian didn't shy away, his charm going into overdrive. Stoic and pristine Sela had come undone at Dorian's attention. She fluttered her eyes at him, giggled uncontrollably, and played with her hair. My stomach was in knots while watching all of this transpire in front of me like a dramatic play. Could no one see what was happening?

Harmony elbowed me, and I looked over at her in confusion.

"What?" I whispered, and her eyebrows were raised and she tilted her head to the prince who was looking at me expectantly. Did he ask me a question?

Oh, he must have, and I was completely zoned out and distracted by Dorian that I had missed the question.

"Have you ever traveled?" Harmony whispered to me under the cover of wiping her mouth with a napkin.

"Oh, uh, yes." I wrung my hands on my napkin. "I've recently been to Florin."

"Really." Evander sounded amazed. "With all of the political upheaval that they just had. King Basil murdered by the daughter of Eville, who overthrew his advisor to help Baist take the throne."

"That's not true," I corrected. Harmony's fork slipped from her fingers to clatter on the plate. Had I just corrected the crown prince in front of everyone? Yes, I had, but I needed to set the record straight. "Princess Rosalie was the long-lost daughter of King Basil and rightful heir to the throne of Florin. She did not overthrow anyone. By the time I arrived, King Basil was already dead, murdered by his chief advisor. If the prince and princess had not stopped the advisor, he would have invaded Baist and then Candor."

The room was silent. No one breathed; no one blinked.

"Why were *you* there during this civil upheaval?" Evander asked suspiciously.

"I had gone searching for my sister. I had been given word that she needed my help, and when family needs you, you go, no questions asked."

"And did you find your sister?" Harmony asked, her face filled with worry.

"Yes, she was being held against her will." I looked right at Dorian, pinning him with my gaze. Challenging him. Taunting him. "By a very evil person." I decided to leave out most of the details, especially that she was the princess. Better stick to the point. "But she is safe now."

"Oh, good." Harmony let out a relieved sigh.

"I heard that Prince Xander's wife has disappeared," Adelle spoke up. "That she is gone and the throne lies empty, for even Prince Aspen is missing. Some think she killed him as well."

"He's not missing," I said.

"Where is he then?" Evander demanded. "How can you know when half the kingdoms don't know."

Evander and Dorian had me pinned with their gazes, and there was no lying.

"When Prince Xander invaded with his army. Prince Aspen escaped on a ship. He headed out to sea. Where he went, I do not know." Even as I said it, it sounded fabricated. Made up.

Evander was rubbing his face and casting dark glances to Dorian. A silent exchange took place between them, and I began to worry. Had I just put my family in jeopardy.

An unnatural silence followed, and Evander cleared his throat and made an announcement. "For our amusement tonight, we have brought the highly sought-after and world-renowned Magical Menagerie and Entertainment Troupe."

Squeals of joy filled the dining room, and I felt the tension in the air lift.

Nessa clanged her glass against her plate, and Tess paled as she shrank in her chair. It seemed that neither girl was thrilled about tonight's activity.

I had heard many tales about the Magical Menagerie Troupe and wonder of their shows. They spent their lives on the road traveling, only visiting a kingdom once every seven years.

For the troupe to be at the palace for a private show was a special treat indeed. The table was cleared, and the room emptied in record time as the girls gathered around Prince Evander. Ever since our discussion, I hadn't caught the prince looking my way, and I began to feel ostracized.

I didn't show it but kept my head up high as I followed the group down the hall, out the main doors, and past the stables to the soldiers' field. A collection of colorful tents in red, purple, and gold stripes were set up around the ground, each one with signs displaying what was within their canvas shells. Controlled bonfires burned along the paths, and performers were already out and about performing. Women in silk dresses and bells danced with swords to the music played on crumhorns, dulcimers, and fiddles.

A male troupe member was rolling around the grass in a circular metal cage, and within the cage with him were balls of fire racing around the perimeter. He ran up the side of the cage, and the flaming trap rolled toward us.

Sela screamed and dodged out of the way. The troupe member jumped up and grabbed the top of the cage, his fingers sliding through the metal bars. He swung to the left, changing the momentum. The flaming ball rolled right past our group.

"He almost killed me!" Sela cried out and grasped onto Prince Evander's arm.

"He wouldn't have hit you," Nessa snapped. "He's been doing that trick for years." Tess elbowed Nessa hard. Nessa quickly added, "I mean, he probably has."

The ladies walked in groups of two and three as we meandered through the tents, each only big enough to fit one or two people—except for the sisters. Neither girl entered a tent, and they both kept their heads down, refusing to meet anyone's eye.

Melisandre inched her way closer to the prince and grabbed his hand. "Look, a fortune teller. Let's have our fortune read." Too much of a gentleman to say no, they both disappeared into the Mystic Madam De Le Cour's tent.

A few seconds later, we heard a scream and Melisandre ran out of the tent in outrage. "An ogre. I refuse to give my money to an ogre." Evander exited a few seconds after.

Many of the fae creatures were still fighting for equality among the kingdoms. Most of the rich could turn a blind eye to the subservient fae creatures. As long as they were shining shoes, mending dresses, cooking or cleaning, it was fine. Because their status was lower than the lowest servant, only a step up from the feral fae in the wild.

All kingdoms except for Rya, Isla, and Kiln struggled with

accepting the fae as equal, and in Baist, fae avoided the kingdom all together.

No one dared to approach the tent, and in a moment of anger, I grabbed my skirts and stormed over to the tent. After turning around to make sure everyone was watching, I went in alone.

I could understand Melisandre's fear. For though the tent was large, the ogress took up most of the space. From her ears dangled multiple gold hoops. Her pale green face had been adorned with makeup to make her appear more human, but it only made her look outlandish. She sat on the ground on a colorful cushion, and gold stars were strung about the tent. Her hair was adorned with colored moss and beads braided into the long, thick strands.

Great pointy teeth shot up from her underbite, and I had to ball my fingers to keep myself from running away. There was barely room to stand up or fit two people within the tent, but I stood in front of the ogress.

"Greetings, Madam De Le Cour," I said, remembering her name from the banner.

"Greetings, daughter of Eville," her voice rumbled in reply.

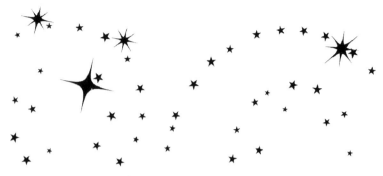

CHAPTER FIFTEEN

I stilled, my hand going to my throat as I waited to see if she made a move toward me. Her black eyes studied me beneath her protruding forehead, and she waved me to sit.

"Sit, child. Your secret is safe with me. I am Ogress De La Cour."

The canvas tent opened up, and Prince Evander entered. "I'm very sorry about Melisandre Fernglass. That was very rude of her."

"Bah! Sit. It is fine. She wouldn't have liked her fortune anyway. She wanted to know if you would marry her, and it is obvious that you won't."

Evander coughed gently and sat down on the cushion next to me. The space was so small that his knees brushed against my curled-up legs.

"Payment first." Her plump hand reached out to us, and I fingered the small silver ring with a blue stone that I wore on my right hand. It was a gift that was given to me by my birth parents—or that was what Mother Eville said. The ring served as a reminder to me that I didn't belong to Lorelai and that my parents didn't want me.

But I didn't bring any money. Who would have thought I

needed it? And I dare not glamour anything into coin in front of the prince.

I dropped the ring into her palm. When her fingers curled around the token, I felt a sense of freedom.

"No, madam, I will take care of the payment." Evander held out three gold coins that were worth far more than my ring. "You can return Eden's ring."

Ogress laughed. "Why would I? What she has given me is far more valuable than your coins. For this was a sacrifice, wasn't it, child?"

"Yes."

"No, keep your money, prince. It has no value here."

Evander leaned close to me and whispered, "Don't worry. I can replace your ring."

"Do you think any ring can replace that which was given by a loved one?" Ogress laughed.

The fortune teller's comments were hitting too close to home. She knew more about me than I did, and I was quickly becoming uncomfortable. What if she knew about my past? What if she knew my parents? Would she reveal my heritage to the prince and would I be cast out or imprisoned?

All the unanswered questions began to worry me, and I felt light-headed.

"What would you like to know?" she asked me.

"Nothing," I whispered and stood up to leave.

"Eden." Evander reached out and gently took my hand. "It's okay if you want to ask about your future."

"No, I... I don't want to know. I don't even know what to ask."

"They loved you dearly," Ogress said softly.

"What? But I didn't even ask anything yet." I tried to keep my tears in check and my hands from trembling.

"I'm a seer. I know the question you will ask before you even ask. But the answer to your question is, yes, they loved you very much. But it was because they saw your future and loved you that they chose to do what they did. It was the only path."

"How could they possibly know my future?"

"Because, dear child, it was in this very tent that your future was foretold."

"When? Where?" I demanded angrily, not caring that I was not being ladylike.

"Here, I say over twenty-one years ago." She smiled cryptically.

I wanted to scream, cry, and vent my rage, let the anger out and destroy all of the Magical Menagerie tents, and I almost did. I could feel myself losing control, feel my glamour begin to lessen and flicker. Then Evander's hand rested on the small of my back. "It will be fine. We should go," he whispered into my ear. "Now, she is just toying with you." But he sounded angry.

"Every seven years," I muttered to myself out loud. "They only come to a kingdom once every seven years. Twenty-one years ago."

The ogress's laugh followed me out into the night.

"Are you okay?" Evander asked, his hand still on the small of my back. Most of the other women were still in the vicinity, trying to listen in on what had transpired in the tent and watching Evander's body language like a hawk.

The slight pressure and heat of his hand seared through the fabric of my dress, and I became extremely aware of his nearness and the fact that he wasn't moving away. I could almost feel the hate radiating from the other girls.

Spurred on by my show of bravery, Helia stepped forward. "My turn next." She spun to Prince Evander. "Are you going to join me and protect me from the ogre? Who knows, I may faint?"

"Who is going to protect the ogress from you?" I mumbled under my breath. Which I thought I whispered so no one heard, but Evander snorted. Apparently, he had.

He stepped away from me and bowed, his arm directing to the tent. "After you."

"I know just what I'm going to ask," she said confidently, giving him a sly wink.

When the tent flap closed, I was surprised that I couldn't hear the ogress's deep voice through the fabric. There must be a spell of some kind.

Now, curious for magic purposes, I stepped to the side of the tent and looked closer at the fabric. Layered within the stripes were thin strands of silver thread. I could see the magic weaved into the thread and followed it with my fingertip. Someone had weaved a silencing spell into the very fabric of the tent. Each side of the tent had multiple spells woven within the canvas. Silencing spell, seeing spell, scrying spell, and foresight—all of them used to augment the person within the tent.

Then I understood. It wasn't that the ogre had the power to see the future. It was the tent, and whoever resided within the tent was blessed with the magic and powers.

"Who?" I wondered, questioning who had the knowledge to do this. Kneeling in the grass, I leaned in closer to the spell for seeing and plucked very carefully at one of the magic threads. Pulling it up to the light, I closed my eyes and tried to listen to the magic, listen as it whispered the name of its castor.

Nothing, I heard nothing. Feeling down and frustrated, I tried again, digging deep into the earth, asking for help. The magic came awake. Slowly, it answered, like an old man being woken from a deep sleep. It yawned, and then the magic trickled up and whispered to me.

The name.

I blinked, listened again, and frowned.

When I came back around to the front of the tent. Helia emerged, her face blotchy and red with tears.

"It's not true," she bawled. "It can't be true."

Evander looked exhausted, and he signaled to one of his guards, who were never far away, and they escorted poor Helia away.

Without waiting, I stormed back into the tent to confront the ogress.

"I knew you would be back." She smiled.

"Tell me about this tent. You are not the original owner of this tent."

"That is correct. For the tent was made by a powerful sorceress, and she graciously passed it and its powers on to our troupe when she left. I have been the Madam De La Cour for the past cycle, and there have been two others before me."

"Then the prophecy about my future, who said it? For you were not the seer at that time. So why say that you foretold it?"

"No, you are correct, but all the secrets that are seen or foretold within this tent are kept within this tent. With each new seer, we have access to those stories and prophecies told before. It is here." She waved her hand along the side of the tent, and it glowed wherever her finger touched. "And then it is here." She touched her own head.

"Who spoke to my parents? Who convinced them to give me up for adoption?" I was shaking. The tears burning at the corners of my eyes were only held back by my outrage.

"You know."

"No. I want you to say it. Out loud."

"It was Lorelai Eville. Your adoptive mother."

I collapsed on the stuffed pillow and buried my face in my hands. Was it all a scam? Did she see my future and then coerce my parents into letting me go?

"Why?" I asked. "Why would she convince my parents to give me up?"

"I cannot tell you everything, for she did not reveal the whole prophecy. I only know what she spoke out loud. But I can tell you that she fully believed that this was the best outcome for you."

"What outcome is that?" I said, terrified of the answer, knowing that I may not be ready to hear it.

"Why the future queen of Candor, of course."

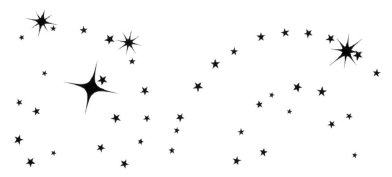

CHAPTER SIXTEEN

My heart dropped into my stomach, and I began to feel ill. This wasn't what I wanted. Or at least, I didn't think this was what I wanted. Evander was really nice, but to what purpose? I would make a horrible queen.

"No, she said I was supposed to come here and get revenge for my mother. That she had been killed by the king. Wait. Was she killed to keep me from being queen?"

"Now you are asking the right questions, but alas I cannot answer any more without payment." The ogress held her hand out expectantly.

"I don't have anything else of value." I patted my dress down.

"I will take your glass slippers," she said.

"I can't. My mother told me that I would need them."

"Your adoptive mother. The one who lied to you. Hmmm?" she said with a wink.

In shock, I stumbled out of the tent and wandered while I tried to gather my thoughts and picture Lorelai Eville as one of the troupe members. Once a lady of high nobility, she gave it up and lived here, among the nomadic troupe. Was it because she wanted to escape and leave everything—her father's death and being a scorned fiancée—behind. Maybe, yes, I could see her trying to start a new life here. And if she was part of the troupe and traveled with them to each kingdom, then of course she would learn about them, their weaknesses, and plot revenge on them.

Or maybe it was more than that. Maybe it was during her travels that she became jaded toward the kingdoms. I could see that. If she foresaw the future of a few of the kingdoms, then she may do everything in her power to fix it, or see to its fall.

What was I then? The kingdom of Candor's salvation or their damnation?

I wandered back to the main group of girls. It seemed, after Helia's fortune, no one wanted to know their future or risk being escorted away. Nessa and Tess had disappeared from the group, and I didn't pay much attention to their whereabouts.

Instead, I quickly became caught up in the show, or should I say glamour.

A sword swallower reveled the ladies by swallowing a long sword, but I could see the shimmer and smell the caramel scent of his glamour, since I knew what to look for. The handle was real, the dagger was all glamour.

"How does he not cut his throat?" Harmony asked. "Surely he would die?"

I grinned as we walked up to a bare-chested man who was pretending to lay on a bed of nails, when in actuality he was on a flat board. When he opened his eyes to look at me, he did a double take. I gave him a knowing wink and nodded to his bed.

"B-But," he stuttered and pointed to me, but I walked away.

A woman in a deep red gown sat by a mirror combing her long beard. Glamour here, glamour there. Everywhere I turned, I saw the shimmer of glamour, the illusion, and I felt at ease. The castor was extremely strong, and I had no doubt that it was all done by one person. For each item had the similar smell of caramel popping corn.

"Come and be amazed. Let your eyes be dazzled!" a man with a graying mustache and sideburns called out to us. Prince Evander slowed before the performer who stood behind a table of colored gemstones. "As we unleash the magic within you!"

"You will not want to miss this," Prince Evander said proudly and gestured for a few of the ladies to step forward. Harmony, Adelle, and Elise were the first to volunteer. I hung back amongst the girls, but the promoter looked right at me.

"You. Yes, you!" he called when I tried to shake my head. "Come here."

I felt a shove from behind as I was catapulted forward to the covered table where four precious stones were laid out in the middle of the table. The edges of the table had four white crystals that were used to keep the cloth from blowing away in the wind.

"Now, ladies, the mind can easily be deceived, but the heart not so much. I ask you to look deep within yourself to find the real diamond on the table.

"May we touch them?" Harmony asked.

The man's mustache curled when he smiled. "Of course, touch, feel, sense, find the real gem on the table. The winner will get a special gift from me."

At the magician's prodding, the girls each took turns picking up the diamonds, holding them up to the light, turning them every which way to see if they could spot the fake.

I frowned at his duplicity and didn't enjoy being played a simpleton.

"This one." Harmony held up one. *It was wrong.*

I had to give it to the magician, it was quite a unique trick.

If I closed my eyes halfway I could see the faint shimmer over the stone in her hand.

"Wrong," the promoter said.

"This one is the real stone." Elise held up the second.

"Wrong again."

Adelle grinned and held the third up triumphantly. But her smile was short-lived as the promoter shook his head.

That left only one untouched.

"That's not fair," Adelle pouted. "Eden wins by default, and she hadn't even touched the stones."

I hated that she was whining, and if I was smart about it, I would have guessed wrong on purpose. But now I just wanted to prove her wrong.

I watched the magician closely, and his mustache twitched. I was right. I could see the glamour on all the gems; they were just pieces of colored glass, but then I didn't know what else I was missing. I studied the table and the four crystal stones that were mere props... or were they? Then I saw it. Everything was glamoured. The four crystals were actually four precious gems. One ruby, sapphire, emerald, and diamond. The diamond was on the corner closest to his left elbow.

"You want me to find the diamond, correct?" I asked.

"Yes, find the real diamond."

My hand hovered over the fourth piece of glamoured glass on the table, and I saw his shoulders drop in disappointment. I should have turned it over. Should have just played the game to lose. But I didn't want to lose. I wanted to win.

I reached past him and picked up the white glamoured crystal and handed it to him. "Here's your diamond," I said triumphantly and tapped the three other glamoured crystals and muttered under my breath so only he could hear. "Sapphire, emerald, and ruby."

I enjoyed watching his eyebrows rise up and his slight nod. "Very good."

"What just happened?" Elise asked, her face a mask of confusion and indignation.

"They were all glamoured," the magician said and waved his hands over the table to release the glamour, and the four diamonds in the middle turned into plain pieces of glass.

"Whoa!" Harmony laughed at the magical reveal.

Feeling pleased with myself for passing the test, I tried to step back from the table, but the magician stopped me. "Don't you want your prize?"

"No, that's okay," I said truthfully. I didn't want a reason for the others to hate me or be jealous.

"Well, for your prize, you've won a tour to see one of the most magical and rare creatures to ever walk our kingdoms."

"Only if we all get to take the tour," I said, feeling good to share the prize.

Again, I must have surprised him with my answer. He bowed his head. "As you wish. Follow me." He beckoned and led us away from the main entertainment tents and into the woods. A white and gold tent stood in the middle of a glade; it was heavily guarded by large, muscular troupe members. One of them even looked like he could be half ogre. I couldn't help but wonder what was inside that needed this much protection.

The magician paused and turned to us. "What you are about to see is a very rare treat, one that I assure you is real and not a glamour."

When he mentioned glamour, I looked away guiltily. He waved us in, and I followed behind Harmony and Elise.

Harmony squealed in delight. Elise gasped, and I moved

around the girls and made my way to the white waist-high corral fence. I forgot that air even existed as my heart was filled with joy at what I saw.

Unicorns.

Two adult unicorns and their colt. Their coats gleamed white, their hair a mix of silvery blue, white, and cream. An albino child tended them. Her hair and skin was almost the same hue as the horses. She was singing sweetly, feeding them sugar cubes and brushing them down.

"Why is a child tending them?" Elise asked.

I couldn't pull my gaze away from the creatures, and my eyesight became blurry with unshed tears at their beauty.

I had to clear my throat to answer. "Only the purest may touch the unicorns."

"You mean virgins," Elise said snidely. "Well, that includes me. I'm not going to let this opportunity pass me by." Elise opened the gate and slipped inside to approach the baby unicorn.

"I wouldn't do that," I warned.

Elise ignored me. I turned to Evander. "Don't let her." But he wasn't watching what was happening. He was in a deep conversation with the magician. It sounded like they were arguing.

The little child tried to place herself in front of the baby unicorn, but Elise gave her a cold glare fit for a queen. The child backed away.

Elise kneeled near the colt that was curled on the ground sleeping. She reached out, and her hand brushed along his neck. "He's so soft!" She giggled. But Elise's giggle turned to a scream as the parents turned to protect their young. They reared up, their silver hooves dangerously close to her face.

The colt became startled. Elise tried to run but slipped and landed on the colt.

I stared in horror as the unicorn's small horn stabbed Elise in the chest. His coat turned red with her blood.

Screams erupted, Melisandre fainted, and Evander was now rushing into the corral to try and pull Elise to safety, but he was met with two dangerous and protective unicorns refusing to let him pass.

The albino child had run away, hopefully to try and get help.

"Move!" Evander called out and tried to sidestep past, but the male unicorn's horn followed him wherever he went.

"Over there!" the magician yelled and tried to lead him over to the other side so he could sneak in, but he was stopped by the mother.

Meanwhile, Elise had passed out on the straw, her face pale, her light blue dress turning purple from her blood.

"Harmony," I cried out to my frightened friend. "It has to be you."

"What?" she said, her hands trembling as I pushed her toward the gate.

"You have to go in there and pull her out."

"I can't. Those things will surely kill me."

I grasped her hands between mine and looked deep into her fearful green eyes. "Listen to me. Being pure does not mean virginal. It is pure in your soul, mind, and body. You are pure. Honest. Loyal. True. I've seen your aura. You can go in there and pull her out."

"Why can't you?" she trembled and looked up at me. "Why can't you go in there?"

"Because I am not good," I stated. "I'm jealous more often

than not and don't think of others. I would not let myself corrupt their young."

"Are you sure?"

"I'm positive. It has to be you."

Harmony wiped her tears away and approached the fence, keeping her hands near her side. "Evander, move away from the corral," I ordered.

"We have to save her," Evander yelled.

"No, they won't let you near their young. Your auras are not pure, but Harmony can."

When Evander saw Harmony and the determination in her eyes, he motioned for the guard to back away, and the unicorns stopped their prancing.

Elise lay unconscious in the straw, and I silently said a prayer over her. Harmony opened the gate and slowly entered. The unicorns' eyes were no longer crazed with worry; they sniffed the air and bowed their heads toward her in subservience. Harmony's slim body was shaking in terror so bad, I thought she would fall over.

She made it to Elise, who was passed out in the straw, and tried to drag her out by her arm. It took quite a few yanks and pulls to get the momentum, but she did it, pulling Elise across the stall, leaving a trail of blood. I waited anxiously near the gate and had almost set a foot inside, but saw the male unicorn lower his horn and take a step toward me.

"C'mon, c'mon," I chanted, beckoning Harmony to pull as fast as the petite girl could. Finally, Elise was within a few feet of the entrance, but Harmony was losing steam. Biting my lip, I raced in, grabbed Elise's other arm, and dug my heels in to pull her out. I was in the enclosure for mere seconds.

The unicorns spun and screamed at my presence, and I

nodded my head. "I know. I know. But you will have to forgive me this time."

I pulled Elise out and quickly assessed the damage. She was losing a lot of blood and fast. I tore a piece of my skirt and tried to staunch the flow.

"The magician went to find a healer." Evander kneeled next to me and pressed his hands on top of mine, adding pressure to the wound.

I knew they would be too late. Her face was pale, and her skin was becoming clammy. I had to make a choice. Do the best I could with my meager abilities and heal her, thus exposing myself? Or let her die?

"Get everyone out of the tent," I ordered.

No one moved.

"Evander, send them away," I pleaded. Looking deep into his eyes, I hoped that he would trust me.

"Out now!" he ordered. The guards that were in the room ushered the remaining ladies out, and then we were alone. Evander and me.

"You too," I said.

"No. If she dies, I want to be able to tell her parents that I was with her," he said nobly.

"She's not going to die," I snapped. "Not if I can help it."

I tried to go over the healing spell in my head, but the images kept getting jumbled up. It was akin to doing a large mathematic equation without seeing it. Once I saw it in my head, I could formulize the correct spell and words.

Evander could see my lips moving, and I kept shaking my head and mumbled, "No, that would be too much," but he wisely didn't say anything. It wouldn't have been an issue, except that he was right here next to me, watching my every move. Silently, judging me.

"Oh, stars guide me," I muttered and pulled the makeshift bandage away and looked at the wound, which was really bad. If only Rosalie was here instead of me. I took a deep breath and closed my eyes, envisioning the wound and sending a trickle of magic into the surrounding area. I used magic to reknit the muscle. For me, using healing magic was akin to running a mile with a lodestone around my neck. Not impossible, just extremely difficult, and I was getting weary quick.

Sweat trickled across my brow, and I tasted blood in my mouth; I must have bit the inside of my cheek. But I couldn't worry about it. I needed to worry about Elise and closing up her wound. I was struggling to breathe, to catch my breath, but I was forcing the magic to work with me, not against me.

"Please," I begged. "Just a little farther."

A soft muzzle brushed against my cheek, and I looked up into the pure blue eyes of the young unicorn, who had come and was leaning against me. My hands began to tremble from pure joy, and I began to cry.

I was scared to go near the unicorn because I felt so unworthy. My whole life I had felt unworthy, less than, and afraid to reach my full potential because I didn't want to fail. But this creature, the epitome of all that was good in the world, approached me, gave me the confidence I needed.

I could do this. I needed to do this. Instead of demanding the magic to help heal, I changed my tactic and tried to coax it. And it answered, rushing to me. My hands grew warm, and the weight lifted from my chest, and I was able to breathe. Her wound closed up, and I continued to pour magic into her, to restore her strength. When I was done, I almost fell over, but instead I turned to the young unicorn who butted his head against me, as if saying, "See, you could do it."

I was still scared, and didn't dare to raise my blood-covered hands and touch the creature. I looked behind the baby and saw that Harmony hadn't left with the others. She stood in the corral; her arms wrapped around the mother unicorn in the gentlest of hugs. Her wide tear-filled eyes watched me. She had seen what I did, and she smiled. It reminded me that she wasn't the only one here.

Evander! I turned to look back at the prince, before he was kneeling over Elise, but now he had leaned back and was giving me the strangest of looks.

His face a stony mask, his eyes narrowed as he studied me. "Who are you really?" his voice was cold, dangerous.

Elise moaned, and her eyes fluttered open. She looked at me and frowned before turning her head to the prince and crying out to him. "Oh, you saved me." Her arms reached for him, and he obliged, helping her into a sitting position. She threw herself at him and clung to him. "My prince, I knew you would come for me."

"Wait, did you do all of that in hopes that Prince Evander would rescue you?"

She ignored me. Evander lifted her in his arms as if she weighed nothing and carried her out of the tent, just as the healer in green robes arrived.

I continued to kneel on the cold floor, my hands covered in blood. The male magician stepped up to me and handed me a towel. "Come with me," he rushed out. "We have much to discuss."

"I'm tired and would like to leave now."

"You can't." He leaned down and put his arm around my shoulders. "You're exhausted and about to pass out."

I stood up. "No, I'm no—"

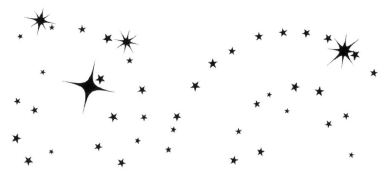

CHAPTER SEVENTEEN

I don't remember how I made it inside the magician's wagon. I must have passed out like he said. But I wasn't out long, for I awoke propped up along a bench with pillows on either side of me. He held a warm drink out to me in a mug with a chip in the handle.

"Drink, you need to gather your strength."

I took a sip and felt the liquid burn on the way down. "What's in it?" I coughed.

"Oh, just an herbal tea infused with brandy. It will warm you up real quick."

I took a wary sniff and pushed it across the hand-carved table toward him.

The wagon was one of the larger traveling wagons. A raised bed with a ladder was at the front of the wagon. Nooks, crannies, and cupboards filled with various scrolls, books, bottles, and jars took up much of the interior. Hung over the side windows were windchimes with handblown glass ornaments that caught the lantern light from outside.

"These are beautiful," I said, reaching up to gently touch one of the glass chimes.

He blushed and shook his head. "It's just a hobby." He rubbed his hands across his knees, and I noticed that he was older than I first thought. His light blond hair and mustache was peppered with white, but at night you couldn't tell. His hands were rough and calloused. His vest, though well-loved, was quite worn.

"Who are you?" I asked.

He laid his hand across his chest and grinned. "I'm Bravado. The proud proprietor of the Magical Menagerie Troupe."

"What am I doing here?"

"You needed to be warned."

"Warned?"

"Yes, warned. What you did saving the girl was reckless and stupid," he chastised me.

"Yeah, that sounds like me," I chimed in.

"No. You have to be careful because of the prophecy."

I froze, a chill racing through my body.

"No," I cut him off. "Stop right there. I don't want to hear it." I waved my hand at him and noticed that all of the blood had been cleaned from my hands. I looked down and saw that my dress was still ruined. "I don't want to know. I need to live my life without being directed by a prophecy. It is lies."

Bravado seemed torn. "But there's more."

"I don't care if there's more. I will not have anyone try and direct my future." I stood. "Thank you for your time and your awful drink—and believe me, that was awful—but I *will* be going now."

"But I've waited all this time to tell you the other half. Because all prophecies must be confirmed. There are always two." He held up two fingers, and I saw the silver ring on his finger. My silver ring that he had already gotten from the ogress.

"No!" I yelled in anger and felt power rip through the wagon. Knocking Bravado back against the bed and causing the wagon to shake and sway on its axles. Whoa! This was the power that came from anger. And why my other sisters' gifts seemed so much stronger. Because they could easily tap into their anger and rage, where I never held a grudge and struggled to hit any deep emotion.

I flung the wooden half door off the wagon open and stepped down the ladder into the soft grass. I stormed back toward the palace and passed an argument between a large animal handler and Nessa and Tess.

"What're you two doing back?" The handler's voice was filled with disdain. The moon reflected off his shiny bald head. His short vest showed the tattoos across his arms and bare chest.

"We didn't come back, Sorek," Nessa snapped. "We got ourselves invited to the ball, and not only that but we were selected as candidates for the next queen."

Sorek let out a great belly laugh and bent over to grasp his knees. "You two? You two weren't even born in Candor. Whatcha do? Steal the invitations. Buy them from a widow who lost her daughter to the plague. Is that it?"

Tess's voice became quiet. "How we got them doesn't matter."

"Yeah, once the king or queenie hear about this, you will be cast out and you will be back here working performances."

"No, Sorek," Nessa snapped back. "We ain't coming back ever. And there's a darn good chance one of us will be queen."

"Why you think that? Don't tell me that you believe in that prophecy?"

"We do," Tess said and pulled a knife from a hidden pocket in her dress. "It could be about us. We were born in the month Nochtember; it could be about but us."

"It's not," he said firmly. "You weren't born in Candor. You don't have magical gifts. The prophecy isn't about you."

"It doesn't matter anymore. We're not coming back," Nessa said.

"We're family. You don't abandon family," Sorek said.

"We're grateful that you found us and raised us, but we don't owe you anything. And if you tell anyone about us...." Tess took the knife and made a slicing motion across her throat.

"We will silence you." Nessa pulled her own knife and, with a flick of her wrist, sent it flying and pinning Sorek's vest to the poster on the wagon behind him.

"Fine, tis a shame to lose you two," Sorek acquiesced. Nessa strode forward, pulled the knife from the wagon with a tug, ripped down the colorful poster behind his head, and flung it to the ground.

Even from where I stood, I recognized Nessa and Tess in matching outfits. Ness in purple holding knives, while Tess stood against a black and white target. The poster called them the Dueling Diva's. The most dangerous show around.

"We don't live in this world anymore. And we would very much appreciate it if you could make all of these posters disappear. Immediately."

Maybe I should have confronted them about lying to me about who they were, but then my conscience overtook me. Wasn't I also lying about who I was? Didn't I help bring Tess here? And now I was just as guilty as them.

Nessa was tucking her knife into her holster and walking

toward me. I waved my hand in front of my body and used glamour to blend into the shadow of the tree.

"I don't like this, Nessa," Tess murmured to her sister. "What if Sorek doesn't hold his tongue?"

"Then I will take care of it. We just need to make sure that no one else recognizes us. At least not until one of us is sitting on that throne."

"Are you sure you heard that prophecy right?"

"Of course. It could just as much be referring to either of us. So shut your yap and let's get back to the group."

"I don't much care for the quiet one. Eden, is her name, I think," Tess whispered. "I swear I've seen her before."

"Ignore her for now. If she becomes a problem, then we will take care of her too."

"Yes, sister," Tess said, as they walked past my hiding place.

They were coming awfully close to me, and as I shifted my weight, my glass slipper slipped in the grass, clinking against a rock. Tess slowed and looked up, right at me, and I held my breath.

"Someone's here." Tess squinted her eyes, her hand reaching for the hidden dagger.

Nessa stopped and looked through the tree line. "No one's there. You're just being paranoid."

"I'm telling you, I heard something," Tess muttered.

Scared that they would hear my heartbeat or the sound of my shallow breathing, I tried to flick my finger and send a burst of magic at a rock twenty feet to my left, to scatter a few birds.

What I accomplished instead was the flinging of a boulder the size of a dog into the tree line.

"What was that?"

"I don't know, but that was bigger than a bird. Let's go." They picked up their skirts and headed back to the group. I sighed in relief. I hadn't meant to startle them that much, but at least my scattered magic worked again.

I looked down at my dress and could see the small embers burning out and ash appearing. I sighed, really wishing there was a better way of controlling how long I was gone for.

I moved back behind the tents on the edge of the troupe and waited for the spell to send me spiraling back to the locked room. As I passed into the tree line, I heard soft moans and saw two people wrapped in a passionate embrace to the right of me. The woman's back was pressed against the tree, her hands wrapped in her lover's hair as they kissed. From the side, I could see his dark hair and heard her mumble, "More."

He obliged. Leaning in, he reclaimed her lips.

Seeing them locked in an embrace made me blush, and I wanted to quickly avert my eyes to give them privacy. Their lips broke apart, and she sighed, "Oh, shhhh."

My head snapped up, and I saw her—Adelle and her secret lover. When he leaned back, I saw his face clearly in the moonlight.

Dorian.

A sour feeling bubbled up inside of me, and pain and jealousy flowed through my body down to my fingertips. I could feel the burning hatred emanating from within me for being so foolish.

I didn't care anymore. I stepped forward and made sure to make my presence known.

Adelle didn't turn, but Dorian saw me standing there watching him with accusation-filled eyes.

The embers were growing, and I broke eye contact. I turned and picked up my pace, walking farther into the woods.

"Sparrow, is that you?" Dorian called out.

"Where are you going?" Adelle called out as Dorian began to chase after me. "Dorian?" she sounded put off.

But the spell pulled me back to the room.

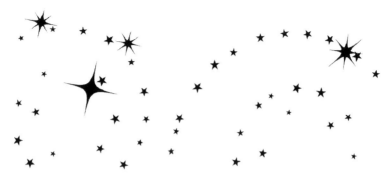

CHAPTER EIGHTEEN

Sleep didn't come easily back in my prison. I tossed and turned and continually ran through the day's events in my head. I had revealed myself to the prince, caught Dorian kissing one of Evander's intended, learned that the two sisters were dangerous, and I was still unsettled about what I was to do here. And to top it all off, it was late morning, almost noon by my calculations, and no one had brought me food or restocked my firewood.

It was as if Dorian was punishing me for escaping, letting me starve and freeze. Or maybe he didn't realize that I came back? If that was the case, I could be locked in here for a while.

I screamed in frustration, letting my anger rage. I stormed over to the door and yanked on the handle. The ward lit up, taunting me about being locked in, but then dimmed. I hated what I was going to do, but I needed help. Needed reinforcements. I needed my sisters.

I searched around for the beetle pin and forgot that I had misplaced it somewhere in the palace. Pulling open the trunk, I searched along the bottom, looking for anything sharp. My fingers found a loose nail, and I wiggled it out of the board and held it up. I pricked my finger on it and stood back up, watching as the deep red drop welled on the tip of my finger. Then I pressed my blood to the mirror on the wall and watched as is shimmered and moved like the drop passed through a plane of water.

"Sisters!" I called impatiently and waited for one of them to answer. Meri was the one who picked up the hand mirror. Her red hair fell in waves to her waist, and her bright green eyes sparkled with mischief.

"Eden! I'm so glad to hear from you. We've all been wondering what the ball has been like. Is it fabulous? Did you meet the prince?"

"Yes, I not only met the prince, but I've been invited to stay at the palace."

Her eyes widened. "How wonderful, but why are you angry? What is the problem?"

"I've run into a snag. I'm locked in a room with a ward on the door."

"Is there another way out?"

"A window that is too small to crawl through."

"What about walls? Can't you just blow it out?" Such a simple question but one that pained me greatly.

"I don't think I could do it. What if I brought the whole house down on me? What if it is a load-bearing wall?"

"What would it matter? You would be free? Unless you're just doubting yourself again. Eden, what have we told you? You are powerful, a sorceress, and are more than capable."

I shook my head. "No, I almost blew up the Rodan's farm last time I tried something like that. I don't think I can. Just help me figure out how to break the ward, and I will be fine."

"No." Meri crossed her arms over her chest and pinched her lips. "There are no ways to break through a ward. If there isn't a ward on the wall, then I suggest blowing out the wall."

"And alert the whole world that a sorceress is here? I'm trying to keep a low profile."

"Why? What is wrong with being a daughter of Eville? You should not be ashamed of your heritage."

I sighed. Meri was a spitfire and one that was not afraid to get into a battle of wits. "Okay, but you know that I'm not as—"

"Poppycock!" Meri snapped. "If I have to hear one more time a woe is me, then I will come up there and drag you back home. You are the most powerful when it comes to glamour. Glamour your way out."

"But, Meri—" I tried to argue.

"No. We all have gifts. Use yours." The mirror turned black as my fiery sister cut our mirror call short.

I grumbled and kicked at the wall in frustration. She wasn't wrong, and I hated that about her.

I heard footsteps coming, and I searched about the room carefully, looking for anything. It wasn't much, but I saw the teacup left by the house elf. There wouldn't be much left of her residual energy, but maybe enough to hold on to the glamour just long enough.

Running the cup between my fingers, I stared at the design and felt my body go cold. I hadn't noticed it before—the design on the teacup, a gold and blue sunburst, wrapped around the lip. It was the same china that was served to me when I had my talk with Queen Giselle and at dinner. It was the royal china set.

Did that mean I was in the palace? Dorian had not taken me to a remote house somewhere in Thressia but straight to the palace. I was hiding here, under the king's nose, this whole time. I chuckled at the genius and the stupidity of the plan. But how did Dorian manage that? Why would he think this was safer than my assigned room up above? He must have his reasons, but I felt even more betrayed and determined to escape.

I focused on the essence left by the house elf. It wouldn't be the same, I could glamour myself to look like any house elf, but it wouldn't truly fool anyone. My living glamours were always stronger if I had a person to mimic.

My reflection in the mirror wavered as I heard Dorian's footsteps coming. I ran behind the door as it swung open, almost knocking into my long nose.

"Sparrow?" Dorian called out and stepped into the room. I carefully slid behind him into the hall, and he spun when he heard me. I was taken aback by his torn clothes and the soot that covered his face. He looked exhausted and worn out.

"Dinky. Have you seen her? Did she come back?"

I shook my head and watched as he went over to the bed and looked under it and then lifted the lid of the trunk.

"I can't figure out how she got out to begin with. She is far more powerful than I thought," Dorian muttered.

I should have ran, taken off, but now that I was in the guise of the house elf, I felt confident. I wanted to see what he would say and do.

"Oh, sparrow." He brushed his hand across his brow, and I saw the bandages on his hands. He was injured. "You flew the nest too soon. If you only knew of the predators that await you out there. They know who you are."

The way in which he said that made me nervous. Was it a threat?

I backed away and fell into a side alcove as he took off running down the hall.

"Dinky, alert the others. Try and find her before Oz does."

I tucked the teacup safely in my apron pocket. I passed two more house elves carrying baskets to a washing room.

Neither one gave me much notice. House elves stature was based on the size and length of their ears. The longer their ears, the higher in the hierarchy they were. And poor Dinky had very short ears, which was probably how she received her name.

The farther I traveled through the maze of dark halls, the more I came to realize there were very few windows. I was in the lower level of the palace.

This changed things. Many of the larger houses in the cities had whole underground structures that were essentially mazes where the "help" lived. The unsightly hobgoblins, house elves, and elementals lived and worked below. Down below, the salamanders heated the boilers for the hot water, while the undines purified the water from the lakes. The gnomes tended to the gardens. Most of the unsightly fae creatures worked at night and in turn received housing and food. While the human servants lived above and did light food prep and served the humans.

In the country and smaller towns, we didn't care about those things, so our hobgoblin, Stankplant, tended our garden, spending most of his early mornings chasing rabbits out of our garden, and the day sleeping in a box by the fireplace.

Never had I ever seen so many fae working together. There was a clear tube system that ran along the top of the ceiling, and I could see air sprites carrying scrolls through the tubes. The clear tubes would congregate into the middle where a large cyclone of sprites were flying together in a dance before shooting down a separate offshoot. This is how messages were sent throughout the palace.

I passed a kitchen that was five times the size of the one I appeared in upstairs. I could smell the most mouthwatering scones and various soups cooking over the fire.

A bell in the kitchen rang, and twenty house elves turned to look at the wall where the intricate bell system was located.

Hundreds of silver bells hung on the wall, and beneath each bell was a room name—Blue Room, Tea Room, Library, etc. The head house elf motioned for me to come to her. I obliged, not wanting to out myself. She placed a tray of tea and the fresh scones in my hand and pointed to the bell that rang for the library.

Okay, but what was I supposed to do? I didn't know how to get out of the basement, let alone to the library. When I didn't move fast enough for the head elf, I felt a swift kick in the bum.

"Youch!" I cried and turned to her, but the house elf glared at me, her worn, brown hands on her hips. I still didn't move. She lunged, grabbed me by my short little ear, and hauled me over to a row of dumbwaiters and into the one marked library. She took the tray and pointed into the small opening.

I obliged. Cramming my overly large human body into a caged dumbwaiter meant for a smaller house elf. She handed me the tray, closed the chute, and hit the button for the elevator to move up.

"Babo!" I snapped back at her in elven and watched her mouth drop open in shock. I guess it wasn't nice for house elves to call their superiors stupid. Dinky may have a lot to answer for whenever she showed back up.

Once the dumbwaiter began to move up, my stomach moved down, dropping into my knees. This elevator wasn't operating on a rope and pulley system, but a much more complicated mechanics using part magic and part machine. I was unfamiliar with this term they call science and didn't think it would stay around long.

The dumbwaiter stopped moving, but I didn't know what to do. I was in a metal box surrounded by darkness, trapped in a wall. *Don't panic. There must be some way out of here.* I ran my fingers along the wall and felt for the handle to open the cage, but even sliding the door up, I was still trapped.

The heavy, dank air was closing in on me, and I was finding it hard to breathe. Was the air getting thinner? What was that smell? Using my hands, I felt along the wall in front of me, scratching, digging my nails in, searching for a ledge. The wall was not stone or wood, but soft and supple canvas.

Running my fingers along the edge, I found the wooden frame and pushed. The wall moved on the left side, and light poured in, illuminating the dumbwaiter.

I could see the stone floors and intricate rugs below and was about to push it open further when I heard two voices speaking on the other side within the library.

"I don't like this, my king," a male voice I didn't recognize said. "My assassin did not return."

"What are you saying, Oz?"

Oz? That was the name Dorian was worried about.

"He was the best. Which means, I can only assume, he is dead and that his mark is still alive."

"Then I need you to find her and handle it."

"I believe it may be handled already. For someone set fire to the Broken Heart tavern."

"What?" King Ferdinand seemed surprised at the news. "How bad is it?"

"I do not know the extent of the damage, my king. Nor do I know on whose order the tavern was destroyed. I only know it burned to the ground and there were—" He cleared his throat. "—casualties."

"Who?" The king muttered, and I heard the worry. Then I remembered the king was once in love with Madam Pantalonne.

"I don't know yet. But casualties are to be expected when we are trying to protect the crown."

"Yes... yes, you are right." The king sighed. "It is to be expected."

My mouth went dry. I hadn't known that the Broken Heart, Madam Pantalonne's home and workplace, was burned down in an act of vengeance to try and get me.

"But what about the reports surrounding from within the palace? I do not like these rumors of a stray witch. I need her found and killed," King Ferdinand growled out. "You must protect my son at all cost. Double the guards."

"For which—" Oz stopped speaking when I shifted my weight and the dumbwaiter in the wall creaked.

"What? Who's there?" Oz said. I heard him draw his sword from its scabbard.

"Relax, it's just the tea I ordered." King Ferdinand's voice drew closer.

The canvas door swung open, revealing me standing in the dumbwaiter, my eyes blinking and trying to focus from the sudden onslaught of light. When the stars disappeared, I looked over at the short, stocky man with the goatee. Oz's lip curled up in distaste when he saw me.

"Ugh, how can you stand having those things running around beneath your feet all the time? And don't you ever worry about them gossiping?"

"They make the best servants. They work for nothing and talk less than the humans. Besides, they are unable to speak of what they've heard."

"Why is that?"

"Because," the king sighed as I carried the tray over to the table, my hands shaking as I tried to pour the tea for the king, "three years ago, their tongues were cut out."

The teapot clattered against the tray, and the king spun on me, his hand raised to strike me down for my clumsiness.

No! I flicked my wrist, and the carpet was yanked from beneath his feet, and he went tumbling to the ground. Hard. His head smacked the floor, and he groaned and rolled over but wasn't in any hurry to move. Oz lifted his sword, and I could see the glint on the steel matched the murderous glint in his eye.

"I'll get you for that, you rat! No one raises a hand against the king."

He swung at my head. I rolled to the right and then under the table.

"Aaahh!" he screamed and tried stabbing me between the legs of the table as I crawled to the other side. I weaved a glamour of confusion over his eyes, so that the room spun and he couldn't focus on me. His aim was off, but not mine. I tossed a glass at his head, followed by another, then the candelabra.

He swung the sword widely, and I ducked. Then out of blind desperation, he flung himself at me, and we became a tangle of limbs and legs as I tried to get up and run. His hand snaked out and grabbed my foot. I face planted hard, my chin hitting the floor, and blinding white flashes of light obscured my vision.

A tug of my leg, and I was being dragged closer to him, my body scraping across the floor. Blinded by rage, I leaned up and bit him, digging my teeth into the meat of his hand.

He screamed, and I was released. I ran for the door. It was locked from the inside, the key missing.

King Ferdinand was holding his head and slowly getting up from the floor.

Oz was cradling his right hand that was now soaked in

blood but was reaching for his sword that had fallen a few feet away.

Out of the corner of my eye, I saw a picture frame move. A brown hand snaked out and waved at me urgently. Knowing that I wouldn't survive this skirmish much longer. I bolted toward the hidden dumbwaiter.

The frame opened. Two house elves were inside. One holding the door, the second one reaching out for me. I scrambled into the dumbwaiter, trying desperately to squeeze my frame inside with two more house elves. The frame closed, and the house elf drew a deadbolt, locking the side of the picture frame.

"That won't hold him," I muttered.

A sword ripped through the canvas, and I saw Oz's face grinning at me cruelly. He reached out to grab the closest house elf by his neck.

"Gotcha, you ugly rat."

The house elf squealed in pain, and I grabbed a sharp knife off the forgotten food tray in the back of the dumbwaiter. I lunged forward and stabbed the man in the chest. He dropped the house elf and stumbled back into the room.

"Go! Go!" I turned toward the elves, who were now huddled in a terrified ball in the corner. I looked at the levers and pushed one, and the cage shot upward and then came to a halt. "Now what?" I asked.

They were quivering and shaking even more. But the one I saved, the one with the reddish-tinged ears, pushed himself up from the floor and began to pull and turn cranks. I heard the cage lift as we moved onto another track. He pushed a button, and we were now moving sideways.

I was completely fascinated by the inner workings of the

system. When we came to a stop, he pointed to the wall. I was too wary to open it. What was on the other side?

The female house elf had a pink string tied to her wrist. She was the one who finally opened up the cage and pushed on the frame.

My mouth went dry as I waited on pins and needles to see where we were. I saw the overstuffed chair and the four-poster bed, and even though I'd barely spent any time in the room, I recognized it as mine. How did they know? I stepped out of the chute that was behind another painting of the palace, this time in spring, and I wondered if behind every one of these series of palace paintings was a hidden dumbwaiter. Probably.

The female elf followed me out of the chute, tended to the fire, and then held her hand out to me.

I stood there dumbfounded. What did she want? She pointed again, this time at my apron and the teacup within it.

"Oh, sorry." I pulled out the cup and handed it to her, and when I did, the glamour slipped away. I became Eden again. "I'm very sorry for the trouble I've caused you. I didn't mean to cause such a mess."

It was then that I remembered. Glamour for the most part didn't work on house elves. They could see right through it— unless they are dim witted. I wondered what that made of the head elf.

I sat down in the chair and felt the tears come. The house elf crawled up onto the arm of the chair and wrapped her arms around me. Her bony hands patted me on the back as if it was all right.

"I didn't mean to get Dinky in trouble. Will she be okay?"

The house elf shook her head no, and the tears came again. Her hand gripped my chin, and she looked right into my eyes and pounded her chest.

"What?" I asked.

She pounded her chest again.

"You. What about you?"

She took the teacup and waved her finger at me. Then removed her string bracelet and handed it to me before pounding her fist again. Realization dawned on me like a rainbow after a thunderstorm.

"If I have to use glamour again, you are giving me permission to become you."

She wrapped my fingers tightly around the string and nodded. Her eyes glittering with unshed tears.

"Thank you, I will. By the way, I appreciate you both coming to my aid. What is your name?"

She paused and held up her hand, and I saw that on her right hand, where there should have been five long, spindly fingers, there were only four. She pointed to the nub that would have been where her pinky finger was.

"Pinky. Your name is Pinky?"

She nodded. Then she pointed to her mouth, opening it up to show me her missing tongue, and I understood. They wanted vengeance, and they saw me as the tool to get them justice. So, even if it meant that they would be beaten, injured, or die, they wanted it.

This was not right. This system was broken, and it needed to be fixed.

Pinky reached into her apron and pulled out my glass slippers, setting them on the carpet by my feet. I had abandoned them in the prison room in my attempt to escape, and now I didn't want to even go near them.

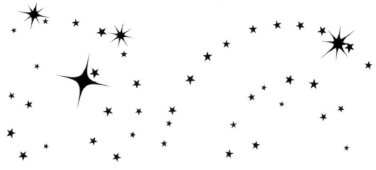

CHAPTER NINETEEN

After my escapade with the house elves and my rumble with Oz, the king's personal assassin, I would have to be extremely on guard. Even being one of the prince's chosen did not keep me safe from the king's wrath.

But I had to go. I had to see what happened to the Broken Heart. Running down the halls in my glass slippers proved useless and only hindered me. I took them off and carried them as I ran out the doors and down the manor steps in my stockings. My feet burned as I ran on the gravel through the streets.

I couldn't believe it. Didn't believe it. I had a stitch in my side and was out of breath by the time I reached the tavern—or what remained of the tavern. Charred black rubble, pools of melted glass, and a spiral of smoke still drifted through the air.

"No!" I breathed out and fell to my knees, the earth still warm beneath my fingers. Tears of grief and frustration fell freely down my face. I wiped at my eyes and struggled back to my feet, looking for any signs of life. I saw the burned enchanted sign, what was the doorframe, and a... a chain.

"What?" I cried out and leaned down closer to look.

"They locked them in," a gruff voice said from behind.

I spun on my heels and saw a weary Dorian.

"Dorian, what happened?" I knew but couldn't believe it. I needed to hear from him.

His hands curled into balls. "Men came in the night and burned the place to the ground. They were hoping you were inside."

"Madam Pantalonne, is she all—"

Dorian shook his head. "She didn't make it out. They chained the doors, locking everyone inside, and set it on fire." He held up his hands, and I could see the angry red blisters on his skin from the chains. "I returned to get your things, and it was already ablaze. I tried to get them out." His head dropped to his chest, and I saw his shoulders shake. "I tried."

Forgetting everything, I reached for him, wrapped my arms around him, pulled him close, and hugged him. I heard his pain in the great heaving sobs as he grieved over the loss of a friend. "It could have been you," he whispered and pulled away.

"No," I said angrily. "I would have stopped the men who did this—no, I would have killed them." I knew then I spoke the truth.

Dorian and I stared at the remains of the fire and the embers that still burned hours later. This was why he hadn't come to give me food. This was why he had wanted to send me home. I just didn't understand why.

A man stepped out of a nearby doorway and walked toward us. The pace and the way he walked, his hand on his sword, made me wary. He wasn't the only one. Two more came from within the shop across the street, three from the alley, and two more stepped out of a carriage that had been parked down the block. All of them wore black clothes without an insignia, and all of them were armed.

"Dorian," I whispered, and he looked up and saw what I

saw. He spun, pushing me behind him, trying to shield me with his body. "Who are they?" I asked.

"They're here to finish the job. To kill you," he said.

"Why?" I cried out. "What have I done? I don't even know them."

"Run," he urged. But there was nowhere to go. Everywhere I turned, there were more men coming toward us, and Dorian was badly injured. I wasn't even sure if he could hold a weapon, let alone fight.

"I won't leave you," I said.

"Now is not the time to act heroic." He pulled two throwing daggers from within his jacket and winced as he tried to grip them.

"Look who's talking." I nodded at his blistered and bleeding hands. "I can fight."

Dorian deftly blocked a knife strike, countered with an elbow jab to the nose, and then kicked his attacker in the stomach. He was doing what he could to keep the men at a distance. He disarmed the second thug, took possession of his sword, and then tossed me his smaller dagger.

I caught it by the handle and looked at the blade. It was well balanced. "What do you want me to do with this?" I called back at him. *I had meant I could fight with magic.*

"Well, for starters, you stab with the pointy end." Dorian was now fighting off his attackers with a dagger in his left hand and the sword in his right, using both with deadly accuracy. He sliced through the front of one man's shirt, knocking him into a barrel. He turned, looked at me, and let the dagger fly. "Like that," Dorian grinned.

I blinked in surprise as his dagger flew passed my ear and lodged into the torso of the man sneaking up behind me. He collapsed in front of me, dead.

There was someone coming up behind Dorian, so I took the blade and tried mimicking his form as I pulled my arm back. Dorian paled. "No, not like that. Not like that."

I went to throw it, but it slipped from my fingers and clattered on the ground behind me.

"Darn it," I fumed at my mistake.

Dorian charged forward, knocking a man into the wall. I heard the crunch of his skull on the brick, and the nameless man slumped to the ground.

"Okay, forget the knife throwing. You good at anything else?"

An arrow whizzed past my head and struck the rubble behind me.

"You missed!" I taunted. With a burst of power, I flung the arrow back at the archer. My aim wasn't any better, as it hit the brick wall next to him. The archer grinned, and I could see his smug face as he pulled the arrow back out of the wall to reloaded his crossbow.

"*You* missed," Dorian shot out and deftly danced out of the way of another attacker.

"Oh, shut up," I snapped irritably. "I tried."

"Can you possibly *try* harder?" Dorian choked on his own laughter.

"This isn't funny!" I growled.

Dorian was full-on laughing. "It kind of is. I can't believe that the king thinks you are a threat to his throne."

"Hey!" I yelled back and was about to send out another retort when Dorian stumbled. He was fighting two men, and blocked an overhead strike, which left his side open. I saw the glint of a knife and could do nothing as the second attacker took the opening and stabbed him in the side.

"Dorian!" I screamed.

Dorian grunted and crumbled. He hunched over as he tried to protect his injured side. The sword was sliding from his grasp. The smaller man took out a second knife and raised it in the air. The knife never dropped a second time.

I flung a decimated crossbeam with perfect precision, knocking him into and through the wall of the building. My head pounded at the use of power, but I didn't care. I screamed and flung out my hand, knocking the swordsman who Dorian was still in a deadlock with into the street in the path of an oncoming carriage. His screams fell on deaf ears.

The arrow, I heard too late, as it grazed my arm. I hissed as the pain radiated through my body. Dorian had crumpled on the ground in front of me and stopped moving. I needed to do something. I closed my eyes and did what I did best. I weaved a glamour over us, hiding us from the attackers, making us blend into the surroundings.

"Where did they go?" one of the men called out and walked forward. If he took a few more steps, he would step right on Dorian's prone form. Even a glamour couldn't hide that. I cast a glamour over one of the assassins to his right, making the shorter man look like me.

"There they are!" The leader pointed his raised crossbow.

"No, no, Reslin. It's me!" The glamoured assassin shook his head, and I heard the thud as the arrow sank into his chest.

I grabbed Dorian and tried to drag him back toward the rubble.

"Leave me," he moaned, blood trickling out of the side of his mouth.

"Hush," I muttered, "or they'll hear us." I found a burning ember and hissed as it burned my fingers. Quickly, I drew out the spell circle. It was funny how I was becoming faster at doing this.

"No, no! What are you doing?" The second glamoured man, who looked like me but sounded older, was now running for his life as they chased him down the alley.

I rubbed out the incorrect symbol as I heard them catch him and he pleaded for his life. Seconds later, I heard his cry as they killed him. I tried to not let his death affect me. Afterall, they were trying to kill us. It was them or me.

The spell was complete. Now I just needed to drag Dorian into the ashes, but the fire wasn't big enough. "C'mon," I muttered as I tried to find any wood that wasn't burned through to add to the embers. But as I tossed more wood on, the ash kicked up and covered me, making my form visible.

"Hey, that's not a witch?" the leader yelled. "It's a trick. It's Pasten. Then where is she?"

They were coming back, and I was working against a dying fire and a dying Dorian.

"There's something moving by the burned tavern. It's a shadow," a third man called.

"Kill it. Kill anything that moves."

Another arrow came shooting my way and lodged near my fire.

"Thanks," I muttered and tossed it into the flames. The fire sputtered to life, and I grabbed Dorian under the arms. "Hope this works." I looked up as three men squinted their eyes and began to swing their blades at the shadows. I felt the nick of a blade on my skirt.

It was now or never. I gathered Dorian close, closed my eyes, and with all the strength I possessed, I yanked him backward with me as I fell into the fire. The heat burned my skin, and I screamed.

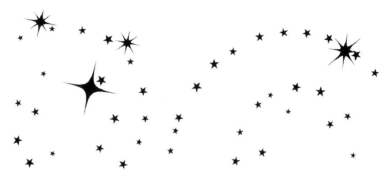

CHAPTER TWENTY

A plume of smoke billowed out of the fireplace as I fell into the bedroom holding Dorian in my arms. My sudden entrance coated everything within five feet in a cloud of black dust. I coughed and heard Dorian moan.

"By the stars!" I heard the high-pitched cry and looked into the startled face of Harmony. "Eden? What are you doing? How did you get in my fireplace?"

"Harmony, I don't have time to answer, but please help me get him to my room."

"A man? You're going to sneak a man into your room?" Her eyebrows disappeared beneath her copper bangs.

"He's injured. I need to help him," I hissed.

"Oh!" She calmed down. "You mean like you helped Elise. I got it." She ran to the door and looked for anyone coming.

I glanced around her room.

"The coast is clear." Harmony rushed over to my side and didn't hesitate to burden herself with Dorian's weight as she slung his arm over her shoulders. Blood and soot covered her beautiful dress.

We quickly carried him across the hall into my room and

placed him on my bed. I turned to assess the damage behind us. We left a trail of ash from one room to the other.

I was trying to figure out how to clean up the trail when I saw the fire salamander scurrying across the floor in a trail of fire. Everywhere he went, he burned up the ash until nothing was left of our trail. When he was done, he ran up the hem of my dress and then across Harmony's before jumping to Dorian, erasing all evidence of the soot and ash before he jumped into my own fireplace and curled up in the logs. With a fiery burp, he started my fire and settled down into a cozy slumber.

"What else do you need?" Harmony asked.

"I need to make sure that no one bothers me while I work."

"Got it." She gave my arm a squeeze. "Good luck." She cracked my door open and slipped out.

I turned to give all of my focus to Dorian. He hadn't made any snide comments in a few minutes, and I was becoming increasingly worried about him. The dark clothes he tended to favor hid the amount of blood he had lost. Only when I unbuttoned his vest and pulled up his shirt did I see the damage. It was deep and didn't seem to have hit any vital organs, but it was taking on an ugly green tint.

His shirt was ruined, so I removed it and tossed it into the fire. Then, using a spell, I warmed the basin of water and used a cloth to clean up the remaining blood from his body, trying carefully to not stare at his muscled chest. His skin was warm to the touch, and as I cleaned around his abdomen, I could see the slight trail of silvery scars that were years old. His whole upper body was covered with the marks.

"What happened to you?" I spoke aloud.

As the water droplets ran across his skin, goose bumps followed.

Feeling confident that I cleaned the area to prevent infection, I reached deep and tried to heal him. I could feel it restoring his energy, giving him strength, slowing the blood flow, but I couldn't close the open wound.

I tried again, but it was no use. My magic was resisting. I could feel it avoid the area.

"I don't understand." I began to panic.

"The dagger was made of iron," Dorian sighed. He opened his eyes, and I was pulled into those deep, light blue pools.

"Iron? But that would mean you're—"

"Fae," he groaned and dropped his head back on the pillow and passed out.

"Fae," I uttered at the same time. No wonder he had such an alluring aura. He was fae, and I wanted to ask him more. Was he part elven like Lorn? Where did he come from? But then I remembered, iron was poison to the fae and was hard to heal.

My fingers strayed to his ears where his dark hair always covered them and pushed the strands away. I sucked in my breath. They were clipped. Someone had clipped his once pointed ears, and now they were round like a human. Only because I knew what to look for and because I was so close to him could I see the silver scars on the backs of his ears.

Who would do such a thing as to maim and hide his heritage? The elves were beautiful and elusive and lived in the northern woods and hardly ever dealt in the ways of man—not since the great war that formed the seven kingdoms. Granted, the only elf we knew was Lorn, and that was because the elves tutored my mother and he was now helping tutor us. This explained so much. How he was able to get past my warded room at the Broken Heart tavern. How he placed a ward on my room to keep me from escaping. But it caused a more complicated problem.

I stood up and paced the room, biting my thumbnail as I tried to think. What to do? I needed supplies, salves and herbs that were readily available from my mother's storage room or a hedge witch, but I had nothing. I needed help. The fireplace blinked at me, and I kneeled in front of the salamander. "Can you find Pinky and tell her I need help? It's iron poisoning. She should know what to do."

The eyes blinked, and he spun in the fireplace three times before disappearing in a puff of smoke. While I waited for help, I continued to clean and care for him. Taking his hand, I held it carefully as I scrubbed the dirt and blood from around his knuckles and fingers, and I couldn't help but ask myself whose blood it was. Whose blood was I cleaning up? His or the assassins?

I poured Dorian a cup of water, coaxed him awake, and pressed it to his lips.

"Here, you must drink to replace the blood you lost."

He took a few sips and groaned. "Do you have anything stronger, like whiskey?"

"Not at the moment."

Knowing what to listen for, I heard the faint creak of a dumbwaiter.

I rushed over to the frame and felt along the edges for the hinge and swung it open and surprised Pinky. She jumped but quickly calmed down and handed me her supplies—bandages and brown packets of herbs and salves. She scuttled out of the cubby, and I closed the frame, and we went to tend Dorian.

She quickly began to mix thistle and a few other herbs in a mortar and pestle. She handed it to me, and I took a quick sniff, nodding in approval before adding a few drops of water to make a thick paste. I carefully packed the wound with the paste and waited for it to draw the poison out so we could seal his wound.

Pinky crawled up onto the bed and put her long nose next to the wound and took a sniff before nodding at me. I wiped up the excess and then turned to the fire, hoping that I would have the stomach for what was about to come next. I could feel my body waver as I tried to steel my nerves. I took the brass fire poker and shoved it into the hot coals, waiting for it to turn white. I was going to have to cauterize the wound and hoped I didn't pass out while doing it.

Dorian hadn't made a sound. He had already passed out some time ago, and I was praying that he would stay that way. I lifted the poker and turned toward his bare chest. Pinky was waving me closer, and I brought the blazing white poker over, imagining it searing into his perfect skin and the inevitable smell that would follow. The floor pulled at my feet like quicksand. The room began to spin, and the poker slid from my hands.

CHAPTER TWENTY-ONE

W hen I slowly came to, I was snuggled into a blanket of warmth. I was so comfortable; I didn't want to move. Then my blanket moved and my eyes blinked open, and I realized I was pressed against Dorian's bare chest. He was on his side facing me, his chin resting against the top of my head. His arm was draped over my waist. His muscled chest pressed against my cheek with each of his deep breaths. I was thankful he was still breathing.

I stilled, too scared to breathe or move. I was on my bed. Somehow Pinky must have put me on the bed after I passed out. But I never cauterized the wound. Dorian could still be bleeding. I tried to glance down without moving and could see the white bandage, and there wasn't any blood leaking. She must have cauterized it for me.

Not only was I a terrible sorceress, but I was a terrible nurse as well. I inwardly groaned. I tried not to move or wake Dorian as I plotted my escape from his side. I was trapped beneath his right arm, and he had thrown his right leg over my left one and hooked it behind my knee—all extremely improper and too close for comfort, especially since he still had his shirt off.

I carefully lifted his arm off of me and tucked it against his side while listening to his breathing. It hadn't changed. He was still in a deep sleep. Hopefully, Pinky had given him something for the pain and it would keep him knocked out for a while.

Out of curiosity, I ran my fingertips up the long scar on his right arm and couldn't imagine how he had gotten it. Another long scar ran diagonal down his chest. I began to analyze the scars and read the story that was written across his body. Years of abuse, but at the hands of who?

My fingers traced over his now nonexistent wound and I heard an intake of breath. Dorian's hand trapped mine against his chest, and I jumped, looking up into his very aware gray-blue eyes.

I sat up and tried to scoot away, but he grabbed me around the waist and pulled me back against his chest so we were eye to eye.

"Where do you think you're going?" he growled.

"To get you some water."

"Lie." He grinned.

"I need to check your bandage and wound."

"Lie. After you so nobly fainted in your attempt to cauterize my wound—I appreciate the attempt by the way—the fire elemental did the job for you. He did an excellent job and didn't burn the palace down while he was at it."

"I did what?" I screeched and sat up to look at the carpet where there was a very distinct burn from the fire poker.

Dorian chuckled. "The house elf and salamander took care of it and your own injury."

I glanced down at my arm to see that the arrow graze had been bandaged and a salve had been reapplied to my palm. It was weird; I had been so preoccupied that I had ignored my burn.

"As you can see, my wound is fine. You have no reason to leave." His arm wrapped around me possessively again and pulled me back down on the pillow. His eyes twinkled mischievously. "I need you close by me."

Now it was my turn to chuckle. "Lie," I said.

The smile fell from his face, and he became serious. "No, I'm not. Your presence makes me feel better. I will heal faster if you don't leave my side." He reached up and brushed his knuckles across my cheek. I was as mesmerized by his eyes as his warm breath that caressed my cheek. His eyes dropped to my lips, and he leaned forward.

I knew what was coming but didn't turn away. He lips brushed across mine in the gentlest of kisses as he waited to see if I would pull away. When I didn't, he kissed me again, teasing my lips with his own. Waiting, asking for permission. My breath caught in surprise at the feeling he stirred within me. He moaned and pulled me closer, deepening the kiss. I could feel his desire, and it matched my own, and soon I was drowning, spiraling down into passion that could burn for hours. He broke the kiss, and his lips brushed against my jaw, my neck, leaving a trail of kisses that left me aching for more.

I couldn't catch my breath, and I knew then how powerful his kisses were, knew that this was how he trapped women, ensnared them within his web to get his secrets. Like Adelle.

The image of him flirting with her and kissing her in the moonlight burned in my mind. I remembered the wager he placed on whether he would kiss me again, and then I remembered he had a fiancée. All of a sudden, the desire left and was replaced by mortification.

"Oh, sparrow." His voice was husky as he leaned forward

to claim my lips again, his hand cradling my neck. It was painful to turn away as his lips brushed my ear.

"Stop," I breathed, feeling the tears of pain pool in the corner of my eyes. I did not want to stop. I wanted to continue to feel his lips on mine, but I couldn't, not when I knew it wasn't real.

"What?" He blinked in confusion, but he released me, and I sat up and moved away. "What's wrong?"

I moved to stand in front of the fireplace, my arms wrapping around myself, feeling lost and lonely without him.

"Everything," I snapped and turned to look into the flames, refusing to let him see me cry. "I do not want to play your games, Dorian."

"Games? I don't understand."

I spun on my heel and lashed out at him, letting all the rage and hurt flow. "You can't play with my feelings to win a bet."

He looked hurt. "I would never play with your feelings." He struggled from the bed, clutching his side. I saw a flicker of pain flash across his face, but he hid it quickly, the mask that hid his true emotions back in place. The one that elves wore all the time. Then I understood. Every time he dropped the mask, he was playing at human emotions, to tease and be carefree, to seduce. That was human. Whereas most elves were stoic in nature, cold and only showed their true faces to family and friends.

My breathing was becoming erratic, and I struggled to regain composure.

"I will not be one of the women you seduce to get secrets from."

He took two steps toward me then stopped. "Is that what you think is happening here?"

"Isn't it?" I asked. "I saw you with Adelle, one of the prince's intendeds, and now me. Are you just trying to destroy us one by one? Ruining any chance we have of becoming his betrothed."

The muscles in his jaw ticked, and I knew he was furious. "So that's what you want? The prince? You would marry him and you barely know him."

"I barely know you," I whispered back, trying to hurt him. He stood there glaring at me.

"You don't know what I'm trying to accomplish here. There are things at play that can either divide our nation or save it."

"Which one are you in favor for?" I asked angrily.

He became really quiet, and I had my answer. "I see. You are not a friend of Candor then."

"Not in its current state. Candor will not survive what is coming if Evander sits on the throne. He hates all things fae."

"You're talking treason."

"I'm talking saving the nation from the threat of war. I made a mistake a long time ago, and now I'm trying to right it."

"What threat? What war?"

He took two steps and towered over me. He lowered his voice, and it became even more threatening. "They are tired of being persecuted, mistreated, abused, and treated as slaves by the crown. They want equality."

"The fae," I whispered.

His eyes glittered dangerously. "The fae."

I turned, and his hand snaked out and grabbed my arm, his fingers pressing hard enough to leave a bruise. I hissed in pain, but he shook my arm. "If you tell anyone, breathe a word, then it will get back to Evander, and he will do anything to protect the throne. He will start a fae genocide. None will be spared. And all of those lives will be on you."

"I don't believe you," I snapped.

"Then you're as blind as the rest of the world. You humans see us as nothing more than cattle or dogs. We are not."

"That's not true. My tutor was fae."

"Oh, so you know one fae that you don't treat as a slave. Good for you," he replied sarcastically.

"You are horrible!"

He gave me another mock bow. "Yes, Your Majesty." He was slow to get up because of the pain in his abdomen.

I was about to make a sarcastic retort when a knock came at my door.

We both stood there frozen in place. Dorian shirtless standing next to an unmade bed. My dress and hair in disarray. I waved at Dorian to hide, and he just stood there smugly. He had no intention of leaving; in fact, he seemed like he wanted to be discovered. Then I would be kicked out of the manor and he would win. I would be sent home.

He took a step closer to the door as if he was going to answer it in his half-naked state. Furious and haphazardly, I waved my hand at him, causing him to be frozen in place. His mouth opened, and I slapped him with the same silencing spell that I placed on the transport driver.

Doing what I did best, I pushed him into a corner and forced him into a chair.

"Sit there and be a good boy," I teased, patting him on the head. "And I may give you a treat." He was not happy. By the angry glare, I knew he would find a way to get revenge. But I would deal with him later. I quickly wove a glamour over him, disguising him as the chair.

Opening the door a crack, I was surprised to see Prince

Evander. He was turned to the side and talking to Harmony. She was doing her absolute best to distract him with idle chatter.

Evander thanked Harmony for her time, and she ducked into her room, raising her hands toward me and mouthed, "I tried."

"Thank you," I mouthed back.

Evander looked worried, his brow furrowed, and so lost in his thoughts that he hadn't heard me open the door. He raised his hand to knock again, and his knuckles wrapped against my face.

"Ow!" I jumped back in surprise.

"Oh my. I'm sorry. I didn't see you there!" He followed me into my room. "Here, let me see." He reached out and cupped both of my cheeks and proceeded to check me over for a bump. I dared not breathe as the prince's face was only inches from mine. I could feel his breath against my skin as he lifted and turned my face right and left, searching for any mark.

I tried to not turn my head and glance at the chair. I could feel Dorian's anger radiating at me from the corner to the point that goose bumps prickled up the back of my neck.

I prayed that Dorian would be good. Because he was fae and had magic, if he tried hard enough, he may be able to knock the chair over, and then my glamour would be revealed.

Evander stopped and looked into my eyes. "I swear sometimes your eyes are green, but right now they're blue. Must be a trick of the light."

His lips parted, and his eyes lowered to my lips and stayed there. "You are beautiful."

A thump came from the corner, and Evander looked up in surprise. "What was that?"

Dorian broke whatever magic spell we had created together, for Evander shook his head and dropped his hands.

"Oh, nothing," I answered and shot a look at the chair, and it didn't move. It seemed that Dorian didn't have an issue as long as Evander wasn't touching me.

"You seem fine. No permanent damage," Evander teased and stepped farther into my room.

He held his hand out, and I stared at it. A wry smile played at the corner of his lips. "Let's go."

"Where to?" I asked suspiciously.

"There's someplace I would like to take you. Just you."

His hand still hung in the air, and I looked at it. I could feel the judgement coming from the chair. "Okay." I didn't take the hand. "Can you give me a few moments to change?"

Evander grinned. "I will be waiting outside." He stepped outside and closed the door. When I heard the latch click, I sighed and buried my face in my hands.

I glamoured my dress into that of a deep ruby red with a low neckline. My hair I spun up into a sleek updo, leaving my neck exposed. I heard a scrape of a chair and turned, knowing that Dorian did not approve of my attire—attire that was meant to seduce.

Slowly, I walked over to the chair and dropped the glamour. His eyes burned like fire. His lips pressed into a thin line. He hated being bound by magic.

"It's not so fun being kept prisoner, is it?" I whispered. "I was your prisoner, and now you are mine. Although, breaking you of your bonds is right up your alley."

This time the kiss was giving me pause. It wasn't like kissing the transport driver. When I leaned in to kiss Dorian to break him of the spell I cast, I took my time, letting my lips linger upon his, drinking him in. Knowing it was a kiss of good-bye. That I was letting him go.

I felt the silencing spell break. It was done. But I was not.

His lips moved against mine, and our mouths parted. He shouldn't have been able to move with the binding spell, but his hands reached up and pulled me into his lap, refusing to break the kiss.

I pulled back, out of breath, my breathing ragged, and Dorian was affected as much as I was. I turned to get out of his lap, and he leaned to whisper in my ear. "Now who's playing games?"

Heat rose to my cheeks, and he grabbed my wrist. I watched hungrily as he lifted it to his mouth and placed another tantalizing kiss on the underside of my wrist. "I'm not done with you," he whispered. "You will help me stop him."

I roughly pulled my hand away. "No, I won't." I changed the subject. "How did you get out of my binding spell?" I asked, pointing to his hands that were moving about freely. "Have you been able to get up and move the whole time?"

"If you don't know the answer, then I won't tell you," Dorian teased.

He didn't say it, but I knew. It was because I was horrible at casting spells. I tried to not let my irritation show. "Don't move until I leave," I hissed.

"Red looks good on you." Dorian's eyes roved up and down my dress before lingering on my face. "And I don't mean the dress."

I turned to face the mirror and saw how flushed my cheeks were from our kiss. I stepped out into the hall and slammed the door.

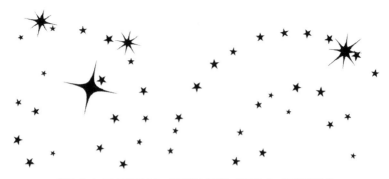

CHAPTER TWENTY-TWO

I stood outside my door, shaking with anger.

"What's wrong?" Evander's voice pulled me back to the present.

I took a deep breath and turned, giving him a full smile. "Nothing. Just nervous."

Evander grinned. "Don't be."

"I'm walking with the crown prince, and you're telling me not to be nervous."

He stopped in the middle of the hall and turned to me. "I've sent Elise home."

"What?" I wasn't expecting that.

"Yes, her heart wasn't pure. The encounter with the unicorns proved that. I've also sent Sela, Helia, and Persephone home." He moved to look out the window over the front of the manor. "I need to weed out the girls that are not compatible."

"I see." I felt horrible that I didn't even know there was a girl named Persephone.

"I'm prepared to send you home too."

"I understand," I said stoically. Too say that my heart wasn't breaking was an understatement. Somehow, I had grown very fond of our interactions, even if they've been random and sporadic, but each one had been very real.

Evander turned and leaned against the windowsill, crossing his ankles. "And that right there is what confuses me."

"Now, I don't understand."

He rubbed his chin. "The others cried, wailed, and threw themselves at my feet. Yet, you tell me you understand. So, despite the coy game you have been playing, I know it's you."

"Who?" My mouth was dry, and I struggled to swallow as I waited for him to call me a witch or the daughter of Eville.

He pushed off from the windowsill and stopped inches from my body. He leaned in and whispered, his voice husky, "I've taken off my mask. You know my secret, but I don't know yours." His breath brushed against my cheek. "Who are you, Eden? Why are you hiding your true self from me? Pretending to be someone you're not."

"I'm scared that you won't accept me for who I am."

Evander stepped back and grasped my shoulders. "You can't deny what happened in the tent."

"I... I...." I wasn't sure how to explain.

"You are special," Evander added. "Don't be ashamed."

My mouth dropped open in shock. He didn't actually say a witch.

"You saved her life, for that I'm grateful."

"Are you going to tell your parents?"

"My mother already knows."

My heart began to thud loudly. They must suspect and will probably be sending someone to kill me right now. My hands trembled, and I went to sit down on the bench. I could imagine Oz bursting down the hall with a sword to slice me in two.

"So I would like to be honest with you," Evander finished speaking.

"Hmm, what?" Oh no, I was so lost in my thoughts that I didn't hear what he asked of me.

"I have to find a bride in the next few days, if I live that long."

I began to choke. I couldn't breathe. My eyes were watering, and Evander rushed to my side. "Please, tell me you're joking?" I choked out.

"No, I'm not." He gripped my hands between his and rubbed his fingers over my knuckles. "There is a prophecy that has been foretold," he began, "that I will be murdered by a witch on my wedding day."

"No," I spat out as I envisioned Prince Evander's lifeless body lay on the floor and a bloody knife in my hand. I was a sorceress, my mother sent me here. Was I the one who was foretold to kill the prince?

"Excuse me?" he looked hurt.

"No. I mean you must be wrong. No one will try and kill you."

He lips twitched as he tried to force a smile. "I hope you're right. But if I don't marry soon, someone may try and take the throne from me."

Now it was beginning to make sense. Why King Ferdinand didn't want me to come anywhere near the palace. But what happens when the reaper of death walked right through their front door.

"What about your father?" I asked fearfully.

"He doesn't know. I haven't told him. He has a different opinion when it comes to people who use magic."

"Like the witch the first night of the ball. What happened to her?"

"Please, let's not talk about that."

"I think we should," I said firmly. "What happened to the witch who tried to come to your ball? Was she not a daughter of Candor? Could she not attend?"

"No," Evander said vehemently. "And you know why. She might try and kill me."

"What about a dwarf, elf, or a dryad? Would they be allowed to attend?"

"Why, of course not." He shook his head. "Why would you be so ridiculous? I can't possibly marry a fae."

"Well, you owe much of your kingdom's wealth to the dwarves, who mine the Dorado Mountains, and the dryads who keep your forests healthy and protect the animals so you have food for your table. And speaking of table, what of the house elves who slave all day cleaning and living in squalor."

"Now you sound like Dorian," Evander accused.

I stopped speaking and had to think carefully about how to approach the next question while keeping my face blank. "Dorian, is he a friend?"

Evander let out a long breath and rubbed his face. "Dorian is complicated. But he, too, is pressuring me to change the way things are, and I can't. I can't risk losing the throne because of a prophecy." I could hear the pain in Evander's voice and tried to think back to the man I had gone riding through the country with, who had no cares in the world and swam in the stream. Now, just a few days later, was a man with a burden, and I understood why he questioned being king. This crown may as well have been made of thorns and blood, for it seemed that it would be hard to bear.

We walked outside through the garden, and I saw where we were heading—back to the magical menagerie tents.

"What's wrong?" he asked when my pace began to drag. He let go of my hand, and I felt my heart drop.

"I wasn't expecting us to come back."

Evander frowned. "They will be here over the next few days in celebration of my forthcoming betrothal."

"Oh," I muttered and looked at the ground.

"But I have a surprise for you, a reward if you will. For saving Elise."

"I don't need compensation," I said quickly.

"Eden," Evander whispered my name, and I looked up and met his kind eyes. "A gift then."

I wasn't used to receiving gifts from anyone other than my family, and that darn blush came back to my cheeks. He took my hand and led me into one of the larger tents.

"This is a magical menagerie, and I wanted to take you through alone. Not with the other girls."

I blinked in surprise at the array of fae creatures that were gathered together. Various tanks of water, ranging from the size of a bread box to one that had to be moved on a wagon, were filled with everything from water dragons to undines, kelpies, alvens, and small water fairies that could float away in bubbles.

My fingers reached out and brushed across the glass, and the water dragon inside followed my finger along the side, chasing it back and forth. I laughed, and Evander watched me. Above the water dragon was a tank, and inside was a feisty grindylow, a creature with long green arms and legs and fins on the side of his face.

A tank was covered with a black cloth, and the dwarf caretaker, Humperstink, gave me permission to lift up the cover. A small, translucent child was floating inside the tank of water.

"What is it?" Evander asked worriedly. He began to look for the lid to open it up and rescue the child.

"It's an ashray," I said.

"What's an ashray?"

"Some would say a water ghost, and this one has, for now, taken the form of a child."

"So, it's not a real child?"

I shook my head. "No, they're nocturnal, and if the sun so much as touches its skin, it will turn into a puddle."

"You know your creatures," Humperstink said.

We walked through the earth terrarium, and I laughed at all of the earth fae. The ballybogs with their round bodies, covered in mud and peat moss and spindly arms and legs, that only communicate by grunts and gestures as they tried to bully the jackalopes.

Evander looked uncomfortable but continued to walk with me through the tour.

We received a tour of all of the larger fae creatures—a harpy, chimera, basilisks. I could have spent all night within the tent and the menagerie of animals. When we came to the end, there were smaller enchanted cages that were not kept out on display with the others. A black bat hung upside down within a cage. I kneeled to get a closer look.

"Who are you?" I asked gently.

The fur shifted and the bat opened his eyes, and I was met with one blue eye one gold eye. I kneeled closer, and the bat disappeared in a flash of smoke and reappeared on the bottom of the cage as a black cat.

"That is different," Evander said, reaching a finger within the cage, and the cat rubbed his face along the prince's hand.

"A puca, I believe." Although, I wasn't one hundred percent sure. There was something odd about this animal.

Pucas, when they shapeshifted, were normally black in every form, except this one. Its leg was pure white and encased in a silver band.

"It's been with us for years, but we can't remove this," Humperstink said, pointing to the silver band around the animal's leg—a silver band with symbols etched on it.

"He should let it go," I said angrily. "A puca should freely be able to transform and not be bound by man."

Humperstink rubbed his long beard and mumbled to himself. At first, I thought he was mumbling to himself, but he was actually speaking to someone on the other side of the tent wall. Another listener. "Yes, yes. You are right. Okay then." He turned to me proudly. "You are right. You can have it." Humperstink came forward and handed me the enchanted cage with the puca. I wasn't prepared for the cage or the black crow that now cawed at me from within.

"I don't know how to care for a puca," I cried and tried to hand the cage back, but Humperstink waved his open palms at me. "Naw, naw. Yours now. Hope it brings you better luck than it did us." I could have sworn he swore at me.

Evander laughed. "Now look what all of your 'free the fae' views has done. It has saddled you with this."

I scrunched up my nose as the puca cawed and screamed in an ungodly way. What had I just gotten myself into? I sighed. "Fine. I will keep it for now. Or at least until I figure out how to get the band off its leg." After my announcement, the puca settled down in its cage and remained quiet as we walked out of the tent.

"I'm sorry," I muttered.

"For what?" Evander asked.

"When you asked me to stay on as one of the chosen, I

became scared. Scared of being myself. That I would inevitably mess up and you would send me home."

"Then you don't understand your value. It is because of who you are that I asked you to stay on."

I held up the cage in front of him and said, "Well, this is what being me gets you."

A white dove flew into the tent and circled Evander before landing on a trunk. Evander rushed over to grab the message tube and read it silently. His face turned into an ugly snarl. He crushed the note in his hand and slammed his fist into the trunk, startling the dove who flew off in a panic.

It was the first time I had seen such a look, and I realized that he was as good as Dorian at hiding his emotions. I only ever saw the calm and amiable side of Evander. He didn't usually lose this temper like this.

"Is something wrong?" I asked.

His anger was consuming him, and he stormed through the cages and kicked the nearest one.

"Evander, stop!" I warned as he was about to topple over a nixies tank.

He looked up at me and realized what he was doing. He quickly cleared his throat and ran his hand through his hair, and I watched as his princely composure slid back into place. "I'm sorry. I just received some disturbing news. I... I...." He trailed off and looked at me with a curious expression. "Actually, I may be able to turn the situation around and use it to my advantage. I have to go and take care of it. Will you be okay on your own?"

I nodded.

He leaned forward and gave me a kiss on the cheek. I was surprised at the show of affection and blushed.

When Prince Evander headed back and was out of sight, I

stood holding the puca's cage and tried to gather the courage to do what I had been avoiding.

I turned and marched over to Bravado's wagon and rapped on the door loudly. The wagon swayed under his weight when he moved. I waited impatiently as the puca's cage began to get heavy. When the door opened, I looked at Bravado carefully, studying his profile, his coloring, and took a deep breath.

"Hello, Father," I said.

His face crumpled as tears began to fall. "Hello, daughter. It is so very good to see you again."

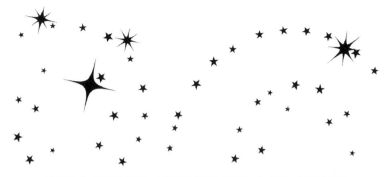

CHAPTER TWENTY-THREE

"You knew I would be coming," I said. "You were in the tent and told the dwarf to give me this." I held the cage up so he could see the puca. I carried it inside the wagon and placed it gently on the table next to me as I took a seat on the padded bench.

"Y-yes, I did," he stammered.

"Why?" I asked.

"Did I give you the puca?" he asked confused.

"No, why did you give me up at all? What happened?"

Bravado's shoulders dropped. "How did you figure it out?"

"I didn't. Not at first. Then it was hard to miss all of the hints. My mother told me I just needed a little bravado. I thought she had misspoken, but she was telling me to find you. Then my ring—my simple topaz ring that I had since I was a child, a gift from my mother—I saw you wearing the same one and thought you wore it to throw it in my face that I gave it up. But there's no way my ring would fit on your finger. Then I remembered what finger you wore it on. The ring finger, which meant it wasn't the same ring. Probably a matching set at one time."

He nodded. "You're right. It was her ring."

"Then there's the windchimes and the shoes."

"Shoes?"

"Glass shoes that Lorelai Eville led me to. Told me where they were buried. Hidden in a fae resting ground. I thought it was just to amplify my powers, but something about my gifts.... It's not just glamour. I can shift into someone, become them when I possess an item of theirs. When I looked in the mirror, I saw—"

"Your mother," Bravado answered.

I nodded. "An older version of myself." I fidgeted with the tassel on the pillow and looked around at all of the glass figurines. "You made them for her, didn't you?"

Bravado answered. "Yes, I crafted them with magic for our wedding day. They brought us lots of luck and love."

"I see. Just not enough love for me." I dropped my head and stared at my hands in my lap. The puca in the cage rattled around and transformed into a mist and then reformed into a squirrel, chattering away at me angrily, trying to gnaw at the bars.

"Ach!" Bravado fell to his knees before me, tears pouring from his eyes. "No, no. Never believe that. We loved you dearly. We have always loved you! Do you see this?" He pointed to the glass windchimes that hung in the window. "Look closer."

I didn't want to look. Couldn't bring myself to stand and see. I wanted to wallow in the truth that he gave me away. But that would be wrong. I stood up, and walked over to the windchimes. Each of the colored glass pieces shimmered as the light streamed through. At night I couldn't see it, but during the day, I could see the magic within. The reflections of myself. As a baby sleeping. One when I was a toddler. Another as I was older and learning to ride Jasper. Another one where I'm holding up a sunflower and smiling. The larger stone had a picture of me and my sister Meri, our faces pressed together grinning. It was a moving picture collage of my life.

I walked over to another windchime and found more of the same. Over a hundred pieces of glass had moving images of me trapped inside.

"How? I mean, how is this possible? I thought you didn't care."

"I did. That was part of the deal with Lorelai. I would send her the glass pieces, and she would enchant them with her memories of you to send back to me."

"The windchime in my room at home," I added. "That was you? You gave that to me, didn't you?"

Bravado rubbed his chest proudly. "Yes, yes. My memories are in there as well. If you only unlocked the spell to show you."

"All this time, and I didn't know."

"You weren't supposed to know. It was safer that way."

"Why? Why was it safer?"

"Because the prophecy."

"The prophecy that you and Mother Eville knew because she worked here for years. She was the one who spoke the prophecy into existence."

"She's never been wrong." He shrugged. "In all the years I've known her, she's never been wrong."

"Well, I'm ready now. I wasn't ready before. It was too soon. Too much that I was struggling to come to terms with, but I'm ready to know the truth and to know how Mom died."

Bravado's chin quivered as he kept back his tears. "And I'm ready to answer your questions."

"Start at the beginning."

Bravado nodded. "Uh, then this will require tea." He got

up and wandered over to the counter where he had a metal pot and began to warm it up on the small pot belly stove. He took down a tin of tea and began to set up a serving tray.

The puca had stopped gnawing at the cage and had turned into a cat and curled up asleep on the bottom of the cage.

"I grew up here in the magical menagerie troupe. Eight generations we have been the caretakers of the fae creatures we come across. We call ourselves a traveling menagerie, but really we are a mobile rehabilitation unit and are part of the U.F.A."

"U.F.A.?"

"United Fae Alliance. Having the magical menagerie allows us across all kingdoms borders because we are a traveling troupe. We spend one year in a kingdom traveling from city to city before we move on to the next. We never cross back until seven years later, or so the kingdoms believe. Our information travels back and forth. We are trying to show that fae are equal, nothing to be feared, and more than just house pets."

"You haven't been to Baist lately, have you?" I asked. "There are hardly any fae there anymore."

"We are trying to rectify that. The last time we passed through, we planted trees and coaxed dryads to live within the woods, but something kept chasing them away. But, yes, that is our goal. My family has the gift of crafting magic and glass. While your mother was the strongest at glamour. Her tent was always packed as she worked her magic. She could make it snow within the tent or make you believe you were sitting on a desert island with your feet in the sand. She performed for kings, making them believe they were sitting in piles of gold or at long banquet tables filled with never-ending wine and food. If she could imagine it, she could make you believe it. And my glass charms only amplified her gifts. Like the shoes."

"But what happened?" I asked.

"Your mother, Amaryllis, kept having nightmares. Horrible nightmares about the future, and it scared her. She went to Lorelai to have her future read, to find the answers to her dreams. But they did not give us any peace. Lorelai predicted that our future child would become a catalyst in bringing about peace to the fae and humans of Candor."

"That doesn't seem so terrible."

"No, not a first. It seemed like great news. Then Amaryllis became pregnant," Bravado said.

"And that was bad?"

"No, not at first. We were so excited. Everyone in the troupe was. It is always a joyous occasion when we are going to add to our numbers. But the dreams didn't subside, and Amaryllis knew there must be more to the prophecy, for she dreamed of blood and death, not crowns or kingdoms."

"That does seem terrible."

"Yes, so by then, Lorelai was no longer with us. She had retired to a small town in a rundown tower. We went back to Lorelai and demanded to know the whole truth. And she told us, 'A child born during Nochtember's light would kill the prince on his wedding night.'"

"It rhymes," I said sarcastically, while trying to hide my panic.

"There's more. She also said, 'That same girl with powers unseen would, by his death, be made queen.'"

That was a whole lot to digest. No wonder the king wanted to kill me.

"Of course, one cannot keep this kind of news quiet. There's always more than one for it to be a prophecy. If Lorelai foretold it correctly, then another in the land would also speak it. For true prophecies come by twos. Eventually word got back to the king. He became paranoid, erratic, and desperate. You were a few weeks old and sleeping in that cupboard—" He pointed to the bench seat I was sitting on. "—when they came for your mother and you. She hid you away, gave you her ring, and glamoured you to look like a stuffed toy."

"When they couldn't find you, she told them you had died of the plague that tore through the land earlier that month."

"There was no plague, was there?"

Bravado shook his head. "No, any girl child born under a Nochtember moon was taken by force under the guise of the plague and killed. It was genocide."

My hands trembled as I remembered my dream of my mother standing over the grave. My grave. Of all the tombstones of girls born the same month I was. My dream was trying to tell me something.

"So, I did the only thing I knew of to keep you safe. I took you to Lorelai. She was the only one powerful enough to keep you safe from the king's wrath, for he dared not touch you while you were under her care."

"What happened to my real mother?" I asked. "She is here. I can tell. I recognize the scent of her glamour. It is all over the troupe. I smell the caramel popping corn."

"She is here," Bravado confirmed.

"I knew it. But Lorelai said the king cut her life short, so at first I thought she was dead."

"Not exactly," Bravado said. "Although, she might as well be. That night when they came looking for you and we told them you had died, they took your mother. My men fought bravely, but they brought a sorcerer with them, and they captured and tortured us and when I would not give up your location. The sorcerer imprisoned your mother as punishment."

He didn't need to say anything. I knew who it was. "Allemar," I whispered.

I surprised my father. "Wait, how did you know? You haven't met him, have you? If you did, Eden, you need to run. Run far away."

"I have, and Rosalie and I sent him to another realm... for now. But where is she?" I asked excitedly. "I want to meet her."

"Uh, she is closer than you realize." Bravado chuckled and glanced at the cage next to me.

I reached out and put my hand on the puca's cage. My hand hit it and disturbed the sleeping puca who shifted and turned into a black parrot. "Are you saying this is *not* a puca?"

"No, no it's not," Bravado answered.

"What is it?" I asked, already knowing the answer because I'd seen the same band once before on my sister, Rosalie, in Florin.

"It's your mother."

The cage rattled as the parrot called out loudly, "Your mother. Your mother."

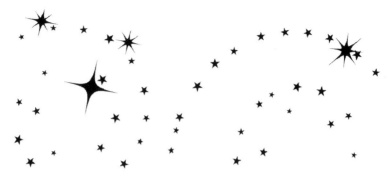

CHAPTER TWENTY-FOUR

After the shock of learning about my mother, that she wasn't dead after all, just entrapped in a puca's body. I imagined having this conversation with Mother Eville at home. She would just wave her hand and say, "Her life was cut short. She might as well be dead because of being trapped in a puca form. Details. Details."

The cage was getting heavy, and I had to stop midway and put it down on the ground. My mother inside squawked at me. "Sorry," I muttered. "But you're heavy." Bravado wanted me to take the cage and see if I could figure out how to free her. But she would have to return with the troupe when they left the palace in the morning.

She squawked her displeasure, and I knew what she was saying. "I'm not saying you're heavy. But the cage is heavy, and I can't just spell your cage with a lighter-than-air charm, because I might just blow you up instead." She puffed up and ruffled her feathers at me in response.

I took the trip back to the palace in stages, taking breaks in between, and by the time I made it up to the hall and to my door, Harmony rushed out.

"Is everything okay? I tried to keep him away, but then I

ran out of things to talk about, can you believe it? Me, of all people. But it was because I was lying, and I don't do well lying to people, especially the prince. I just clam up. Oh, what's that?" She stopped talking when she noticed the black puff of cloud, as my mother decided to show off just then and reappear as a poisonous Sion adder. Its hood opened threateningly. She was trying to scare the girl away.

"It's my mo—pet," I corrected myself.

"Oh, I love adders." Harmony leaned down undaunted, and my respect for her grew tenfold. "Well, you better put it away. Those are poisonous, you know. And dinner was sent to our room. We are supposed to dress and meet Prince Evander down in the ballroom for another surprise. I'm so excited. I wonder what it will be."

"Thank you." I opened my door and rushed inside, using my foot to close the door behind me, and dropped the cage on the floor.

My eyes searched my room carefully, looking for signs of Dorian. He was gone. He must have slipped out, but yet Harmony never mentioned him leaving. I shook my head. He wasn't my concern right now.

I carried my mother over to the table and looked at her cage and the spell on it. She couldn't shift into anything bigger than the cage or small enough to get out.

"Do you mind?" I asked. She turned into a bird and tried to hold her foot out for me to look at. The symbols were different than on the restraints that were put on Rosalie. It seemed that Allemar studied each sorceress and then made a band specifically for them to bind their powers. For my mother, it was to bind her glamour and shifting ability. And with Rosalie's, there was a counterspell that Aspen had to do to release the band.

"I'm sorry, Mother. I don't think I can break your bonds without the key, and Allemar is locked in another plane. Unless...?" I sighed at the impossible thought. *What if I broke him out? Then maybe he would give me the key to free my mother?*

It was a thought. A slim hope. After all, I wanted to save my mother.

A knock at the door came, and Cristin entered, her face pale with worry. "Miss Eden!"

"Yes?" I stood up and turned to look her way.

"It's time. All the ladies are being summoned downstairs."

"Okay." I took a shawl and tossed it over the cage and followed Cristin down, being careful to change my outfit little by little as we walked so Cristin didn't notice my bright red gown turning into a more modest plum that covered more of my neck.

When we came to the ballroom, I was surprised to see King Ferdinand and his wife Giselle sitting on the throne, and there were only five girls left—Adelle, Harmony, Tess, Nessa, and me.

Where was Evander? I looked for him but couldn't find him, and my heart dropped. This might not be a good omen.

"Welcome, ladies," King Ferdinand said. "You are the final five that Evander has chosen, but it has come to our attention that we need to move the process along a little quicker. So we are going to speak to each of you and narrow it down to three. Then, by tomorrow, he will have to choose who he is going to walk down the aisle with, and one of you will be made his wife and future queen."

I heard the gasps of the girls at the announcement.

"So soon?" Harmony said. "I can't believe it."

"Finally," Adelle muttered.

Harmony even reached over to give my hand a squeeze, but I couldn't rejoice with her. I found myself staring daggers at the king. I couldn't hide my hate and resentment and decided that a crown wasn't worth it. I would take my revenge right now. Kill the king. Wipe the slate clean for Evander. Give him a chance to rule a nation and screw the prophecy.

I stepped forward, my hand curling as I began to draw power. One blast of magic, and that would be it. It would be over. Someone appeared between the thrones. It was Prince Evander as he leaned over to surprise his mother with a quick kiss. He came and sat next to his father on the lower throne on his right, and my hand fell to my side.

Do it! my subconscious yelled at me. *Finish the prophecy. Kill them both with one blow. Then you'll have your revenge. The prince is killed and you will be queen.*

I could feel the darkness, the voice in my head yelling at me, but I couldn't do it. "No," I breathed out.

"What was that?" Harmony asked.

I shook my head. "Nothing."

Queen Giselle stood up. "We will now speak with each of you privately in our parlor. Miss Harmony." The king and queen stepped off the dais and moved to a waiting room a few feet behind the throne.

Prince Evander came down to speak with the remaining ladies. Tess looked extremely nervous, as she would soon run out of glamoured items to fool the king into thinking they had money. She was avoiding Nessa. In fact, the sisters were on opposite sides of the room and kept giving each other odd glances. Something was up, but I was distracted by the sudden arrival of Dorian.

My heart skipped a beat in excitement, and I found myself stepping his way, but then paused when I saw that Adelle beat me to it. She didn't seem inclined to hide her infatuation with Dorian while Evander was in the room. Either that or she was counting on the fact of trying to make him jealous.

When I heard her annoying laugh and saw Dorian's serious face, I decided it was the latter. Dorian had obviously not said anything remotely funny. He raised an eyebrow and looked up. Our eyes met across the room, and I could feel the heat rise by three degrees. I broke eye contact first and turned away.

Dorian moved away from Adelle and tried to cross the room toward me, but he was waylaid by the persistent woman. There was something wrong. I could tell by Dorian's expression. He mouthed the word across the room, and I tried to read his lips.

Mister?

Twister?

Sister!

I looked up at the two sisters and saw Nessa's hand slip into the hidden pocket of her skirt. She carefully pulled out a throwing knife and hid it among the folds of her dress. Across the room, I saw Tess—her face pale, her hands shaking—doing the same, and in the middle of their crosshairs was Prince Evander.

Nessa gave a nod, and Tess's face glistened with sweat. They raised their hands in perfect unison, their throwing knives balanced on the tips of their fingers as they took aim.

"No!" I screamed and flung my hands up in the air. Using glamour, I caused a great black cloud to appear, hiding him, and then with a blast of power, I flung him to the ground as I heard the sound of the knives connecting with something soft.

It wasn't pretty when I knocked Evander down. I ran across the room and kneeled near him. His eyes were closed.

"Evander!" I cried out. "Please, don't be dead. Evander!" I patted his cheeks and waited for him to respond. He blinked in surprise and looked up at me. I was never in my life happier to see those big, beautiful amber eyes.

"Eden? What is going on?" He leaned up on his elbows. I tried to untangle myself from him, but he was leaning on my skirt, so as I flopped back down on top of him.

Someone roughly grabbed me by the upper arm, hauling me away. I heard my dress rip as it was caught under Evander.

"Ouch!" I cried as I saw Dorian's angry look. He was the one who yanked me away and roughly placed me down on the ground on the other side of him. I looked back and saw the two lifeless bodies that lay sprawled on either side of the ballroom. Two piles of colored silk and lace and the red pool of blood that coated it.

Nessa and Tess.

When I had removed their target, their knives crossed each other midair and hit the other sister.

"What? Oh no! No. They can't be dead?" I got up and tried to run to them, but Dorian held me back.

"There's nothing you can do, sparrow. They made their choice. They're dead."

"No!" I crumpled and began to cry. Not over Nessa, but Tess. I was the one who made it possible for her to be here. I was the one who gave her the glamoured dress and invitation. If it wasn't for me, she would be safe. Alive.

Great sobs of guilt tore through me, and I buried my face in Dorian's shoulder. It wasn't until I heard a clearing of a throat that he pulled away.

Prince Evander was there offering me a handkerchief. "If I didn't know better, I would think you're crying because I'm the one *not* dead." His voice was cold.

225

I took the handkerchief and wiped my eyes. Dorian stepped back and let us talk. "No, I'm very glad you're alive."

"Even if their aim had been true, they would not have survived for very long."

I blinked in surprise. "You mean their punishment would be death?"

"Of course," he said. "That is the punishment for trying to kill a member of the royal family. It's treason. But I have to wonder who saved me. Someone conjured a black cloud, and a great gust of wind knocked me to the ground. It was more than healing magic. It was real magic." He looked at me through narrowed eyes, and I looked away, unable to keep eye contact.

"Does it matter how as long as you were saved?" I whispered.

"Eden, tell me the truth. No more lies. What month were you born?"

"I, uh... Evander, it's not what you think."

"Come, Your Majesty," Evander's guards interrupted me and abruptly pulled him away. "We need to keep you safe."

The whole time they escorted him away, he stared at me, and I felt my heart thudding in fear. He knew.

Dorian stepped near me. "That was very foolish of you to save him."

"It was the right thing to do," I said.

"Now there's no denying who you are. He knows. And you will have to live with the consequences."

"I know." I sniffed and wiped at the tears that were continually falling.

"Come." Dorian grabbed my hand and led me behind the throne where he pressed on a hidden panel in the wall. "You will be safe here until they clear the palace."

Dorian opened the door to a hidden room where Adelle

and Harmony were already waiting. Harmony was sitting on a settee, her hands clutched with worry. She must have been escorted here, when the skirmish started.

When I stepped through, she flew from the couch and ran to me. The door closed behind me.

"Oh, Eden, what happened? We heard there was an attempt on the prince's life? We were escorted out and kept in the dark." She grasped my elbow and pulled me over to the seat next to her.

"It is hard to believe, but someone tried to kill Prince Evander."

"No!" Harmony gasped.

Adelle was pacing the windowless room. Her hair was down in one long braid, simple yet elegant. Her dress was not a deep red like she normally preferred but a soft yellow. In her current attire, she seemed younger than I originally thought she was. She looked scared, timid, and, for once, real.

"Adelle," I called and reached out my hand. She glanced at it and walked over to sit on the other side of me.

"There's something odd going on here," she whispered. "I was there. I saw a dark cloud before the attack. It covered Evander. Just before you"—she turned and raised a finger at me— "saved him. I don't think those two girls conjured the cloud. It didn't help them; it hindered them."

"What are you saying, Adelle?"

Adelle waved her hands in the air. "I don't know exactly. But I had the room next to Nessa, and once I accidentally walked into her room thinking it was mine and she was speaking to someone."

Harmony shrugged. "That's no big deal."

"There was no one in the room," Adelle hissed. "She was

talking to someone, calling them master. I saw a shadow in her mirror, but it disappeared when I stepped in the room."

Harmony let out a frustrated breath. "Magic mirrors, most everyone has one."

Adelle shot Harmony a frustrated look. "No, this wasn't someone talking in an enchanted mirror. The mirror was dark, filled with smoke. When she turned to look at me, her eyes were black. Like dead black. I think she was being controlled."

"Controlled by a mirror?" Harmony asked.

"No." Adelle looked to me to help explain. "Am I losing my mind? Can someone control another's actions through a mirror?"

I had to be careful of my answer. I didn't want to scare her any more than she already was with how much I knew. I played it down. "Maybe. How would I know?"

"You know more than you let on." Adelle narrowed her eyes at me, her voice lowering. "I know what I saw. That black cloud, I think it was you."

"You must be mistaken in what you saw," I said quickly. Too quickly. I gave myself away.

Her lip curled up in a knowing smile. "I thought I was good at court intrigue. Where I am devious, you are dangerous." Adelle got up from the settee and moved away from me to stand against the wall. She crossed her arms over her chest and watched me closely. "I think you are a sorceress and you were controlling them. Like a puppet."

"What? No, I wasn't. I was Tess's friend."

"Liar," Adelle sneered. "You never once talked to her. Yes, she droned on and on about a stupid fairy godmother, but not once did she mention you. I think you are the liar. I think you will be the next one to go."

I blinked and tried to keep my face neutral. "You're mistaken, Adelle. I'm not going anywhere."

"We'll see about that. Once I take my suspicions to the king, you will be gone." She knocked on the wall but hadn't hit the hidden door. She moved along the panel, knocking until she heard the hollow sound. Her fingers followed the wallpaper and under the wainscot until she found the hidden handle and let herself out.

"Don't worry," Harmony said. "Prince Evander likes you. He won't send you away."

"I hope you're right." I watched the swish of Adelle's dress as it disappeared down the hall, and I wondered how much of what she said was a lie and how much was the truth.

Was that all for show or did she really catch Nessa speaking to a shadowy figure in the mirror?

Harmony was putting on a brave face but was quietly crying.

"What's wrong?" I asked, handing her Prince Evander's handkerchief.

"I'm scared to get married, Eden," she whispered. "I don't think he is the right man for me. Even though he's nice and it's what my family wants. I'm just not sure."

"Oh, Harmony." I gave her a hug. "If he asks. You will know deep in your heart if he is the one or not. You have to stay true to yourself, and your heart," I said.

And wondered, if he asked me, what would I say? For the first time being married became a real possibility. One that I had never before considered because I was a hated sorceress. Could I have a happy ending with a prince? It was something worth thinking about.

~

A few candle marks later, Derek came and escorted us back to our rooms to await further details. I felt a moment of sadness that it wasn't Dorian.

"Where's the other one? The loud one?" Derek asked, looking around the room.

Harmony giggled at his description of Adelle.

"If she's the loud one, what am I?" she teased.

He gave her a charming grin. "Why, the pretty one, of course."

Harmony blushed and pointed to me. "And Eden?"

Derek gave me a cursory look, his brows furrowed. "The odd one."

I shrugged my shoulders. "Can't argue. Seems about right."

Harmony's giggle was contagious, and I found my shoulders shaking along, and then I couldn't contain it anymore. We both began to giggle, and the stress released with our laughter.

Derek and Harmony walked arm in arm back to the rooms. Their laughter echoed down the hall and brought a smile to my face. It may not be obvious to some, but it was obvious to me that Derek was smitten with the young Harmony and the feelings were mutual. If Prince Evander didn't propose to her first....

When I came to my room, I saw that Evander was standing in the middle of the hall waiting for us. His hair was disheveled, and he looked weary.

Derek quickly released Harmony's hand and turned on his heels and left. She curtseyed to the prince, who didn't even acknowledge her, and headed into her room. The soft click of the lock seemed to wake up Evander.

He cleared his throat. "Can we go somewhere and talk?"

"Of course," I said, trying to hide my nervousness.

I followed in step with Evander as he slowly walked away

from my door. I had a feeling that Harmony was pressed up on the other side of her door listening in to hear what he had to say, but Evander was silent. He didn't speak at all until we walked outside and were back on the wooden bridge.

"I know your secret. The one you've been trying so hard to hide. You were born in Nochtember. You're her. The daughter of Eville. The one that will kill me."

"I—"

"There's no use denying it. I figured it out a while ago and was hoping you would tell me yourself. But you never did."

"I'm sorry," I blurted out.

"Are you here to kill me?" he asked, a somber expression on his face.

"No. Never. I hoped I would have proven that by saving you earlier."

"Then why did you come here?"

"I told you, my mother sent me. She wanted me to learn the truth of what happened to my parents."

"And did you do that? Find the answers you were looking for?"

"Yes," I said softly. "And I promise that I would never harm you. In fact, now that I have my answers, I can leave and not burden you with my presence."

His stony face slowly turned into a smile. "Well, actually, I was hoping to ask you a favor."

"Anything. What do you need?" I asked, worried that he may need help.

Evander took a deep breath and met my eyes. "Will you marry me?"

"I don't understand? If you believe that I'm the one that will kill you, why are you asking me to marry you? Are you mad?"

Evander's head fell back as he laughed at my insult. He wiped at his eyes and grinned at me. "I can guarantee that you will not touch a single hair on my head. That I will be safe from harm on my wedding day, and every day after. Because I believe the prophecy was wrong. Think about it. You saved me."

I was numb.

I was shocked.

They were wrong.

My mother was wrong.

The prophecy was wrong.

Evander wasn't killed by a sorceress. He was saved by a sorceress. My heart soared at the idea that they were wrong. That Evander didn't need to die, because I had saved him. I was so thrilled at the idea that he wasn't going to die that I threw myself at him in a hug and gave him quick kisses across his face.

"I'll take that as a yes." He laughed and kissed me back, capturing my lips with his.

It was a rough kiss, possessive and completely different than Dorian's, and I found myself pulling away.

"You won't regret this," Evander said. "I will take care of all the final details."

My stomach fluttered, but I wasn't sure if it was from nerves or excitement. I hadn't exactly said yes. But the more I thought about it. The more it seemed like the right choice. It would make my mother proud. Maybe, this is what she had planned all along. This was the greatest act of revenge—to marry the crown prince. Suddenly, my duty became clear. I couldn't trust Dorian or the emotions he stirred within me. He was manipulative and deceiving. Evander was kind. I could have a future with him. I could learn to love him. The doubt faded away, as hope of a future with Evander began to form. Yes, I could marry him. No, I *would* marry him. Then I could ban Dorian from the palace and I would be safe from him and those uncomfortable feelings. I could do good with my life. It would have a purpose. I would support Evander as he became King and I his Queen. It was the perfect revenge.

He placed me back down on the bridge. "You just make sure to stay away from Dorian until tomorrow."

"Dorian? I don't understand. He's just a servant."

Evander's eyes darkened with anger. "He's not just a servant. He's jealous and petty and always tries to steal what is rightfully mine. Do you understand? Promise me that you will not go near him till tomorrow."

"I promise," I said.

"He is going to try and take you from me. Turn you against me. I can't have that." Evander looked frantic and grasped my hands.

"I won't let anything come between us," I promised.

"Good, good." He kissed my hands that were tucked between his. "I have a few more details to go over before tomorrow. But I will come to you later with more instructions. Understand?"

"Yes," I said, frowning at all of the instructions and demands and wondered if this was how our marriage would be. But I pushed the thought to the back of my mind. He had almost been assassinated a few hours ago; he was probably still shook up and needed reassurance. "I can't wait to be your wife," I said.

"Don't you mean queen?" Evander quipped, but I didn't think it funny.

"Well, I guess now that you mention it," I smiled.

He walked me back to the second floor, but we parted at the top of the stairs.

When I made it to my room, I had a heavy heart and I wasn't sure why. Maybe because I had just agreed to be queen. I opened the door and stepped into my room.

An eerie voice echoed around me.

"Kill. Kill. Kill."

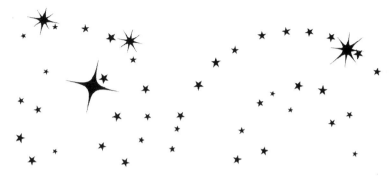

CHAPTER TWENTY-FIVE

I spun around and froze.

The mirror on my wall was filled with smoke and cast a red glow over my room. I heard the voice repeat in my room, "Kill. Kill. Kill."

"Who's there?" I called out.

But no one stepped forth. I moved toward the swirling, foggy mirror. I could see a darkness beyond. Unlike my mother's mirror when we scried, this mirror revealed smoke. I had a clue as to who the speaker was.

"I know you're there!" I called out to the mirror. "I can see you."

"And I s-s-seee you," the voice from the mirror called back.

"What do you want?" I asked.

"Freedom!" It called back through the mirror.

"I can't do that. I don't know how to release you. And, even if I could, I wouldn't."

"Kill, kill, kill," the mirror repeated.

"No. Did you command Nessa and Tess to try and kill the prince?"

"Yesss," the voice answered.

"Why?"

"Death equals freedom."

I knew that from wherever the plane was that we had sent Allemar, he was struggling to get back. He was not as eloquent as I had heard him. In fact, he was very short.

"That isn't true," I answered.

The shadowy figure moved to the mirror, and I saw something touch the glass, but I dare not move. I didn't know what it was and had no desire to get any closer to the mirror.

"Kill, kill, kill," the voice commanded again.

"Stop it. That's enough."

"Obey me," Allemar whispered through the mirror.

The hair on the back of my neck rose as I felt the power of his compulsion through the mirror. He was an extremely powerful sorcerer. I grabbed the brass fire poker and swung it with all my might, shattering the mirror. When the glass broke, the voice disappeared and I was left standing amidst a mess of broken shards.

My hands trembled as I kneeled down to pick up the pieces. My finger slipped, and I cut myself on the glass. A drop of my blood soaked into the mirror, and I saw an image of a woman with red hair in the glass before it disappeared.

"Meri?" I held up the glass, but she never reappeared. Maybe it was just my imagination.

Taking most of the glass, I dumped it in the ash pail for the fireplace and went back to cleaning up the rest of the pieces. Among the shards I found a glowing key. I tossed it into the ash pail as well. Then I remembered my mother.

She hadn't made a sound since I came back. I ran to the cage and saw that part of the shawl I had thrown over the cage had slipped off and left her in full view of the enchanted mirror.

The bird was sprawled on the bottom of the cage, her eyes

rolled back in her head. I could see her heart racing under the thin feathers. I stood back and tried to cast a spell to open the lock on the cage.

"*Incendium.*" There was a poof of smoke.

"*Lochen.*" The lock shook but didn't unlatch.

I needed the counterspell. I had seen Aspen weave it once in the air, but I didn't have the mind to remember those kinds of spells.

In a moment of panic, I rushed back to the broken shard and pinched a drop of my blood on the glass. It glowed and hummed, and I prayed that Rosalie was near a mirror.

"Rosalie," I called out. The glass pulsed, and I saw my sister pick up the mirror.

Her face was fuller, and her dark black hair was styled to cover her cheek, hiding her scars.

"Eden, is that you?" Rosalie asked.

I lost it. I began to cry. "Oh, Rose, I messed up. In so many ways."

Her eyes narrowed and she stiffly said, "Tell me."

"I found my mother. She's alive but trapped in the body of a puca in an enchanted cage."

"All cages have a key," Rosalie said. "You need to find the key."

"Yes, but she has a band, the same one that bound your powers."

She blinked, and her head dropped as she battled her own memories of being imprisoned. "I see."

"I don't remember the counterspell."

Rosalie became very still as she thought. "Eden, that counterspell is extremely dangerous."

"I know."

"One wrong word, one wrong finger weave, and it recoils back on you. Killing you."

I swallowed. "That I did *not* know." Maybe I wasn't as confident as I thought. "Can you come? Maybe if you come here you can cast the counterspell and free my mother."

"Eden, I can't," she said softly.

"Please, Rosalie. I need you. I'm nothing without your strength. My thoughts are always jumbled and frayed. I can't focus, and ever since you left, I feel like the center of my world is spinning and I'm going to lose control."

Rosalie listened to my ramblings like an older sister should. "Eden. Eden, my darling sister in spirit, I love you. Listen to me. You don't need me. You have all you need. Your life will not spiral out of control. You just have to find your center."

"Rosalie, please just come. Use a traveling spell. I've become very good at using the fireplace. You can just pop over here and do the counterspell and then go back to wherever it is you've decided to hide." I knew I sounded desperate.

"Eden." Her voice became soft, and a smile fell on her face, lighting it up. "I can't. It is too dangerous for me to travel right now. And I wouldn't dare to be the one to try the counterspell in my condition."

"I don't understand," I said numbly.

The mirror moved as Rosalie set it on a table and backed away. I could see that she was in a very small cottage, and when she stepped back, I could also see that she was very, very pregnant.

She rubbed her hands over her protruding belly and then came back to the mirror. "As you can see, I have found the center of my world. And I would do anything to protect her."

"Her?" I gasped.

"Her." She nodded. "So, I can't be the one to do the counterspell. If I mess up, it is two lives that I'm risking."

"I understand." I did. I truly did and let the tears of happiness flow for my older sister and my niece.

"But I will walk you through it step by step. Just remember, whatever I show you, you have to reverse it in the mirror. Okay?"

"Okay."

The next candle mark was grueling, partly because I had to learn the counterspell out of order, so as not to cast it accidentally, and the other was because I couldn't focus because I was watching my mother slowly die.

When I believed that I had perfected the counterspell, I was still left with one problem. I didn't have the key to the cage.

"Bring the mirror to the lock please," Rosalie said. My fingers fumbled with the glass, and I held it up so she could see the lock more carefully. "It just needs an enchanted item more powerful than the lock to shorten it out."

"Where do I get that?" I asked.

"You'll have to figure it out."

"I don't know if I have time."

"Make the time," Rosalie said. "You are stronger than you believe."

I hung up with my sister and looked back at my mother. Her breathing had become more ragged, and she didn't seem to be getting any better. In fact, she looked worse.

"Oh!" I began to panic and pace up and down my small room. "Key. I need a key or a way to—" My eyes fell on the key I tossed in the bucket. The one that had fallen from inside the mirror when I shattered it. *I wonder if...?*

Allemar had mentioned freedom. I wondered if he was

referring not to himself but to my mother. Was this the key? I picked up the key and carefully took it over to the cage. With a deep breath, I pressed key into the lock, closed my eyes, turned, and waited for the explosion.

A click as the lock unlocked... and then nothing.

I swung open the door and reached in to pull the now barely breathing bird out of the cage.

"Okay, Mother, you gave me up to save me. Now I'm going to do my best to repay you, and I'm going to try and not kill us both in the process. Okay?"

She didn't say anything.

Not having my chalk, I reached back for a charred piece of wood from the fireplace and began to write out the counter-spell. One day, I would be confident enough to weave it in my head. But today was not that day. When I was sure that it was in the right order, I quickly breathed the words under my breath and waited.

A flash of light blinded me, and power hit me so hard in the chest it sent me spiraling through the air to land on my bed before I rolled off the other side and to the floor.

Coughing, I got to my knees and peeked over the top of the mattress. Feathers, feathers everywhere, on the bed, floor, and floating down from the ceiling. And in the middle of the floor where my mother had been was nothing but a flash of white char.

"No!" I moaned. I failed again and killed my mother. I buried my face into the mattress and wailed. The wailing continued until I could hardly breathe, and when I decided I didn't need to breathe anymore. I passed out, sliding off the bed and onto the floor.

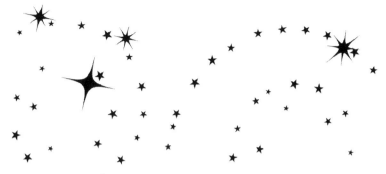

CHAPTER TWENTY-SIX

"**E**den!" a familiar voice said as someone shook me awake. "Eden, wake up."

I curled up on my side and tried to ignore the annoying voice. "Eden, what did you do?"

Slowly coming awake, I saw Dorian hovering over me.

"Go away," I mumbled and feebly tried to push him away.

"No, you need to get up now." He lifted me up off the floor and wrapped his arms around me. When he did, I saw my room and the feathers, and then I remembered what happened. My spirit broke.

"No, I need to lie back down." I pushed away from him and tried to hide from the evidence of what I had done.

"Eden." Dorian's voice became low. "If you don't get up right now, I'm going to kiss you."

The floor instantly became my enemy as I leaped up and tried to scramble across the bed and to the other side, putting as much distance as possible between us. "You stay over there." I pointed to the far side of the bed.

"I will, but you have to explain what in the world happened here." He looked around, and I took in my room from his perspective.

It looked really bad. Broken mirror with pieces still scattered across the room, furniture toppled over, the remains of my botched spell, and not to mention the feathers. The black feathers that looked like black snow over my room.

He came and stood over my handiwork and then shrugged his shoulders. "Were you summoning something?"

"No," I pouted. "I was trying to free my mother from a binding spell." I pointed to a cage.

"Your mother was in that cage?" He looked like he didn't believe me.

"Long story. But it backfired and instead I... I... k-killed her." My lower lip began to tremble, and I turned to hide my mortification and pain. I would not cry in front of him.

"Aw, sparrow." Dorian came and wrapped those long arms around me, and I felt safe and whole. Then I remembered what I had promised Evander. I would marry him and needed to stay away from Dorian. It pained me to step out of his embrace, and I saw the look on Dorian's face. He was hurt.

"What's wrong?" he asked.

"I can't."

"Why?" he asked. "Is it because of Evander?"

I nodded.

"So, this is how it's going to be. You've made your choice," he said softly.

"Choice?" I scoffed. "There was no choice. You don't say no when the prince of Candor asks you to marry him."

"You could have said no."

"Why?" I turned and glared at Dorian. "Why should I?"

He looked perplexed. "I mean, I thought that we—that you and I...."

"What did we have, Dorian? Because I'm confused at what it is exactly. You kissed me. But we both know that's how you play the game, how you get your secrets. You seduce women. You seduced Adelle. I'm just another one of your conquests. So how should I expect anything different when I've only seen one side of you?"

Dorian wouldn't make eye contact with me. He stood in the middle of the room while I scolded him, letting my anger rake across him as I tried to hurt him with words, because I was hurting deep inside.

"I never tried to hide who I am from you. I collect secrets and, yes, I seduce women to get them. But you were different than the others." He looked up, and I fell into those deep pools of blue.

"I know. I'm odd," I interrupted.

"No. There's more—"

"I'm just another one of your girls you flirt with." I ticked off my fingers. "What about Sisa, Adelle, Nessa? I do not want my name on that list."

"You know nothing of my past or Sisa," he growled.

"And you know nothing of me or my past... or my future."

"I could have, if you let me." He reached up to brush his knuckles down my cheek, but I turned away and he got air.

"Never once did you declare your feelings for me. So, I had one choice. When the prince asked, I said yes."

"Are you saying that you would have married me if I asked?" He seemed perplexed by the idea.

"No." I stepped close and leaned up onto my tiptoes as I ran my fingers over the button on his jacket. "Because you would have never asked," I whispered into his ear. I stepped back, my hand sliding into the folds of my skirt, the button I stole tucked in my fingers.

His head dropped, and his hands balled into fists. "Is it because he is the crown prince?" He looked up at me, and his eyes looked misty. "Are you only marrying him because he is the prince?"

"I have been fighting my fate since I came. Since I first heard it," I admitted. "It has been foretold that I would be queen."

"Answer me one more thing. Do you love him?" he asked, his eyes dark and stormy as he watched me closely.

"I... I don't know."

Dorian's eyes glittered dangerously. "You paused." He laughed darkly. "There's more than one way to become queen, and it doesn't involve marrying Evander." He rushed toward me and planted his lips on mine.

"Dorian, stop. It is done. I gave my word. I will marry him tomorrow."

"It's not done. Nothing is said and done. Unless I'm dead." He turned on his heel and headed for the door.

"He said you would do this!" I called out, and he paused. "Evander said you would try and take what is his."

Dorian's eyes glittered with anger. "He's wrong. You were never his, and I'm going to prove it."

"Stop it!" I cried out in frustration and stomped my foot. "I am not a prize to be fought over."

Dorian shook his head. His voice became a low growl. "It is not I who takes things from him. It is Evander who steals things from me. And I won't let that happen again."

"Dorian. Please, just stop whatever you are planning on doing."

"You should have just let those daggers find their mark," he said, and I gasped.

"How could you say something like that?"

"Because he is not a good person."

My face curled up in disgust at what he was saying. He

had mentioned before about usurping Evander; now he was talking treason. "And neither are you," I snarled.

"I never pretended I was." Dorian shrugged.

"I'm going to report you to the guards. You will end up in prison."

His face turned ugly. "Now you sound like a queen." He turned to leave the room but paused and looked back at me thoughtfully. "By the way. I have to ask. How did you know?"

"How did I know what?" I snapped.

"How did you know that the two girls were going to kill Evander?"

"Because of your warning," I said.

His eyebrows rose up, and he shook his head. "What warning?"

"You mouthed the word 'sister' to me. I ran with that."

"The two girls were sisters?"

"Yes. You didn't know?"

"No, no one did, but you knew?"

"Yes, I had met them the other day in the market and helped one of them with dresses to come."

Dorian's face became stony.

"But I had no idea they were going to try and kill Evander."

"I didn't either," he admitted.

"Then what in the heavens were you trying to tell me in the ballroom?" I yelled.

Dorian's hand dropped from the door, and he looked sick. "I thought you knew already. That you had heard the news from the house elves."

"What news?"

"They apprehended a woman trying to sneak into the

palace. She used magic to try and break free, so they've imprisoned her below."

"And?" I said angrily.

He looked at the ground and then back up at me. "It may already be too late. I tried to tell you."

"Dorian, for the love of all that is holy, if you don't spit it out, I may fry your tongue on a spit and feed it to the dogs."

"It's your sister."

"My sister?" I felt faint. Dizzy. "How can you be sure?"

"Because she was asking for you by name. No one else knows she is your sister. I was able to get a message to her that, to keep you safe, she mustn't let your heritage be known."

"Where is she?"

"You can't go to her," Dorian said. "You must let her be. If the king finds out that you are her sister, there will be nothing anyone can do to save you."

My mind was frantic. I rushed past Dorian, pushing him out of the room, and headed down the hall. I didn't know where to go, so I just started running.

"Eden." Dorian raced after me and grabbed my wrist. "Stop it."

"No. No. I have to save her. It's my fault she is here. I called her on the mirror. If I didn't call, then she wouldn't be here." I began to panic.

"Calm down."

"I can't calm down. I can't have another death on my conscience. Everywhere I go there is death. I caused this."

"No, you didn't." He grabbed both sides of my face. "Listen. I will take care of it. It will take some time, though. Do you understand? Do you trust me?"

My head nodded between his palms.

"Good girl. Now go back to your room."

I shook my head. "I can't. I won't go back there. I can't go back to that mess where I murdered my mother."

He let out a loud sigh before waving my servant, Cristin as she passed by.

"Yes, sir?" She paused and smiled at him.

"Take her to my room while her room is cleaned. Do you know where that is?"

Her smile lit up, and she gave a knowing smile. "Why of course I do."

"Good, go with her." Dorian released my face and nudged me toward Cristin.

I watched as he rushed off down the hallway, and I wanted to go with him.

"Come along, Miss Eden," Cristin said and began to walk up a flight of stairs to the third floor.

"I didn't know he had a room up here," I muttered. "I thought he lived in the basement with the house elves."

"That would be silly," Cristin said simply but didn't elaborate. On the third floor, we passed the royal suites and then stopped at a door that led to one of the towers in the palace.

She opened the door, and I was met with curved stone steps. Cristin didn't follow me up the stairs, which opened up to a sizable study containing a long wooden table covered with books and half burned candles, bookcases overfilled with books, journals, and scrolls. Rolls of parchment were stacked on the table, and he looked to be in the middle of studying. I picked up a few of the books and noticed they were on fae— elves in particular and their magic. There were glass jars filled with paint and another with paint brushes. Through the study, there was another room, and I peeked in to see his bed. All the curtains had been pulled closed. I went to open the window, and when I did, I revealed a floor-to-ceiling mural behind me.

Every inch of the walls had been painstakingly painted of the northern woods with their white gnarled trees that many believed were haunted. The artist had used great detail in capturing the fae creatures that were hidden among the boughs—fauns, dryads, ballywogs, gnomes, house elves, and more.

That was what he was studying. He was recreating a world to include the fae. My breath caught as I saw an easel in the corner of his room where he had begun a charcoal sketch. Even though it was in the early stages, I recognized myself.

"It's quite beautiful, isn't it?" a feminine voice said.

I turned and dipped into an ungraceful curtsey as Queen Giselle entered the room.

"He gets the gift from his grandfather."

"Who?" I asked, confused by what she was revealing.

"Why, Dorian of course."

"I don't understand?"

"And here I thought you were the smart one among the girls."

"No, I'm just... me."

She smiled sadly. "I see that." As she moved across the room, I could see her noble grace for her steps didn't make a sound. She paused to look at the charcoal sketch of me. "He is quite fascinated with you."

"I know," I said. I was struggling to follow along. Was she referring to her son Prince Evander or Dorian?

"Now, we need to clear the air of some things. You will marry Evander and be done with Dorian?" Her voice was cold. "I see the way he watches you, and it is unhealthy for one to be so infatuated. You must be loyal to my son Evander and Evander alone."

"I understand."

"Really, then why are you in Dorian's room? I was just informed that you agreed to marry my son."

"Because, my... I, uh...."

She waved her hand to dismiss me. "It is forgiven as long as it doesn't happen again. You have proved to be quite useful and will continue to do so."

"Of course," I said.

"Good." She smiled, though the smile did not reach her eyes. "I need you to prove it now."

From the bell sleeve of her gown, she pulled out an enchanted mirror. She whispered a few words and an image came into focus. She turned the mirror toward me so I could see it. "Do you know this traitor?"

It was Meri, my younger sister, who was locked in a warded cell. I was unable to hold back my quick intake of breath.

"Ah, yes, I see you do. Either way, her life is in your hands."

"What do you want?"

"Easy." The queen held the mirror up and walked closer to me. "I saw it the moment you let your anger slip in the garden and caused the storm. I know you are one of the adopted daughters of Lorelai Eville."

"I can explain—"

She waved her hand through the air, silencing me. "I know that my husband is truly thrown off by that stupid prophecy that the seer spoke into existence years ago, and since then it has driven him to do unspeakable acts of evil in an attempt to protect his son. I, too, have studied the prophecy. I, too, have prayed for guidance and searched the stars for answers, and it has come to me in the form of you." She pointed and slowly circled me, looking me over from head to toe.

"I believe that you are indeed part of the prophecy. It's just that a prophecy can be interpreted many different ways. They said a girl with power will kill the prince on his wedding day. No one said which prince."

"I don't understand. I thought Evander's older brother, Vincent, is dead."

"Vincent is indeed alive and well... for now. But I want to make sure that he doesn't remain that way. You kill Prince Vincent, and I will make sure that no one will harm a pretty red hair on your sister." Queen Giselle tucked the mirror back into the folds of her bell sleeve. "Then the prophecy will be fulfilled. A prince is dead. My son is alive, and you will be the future queen. That is as long as you don't betray us."

"Then you will let my sister go?" I asked.

"Of course, you will have what you wanted, and I will have what I wanted. My son on the throne and you will be by his side."

"And if I don't?"

"Your sister will be dead within minutes, and you will follow in her footsteps."

My hands shook as I tried to come to terms with what she was asking me to do. Murder a lone prince I've never met and then save my sister and become queen.

"Where can I find Vincent?" I asked, my head dropping to my chest in subservience.

"Why, you are already acquainted with Prince Vincent. Or do I need to introduce you to Vincent Dorian the II?"

"Dorian?" I couldn't swallow. My mouth went dry, and the world swayed. "But I don't understand."

"You don't need to understand. Just follow orders," she hissed. "Kill Dorian, save your sister."

"I... I will. On one condition."

"You have no business asking for anything."

"I would like to see my sister. To make sure what you say is true."

The queen's eyes glittered dangerously. "Very well. I will make sure that Oz finds you and brings you back. He is loyal to me. If you so much as try to help her escape, he will cut her down. Do you understand?"

I nodded.

Queen Giselle stepped closer to me, and her finger glowed with power as she drew a sigil over my mouth. "In case you get any crazy ideas to tell anyone my plan. You can speak, but you will be unable to warn anyone or speak my name."

My mouth burned as I tried to cry out, and my lips automatically closed. Tears burned in the corner of my eyes. I never would have suspected that Queen Giselle knew magic. She was a sorceress too. Now it made sense how she wooed and married a king.

"Now remember, dear Eden, kill Dorian and save your sister." Queen Giselle clapped her hands and the man from the king's study stepped out of the shadows. He bowed his head to me, and I felt sick to my stomach. I could see the remains of a bandage under his vest. I hadn't stabbed him hard enough.

The room became blurry as I followed him out of Dorian's bedroom, through the study, and down the winding steps. My tears almost caused me to fall multiple times, and I slowed when I came to the hall. Oz never spoke but kept his hand on his knife as he escorted me into a private sitting room. It looked exactly like one of the three other sitting rooms in the palace, but I didn't understand why this one was so special. I didn't see my sister.

"Where is she?" I asked.

He turned those deadly eyes my way and moved to stand in front of a cold fireplace. Reaching his hand inside, he felt around for a switch, and I heard the click as it activated. Gears began to grind as a hidden door opened inside the fireplace. He gestured for me to go first into the darkness and I did. If Meri was down there, then I would go after her.

It was a long tunnel with cold metal doors on either side with slots on the bottom big enough to fit a plate of food through and a peephole to check on the prisoners. He stopped in front of one, and I heard someone cough inside.

"Meri?" I called out.

"Eden?" I peered through the hole and her hand reached through and began to paw at my face. She was checking for a glamour, and I let her. I was thoroughly poked and prodded in the eyes and nose before she said, "It is you. I'd recognize that scowl anywhere."

"Are you doing okay? Are you injured?"

"No, it actually hasn't been so bad. Except for the food. The food is terrible."

I couldn't contain the snort. That was one thing about my sister Meri. She loved food and eating.

"Meri, how did you get here so fast and why did you come?"

"Well, I wanted to make sure you were okay. I felt bad for refusing to help you, so I used a traveling spell and... well, here I am. I came to rescue you." Her hands waved through the bars. "Although, it looks like you were able to get out of the ward after all."

"And now, it is you who needs rescuing." I laughed as tears silently fell down my face.

"No. I'm just here as a backup. You know, in case you need me," she said bravely, but I could hear the worry in her voice.

"Oh, Meri," I sighed. "Have you kept your spirits up by *singing?*" I asked the hidden question about using her powers.

"Uh, no. I'm too scared too. There was another woman down here, Bellamy, and she *tried to sing*," Meri hinted, "but she's gone and hasn't returned."

"Well, don't you worry. I have it on good authority that you will be released soon. I just have to do a favor for the queen."

"Really, then what is taking you so long?" Meri whined. "I'm starving."

I chuckled. "Uh, we just have to wait till tomorrow. All will be well by tomorrow. I promise."

A dramatic whine came from Meri. "I will be skin and bones by tomorrow."

"You will be fine."

"Cake! Send cake and all will be forgiven."

"I think we can send you some wedding cake."

"Ooh! Who's getting married?" she asked.

"Me to Prince Evander," I said softly, no longer excited about the prospect.

The musical laughter that poured out of the cell at my expense didn't stop until I heard Meri slapping the door and trying to catch her breath. "Oh, that's great. Two for two. Mother Eville sure knows what she's doing. She sent two daughters out and gets them married to royalty. Well, that's not happening with me. I guarantee it."

"Maybe this isn't the best time to talk about it," I whispered.

Meri didn't hear me but began to rant out loud at why she wasn't in a hurry to get married. "I would rather die an old hedge witch with tons of orange cats, not black ones because everyone always thinks witches have black cats. Or a boat. I will stow away on a boat!" she yelled out after me. "Let's see

Mother marry me off to a prince if I'm in the middle of the ocean!"

Oz gave me a curious look as he reached up and slowly closed the grate over her rant, which only muffled her outcries. I would have laughed at the cold-blooded killer, if he hadn't tried to take my head off.

But it seemed that Meri was in fine spirits for now, especially since I gave her something new to worry about. She was right. Rosalie was married to a prince, and I was engaged to one. It seemed that we were following a pattern.

As we were leaving, I was distracted by a familiar house elf that was missing a pinky and was carrying a tray of food. Pinky stopped outside of Meri's cell and slid the food under the flap. I tried to not stare but wondered if that was Dorian's spy. It would make sense that he would use the house elves. No one ever noticed them.

I came to the end of the tunnel and waited for Oz to hit the hidden switch again to open the wall and let us back into the upper room. But the switch wasn't on the wall where I was watching, and I missed how he made the wall move.

When I stepped through the fireplace and back into the sitting room, I was surprised to see Evander waiting with his mother.

Neither one of them were surprised to see me exit from the secret fireplace. "Why hello, dear." Evander gave me a grin. "Did you have a good visit with your sister?"

"You knew she was here?"

"Of course, I knew." He gave me a sly smile. "And I knew who you were the very first night of the ball."

"How?" I asked, perplexed.

"Who knew that my new acquaintance Derek was also truth seer? He told me that there was something off about you.

Then you showed your hand again and again—with your thunderstorm antics, choosing the glamoured stone, which was a test, saving Elise. I would be dumb not to have figured it out. Now, I can use your sister to control you, and therefore control the prophecy. Isn't that right, Mother?"

"It is a good plan," she cooed and gave his shoulder a squeeze.

My hands became cold, and I reached for the top of a chair to steady myself. "Why do you want to kill Dorian?"

"Because as long as he lives, he stands between me and the throne," Evander answered.

"But I thought you didn't even want the throne, that you were only taking it because your brother had died."

"That's what I want my father to believe." Evander shrugged. "Dorian is his favorite son. He is obsessed with the fae. Of course, I want the throne. Always have. It is rightfully mine. My half-breed, bastard fae brother should not wear the crown of Candor. He can't."

"But Dorian abdicated and is dead to the world. There's no need to kill him."

"There wasn't until you came along." Evander came up and walked around me, his hand trailing along my shoulder and golden hair. "He was obsessed with Sisa, his first love, and swore to never love or marry out of respect, and therefore abdicated the throne. Because he can't become king if he refuses to marry or have heirs."

"I don't understand what this has to do with me," I said.

Queen Giselle held her fan and was using it to fan away a large bug that kept trying to land near her. "As I said before, Dorian is infatuated with you. He is forgetting his place, the place he has banished himself to—that of a servant. He is acting irrational, and we think he may be questioning his choice."

"He made it obvious the night of the masquerade ball when he couldn't take his eyes off of you the whole time we danced," he sneered.

"That's the reason you asked me to stay on, isn't it? To infuriate Dorian and rub it in his face. Not because you liked me."

Evander sneered. "Yes, you should have seen the panic in his eyes when I asked you to stay." He laughed. "And then I did everything I could just to woo you to hurt him. It was obvious the way he felt about you. He couldn't hide his feelings during dinner, and when I confronted him about how he favored you, he tried to throw me off by seducing Adelle instead."

My cheeks burned, and I realized now what Dorian was doing that night. He was trying to hide his feelings for me.

"Frankly, I don't understand what he sees in you. You're ungraceful, uncoordinated, not eloquent. You're kind of a mess. It was a struggle to find a reason to keep you on and even harder to pretend to be attracted to you. But I did it to upset him."

"I thought you had feelings for me," I whispered, feeling my heart break again at being rejected, learning it was all a lie. "Why then did you propose to me?"

"To hurt Dorian!" Evander said. "I already decided not to marry for love. I would marry to strengthen the crown, and your powers could do that. You are already invaluable to me, as soon as you take care of Dorian."

"Why do you need to hurt him when I said I would marry you?" I looked up at Evander. "Why don't you believe me?"

Evander slammed his fist into the coffee table. "As soon as

Dorian found out that we were engaged, he rushed off to father to try and stop it. Right now he's petitioning father to have him redeclared crown prince."

"Really?" I couldn't hide the excitement in my voice.

Evander's eyes darkened. "We can't have that! I didn't go to all that trouble to poison Sisa for nothing," he yelled.

I began to tremble at his outburst. "No! Tell me you didn't. You wouldn't kill your brother's love just to take the throne."

"Half brother," Evander spat.

I turned to Queen Giselle for answers. "During Ferdinand's royal ball, he had fallen in love with a fae woman," Giselle scoffed. "He even proposed. But I couldn't let that happen. I couldn't let a fae women sit on the throne of Candor."

"You used magic. What was it? A love spell? Forgetting charm?"

"A little of both," she said. "He forgot all about her and his promise. Then we were married. But I wasn't expecting him to remember her. Ten months after our marriage vows, he had the nerve to bring his bastard son under our roof and declare him as his heir." She looked sickened. "He is not my son. That thing is not my son."

Evander went and rubbed his poor mother's shoulders because she looked like she was about to faint.

"You clipped his beautiful fae ears," I accused. "Whipped him and beat him."

"It was for his own good," Queen Giselle said. "I knew he wasn't king material when he spent all of his free time at that stupid tavern with his whore of a mother."

A light went on in my head, and it all made sense. The story that Madam Pantalonne said about falling in love with a king. She was in love with the king, and her big cotton-candy-colored wigs covered her ears so no one ever saw her true heritage, and Dorian was *her* son. No wonder she had a soft spot for him, and he was so torn apart when the tavern was destroyed.

My heart ached, for in the span of a day, we had both lost our mothers.

"Why don't you do it?" I snapped. "Why haven't you killed him? I've seen his back; you've had the chance to do it multiple times."

"Don't you think I've tried?" she hissed. "My husband has threatened that, if anything should happen to Dorian, that if we harmed him, that Evander and I would be cast out of the palace."

"Then why tomorrow?" I asked.

Evander walked over to the portrait of King Ferdinand and looked up at his father. His face turned down in a sneer. "We can't take the chance that he would reinstate Dorian as his heir. This is your fault that we must kill them both."

"Now, you will be a good little sorceress and go to the room that we have prepared for you and will do as you're told. Tomorrow, under the guise of marrying my son, you will kill my husband and his favorite bastard son." Queen Giselle's smile was viperous.

"No, I won't do it," I declared.

Evander came up and took my hand, giving me a sweet kiss on the top of my knuckles.

"You forget I have your sister and I will kill her in a heartbeat," he threatened, his hand crushing my fingers in his grasp. "I've done it before." He dropped my hands and held up his fingers. "Now the board is set. All you need to do is kill two birds with one wedding."

I was going to be sick.

CHAPTER TWENTY-SEVEN

E very part of my soul wanted to lash out and hurt
Evander and his horrid mother, Queen Giselle. I had
begun to fall for Evander's quiet temperament and his deep
questions about ruling. I thought that it was King Ferdinand
who was the vile one, but I was wrong. It was the queen and
her son.

King Ferdinand had a soft spot for the fae and had gone
crazy out of desperation to protect his fae son.

My room had been cleaned up and put back to normal,
minus the rug with the burn stains that had been rolled up and
removed and the blank wall where the mirror had hung only
hours before. I sat on my bed staring at the floor, trying to
figure out how to fix everything that I had broken. If I hadn't
come, the Broken Heart tavern and Madam Pantalonne would
still be alive, as well as Nessa and Tess, my mother—alive
though still trapped as a puca—and, of course, my sister
wouldn't be imprisoned.

A knock came at my door, and I ignored the persistent
tapping. When it didn't cease, I called out, "Go away!"

The door opened and Adelle slipped inside, closing the
door behind her.

"Adelle, I'm sorry. I'm just not in the mood for visitors."

Her normally pristinely styled hair fell in disarray around her shoulders as if she had just woken up from a deep sleep. She looked horrible.

"You... you...." Her voice trembled, and her finger raised at me accusingly.

I stood up, my hands dropping to my sides, and I looked down at my feet. "You heard the news. I'm sorry, I wasn't supposed to tell anyone."

"Y-You," she stuttered as she struggled to walk over to me.

"Adelle, are you okay? Have you been drinking perhaps? You don't sound like yourself." I moved to her side and reached out to touch her sleeve. Her skin beneath my fingertips was burning up.

She attacked. Adelle grabbed me by the upper arm, swung me around, and slammed my head into the wall so hard the paintings shook. Her eyes were dark and filled with hate.

"Free me," she hissed out, and I could smell the sulfur on her breath and knew that it wasn't Adelle anymore but Allemar controlling her.

"Free me. I freed your mother." Her mouth twisted into an un-Adelle smile. This one was crooked and her lips twitched.

"Adelle, listen to me," I said calmly. "This isn't you. Remember, you are being controlled by someone else. You were right all along."

Her hands reached up to my throat, and she squeezed. I started to choke and struggle for air. She was much stronger than I had anticipated.

"Adelle," I grunted. But it wasn't her eyes that looked back at me. I saw only darkness. I reached out, closed my eyes, and felt the warmth of my glamour spread over my body as I became

Adelle. My hair became longer, darker. My dress mirrored hers. I was her, except for my eyes. I made sure that she looked into her own star blue eyes and not the black pools that I saw.

The pressure on my own neck faltered as she was confronted with herself.

"No!" Adelle cried and stepped away, her hands going to her ears as she kept mumbling to herself over and over. "Stop it. Go away. I can't hear you anymore."

I gasped and clutched my throat, feeling the burning sensation return as she had pressed on my earlier bruises. She was becoming frantic, and I needed to act. I had to save her. I walked over to her and touched her forehead.

"*Somnus,*" I whispered confidently.

Adelle's eyes blinked and slowly closed, and she began to collapse, but I caught her midfall.

"Whoa!" I grunted and carefully laid her on the ground. She rolled over to her side, and I heard a contented snore. Then faltered. What was I to do with a possibly possessed woman? Who, when she woke up, may try and kill me a second time? "Oh drat."

Another knock came at my door, and I looked at the collapsed girl in panic.

"One minute," I called out and decided to roll her under my bed.

The person didn't wait, because no sooner had I rolled Adelle under the bed then my door opened and Dorian walked in. When his eyes met mine, lighting up with excitement while my heart dropped in dread.

"Ah, you came back here. I expected you to stay in my room. There's good news." Dorian came over to me. "Your sister is still alive and in good health." He reached out and grasped my upper arms. "I also have something I need to tell you. I'm not who you think I am."

My heart was breaking at what I was about to do.

"Stop," I whispered.

"I've lied to you, kept things from you."

"Stop," I said more firmly. "It doesn't matter."

Dorian frowned. "You don't even know what I was going to say. It changes everything."

"It changes nothing," I snapped. "I promised I would marry Evander in the morning. And nothing you say will change that."

"Yes, it will." He reached out, cupping his hand behind my head and pulling me close in an embrace. "I can be your prince, if you will let me."

His words so cryptic yet so poetic, but I needed to tell him. To warn him.

"Dorian, I—" My mouth began to burn and the words wouldn't come forth. The spell made it impossible to speak of what was coming. I took a deep breath. "I'm going to ki—"

"Kiss me," he interrupted me and pressed his lips to mine, silencing me with his kiss. He teased at my lips and tongue, making me weak in the knees.

I pulled away, and the tears began to flow. "No, you must leave. Go, run away from here." I pushed him in the chest.

"Only if you come with me." He grasped my hands between his. "I don't want to be apart from you."

"That will be awkward when I'm married to your brother," I spat out angrily and watched as the smile fell from his face.

"You know?" He became very still. "That he's my brother. That I'm Prince Vincent."

"I know."

"And yet you will still marry him?"

"Yes." I closed my eyes so I couldn't see the pain in his eyes that was mirrored in my own.

"Why?"

I had to think hard and fast, because the spell would not let me warn him but didn't have a problem with me telling him to run away. I had to dig deep and bring out the claws and the words that I hoped would wound him. I was going to dig at his scars.

Angry tears of self-loathing poured down my cheeks, and I used the hatred to fuel my words. "Because he is not you. For how could I ever love a half-fae like yourself?" I watched as my words began to cut into his stony exterior. But he stood there nobly and didn't move.

"Evander is twice the man you will ever be. You are nothing. A nobody. A bastard son that runs away from his duty and crown. A coward."

"Don't do this," Dorian warned.

"You ran away then. You should run away now. Leave here, for I never want to see your face again. I love Evander. I will marry Evander and be queen. And you will do nothing but tarnish my wedding with your presence." His face became cold, hard, unreadable, and he stormed out of the room, and I prayed that I had done enough to make him leave. Run far away.

I collapsed in a swirl of skirts on the hardwood floor of my room and buried my face in my hands and cried. Cried tears of grief, sorrow, pain, and relief. Because I had found a loophole in the contract with Evander.

They said I must kill Dorian tomorrow, not tonight. I only prayed that he wouldn't show up for the wedding, because if he did, I might have to kill him.

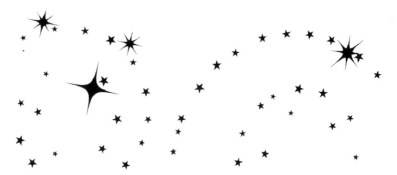

CHAPTER TWENTY-EIGHT

Morning came rolling in under the cover of gray clouds and thunderstorms, very much like my mood. At the crack of dawn, servants were jam packed in my room as they prepared me for my wedding day.

Harmony didn't seem the least disappointed that she wasn't the one marrying the prince. In fact, her cheeks seemed rosy and there was a sparkle in her eye.

"I'm so happy for you," she gushed over morning breakfast in my room. "I just knew there was something special about you, and it seems I was right." She broke her croissant and dipped her knife in raspberry jam and spread it over the soft, warm bread.

"Really, you're not at all sad?"

"Nope." She grinned mischievously at me. "In fact"—she held up her hand, and I could see the teeniest hint of gold-colored string around her finger—"I'm promised to someone too."

"Who?" I asked, but I had a feeling I knew.

"Derek," she sighed his name dreamily.

"He is perfect for you," I said, meaning every word. There wasn't anyone else here as pure as him.

"Of course, you will be invited to the wedding." She grinned.

"I'll be waiting for the invitation," I said, turning back to my untouched breakfast. I had no appetite and doubted I would until the wedding was over.

"Too bad Adelle can't join us," Harmony said. "I knocked on her room, but she didn't answer."

"I think she's a bit strung out by the news. I bet she's just oversleeping." I glanced at my bed. From where I sat, I could see her foot sticking out from under the covers. Carefully, I got up and moved over to the bed, and in a facade of adjusting the pillows, I pushed her foot back under the bed. She would sleep for a while longer as I had rewoven my sleeping spell over her. I only hoped she didn't start snoring.

"It's time," Cristin said and waved in a group of dressmakers, all of them carrying various dresses in white and holding them up for my selection. "Which one do you like?" she asked. "They were all selected by Queen Giselle herself. You have gowns made from imported silk from Rya, pearls from Isla, and diamonds and gems from the mines of Kiln. All gifts from the other kingdoms for your wedding." Cristin clapped her hands, and boxes of veils were brought in and laid out on the table.

"Can you give us some privacy?" I asked.

"But you will need help getting ready. The queen was adamant that you not be late."

I gave her a cold stare. "Do you really think I would be late to my own wedding? Besides, Harmony will help me." I reached out for Harmony's hand.

Harmony fluttered and preened. "Of course, I will."

Cristin curtseyed and left, taking all of the servant girls and dressmakers with her.

I turned to the pile of the most gorgeous dresses I had ever laid eyes on. They brought me no joy, only despair. For I would wear one of them as I walked down the aisle to marry a man I did not love to save a sister that I did love.

Harmony begin to sort through the dresses. "Nope, not that one. Yuck. Ew. Okay, what about this one? It's timeless." She spun, holding an A-line, high-neck dress covered in lace that ran all the way down the arms with silver rings that attached to my fingers.

I became excited. "Yes, and a veil. I need a veil." A plan began to form in my head, one that seemed to have been in the making since the very beginning.

I scoured through dozens of veils until I found one that would work. "This one." I pulled it over my face and could barely see anything.

"Are you sure?" Harmony frowned. "It will hide your face."

"I'm sure," I said. "It's perfect."

"Well, if you say so." She flipped the lace back over my head and gave me a hug. "You will make the most beautiful bride."

I grabbed the dress and tossed it to her. I slipped off my glass slippers and handed them to her with the veil. "No, Harmony, you will," I said, and quickly explained my plan.

My stomach was in knots as I walked down the carpets toward the royal suites, trying to remember to keep my head up and my shoulders back and to not look like I was about to puke. I only had an hour to get my plan put into action, and even now I didn't know if Harmony would be able to pull off the charade, I asked her to play along without giving her the full explanation, for the spell kept my lips sealed.

I tried to put a little sashay into my hips as I walked toward Dorian's room, glancing at the mirror. I waved my hand and adjusted the shade of rouge on my lips to a darker hue. As I climbed the stairs, my heart rate climbed with each step, beating faster and faster as my nerves began to get the better of me. I opened the door into the study and saw that it was empty, other than the normal scattered mess of books and scrolls. Moving through the study into his bedroom, I saw that the easel was knocked over and the painting of me gone. Destroyed or tossed out, it was evident that it was no longer in the room. His wardrobe was open and looked like clothes were missing.

My plan was to come up here as Adelle and turn the tables on him. If he was here, I was going to seduce him, convince him to run away with me—Adelle. But it seemed I didn't have to. He was gone.

I turned around and almost screamed as I saw Evander in the doorway of Dorian's room. "How very interesting that I would find you here," he said. "After you swore your undying love to me."

My feet were frozen to the floor, unable to move as Evander walked toward me. He stopped inches from my face as his hand reached toward my neck. He brushed my hair over my shoulder, and his hand clasped my face roughly.

Then his mouth was on mine and he was kissing me passionately, unlike the one we had shared before. I was shocked by the aggressiveness of the kiss and how his hands wandered to my lower back, pressing me close. "My father told me to marry for money. But with you, Adelle, I get the whole package."

I stiffened and turned my face away.

"What's wrong?" I could hear the frustration in his voice.

"You're getting married today," I said.

"And why should that stop us? I don't plan on being married for very long. Just long enough to fulfill the prophecy and become king. Then there will be an accident. You did say you wanted to be queen." He ran his lips across my cheek and whispered in my ear, "I can make that happen. Be my queen."

I felt queasy. He just admitted that he was going to kill me. My stomach lurched, and I pushed him away from me as I wiped his kiss away with the back of my hand.

His normally handsome face turned sour. "Let me guess, you came here because of him. You're choosing Dorian over me?"

I didn't say anything out of fear. Just nodded my head.

"I have to get ready," I said in my best imitation of Adelle. "For your wedding."

"Again, he steals what's mine," Evander began to vent and pace the room, his anger rising and my fear with it. He followed me to the study, and I opened the door to head down the stairs.

Evander came up behind me suddenly, his voice a low growl. "Well, if I can't have you, no one can."

He shoved me from behind. I felt air rush past me, and the floor dropped out from below as I fell forward, my momentum carrying me into nothing. The steps rushing toward my head. I covered my face and felt a soft cushion of air surround me, but it didn't stop my forward fall. I rolled, tumbled, and fell down the curved stairs, but instead of a sharp jab, I was encased in warmth. When I hit the floor, I lay sprawled out and played dead. Closing my eyes, I used glamour to make a pool of blood cover my dress and accentuated the angle of my head. I heard

Evander's steps as he sauntered down each one, not in a hurry to check on me. He slowed, I assumed when he saw my dead body. He leaned close, and I felt the nudge of a boot on my leg.

"What a waste." He clapped his hands, and I heard the soft shuffling of feet, probably a house elf. "Get rid of the body."

The boots continued down the hall, and I waited, my chest screaming as I held my breath. A soft nudge came on my shoulder, and I peeked through lowered lashes. It was Dorian's house elf Dinky. She must have used her magic to slow my fall and save my life.

She waved her fingers at me and gestured to hurry, pointing toward my room. I got up and glared after Evander. My fingers curled into fists, my nails biting into the palms of my hands. I was shaking with rage.

"Is Dorian gone?" I asked.

Dinky nodded.

"Good. I wouldn't want him to see me murder his brother."

The orchestra played a light and airy sonata, and I had to admit that the chapel was decorated beautifully for my wedding. Long, silk streamers hung from the ceiling, and vases of cream-colored roses lined the altar. The ceremony was small. The king and queen sat on smaller portable thrones, and Evander stood in front of them waiting eagerly for his bride. Long, wooden boxes lined the sides of the chapel, and the very few guests sat on raised benches within. Guards were scattered in groups of two throughout.

I adjusted the white silk gloves and checked to make sure Dorian's button was still tucked against my palm and that my glamour was securely in place. The double doors opened, and I walked down the aisle.

I looked beautiful. The dress Harmony picked out hugged my curves, and the veil was thick and beautiful. From this distance, I could see her hands shaking, and she kept glancing over to me.

Very slowly, I shook my head no. Not yet.

Evander lifted my veil, and my smile was too bright, too forced, but he didn't notice. The wedding continued as the priest began the vows, and I waited—waited for the right moment for the cue. For the priest to ask the right question. It was what we rehearsed.

My hands clutched the button in my glove, and I shifted my weight from one foot to another.

The priest began, "If anyone has just cause as to why these two should not wed, then spea—"

"I object," I called out in my best Dorian impression and stepped from the bench seat on the side of the room, where I had been observing. Harmony, in my wedding dress, holding Evander's hand, spun and looked relieved.

"I object," another voice called out from the back of the chapel, and I turned and faced down the real Dorian.

"Oh, by the stars," I groaned.

"Two Dorians." Evander turned to glare at the woman on his arm and Eden's shocked face. Harmony was wearing my glass slippers and my glamour held strong. "What is the meaning of this, Eden?" Evander shook her arm hard. "You were supposed to take care of this."

Poor Harmony looked so puzzled, and she tried to run away. "Do something now." Evander pushed her, and she stumbled down the steps. One of the glass slippers slipped off her foot as she tried to catch herself. The glamour disappeared, revealing Harmony in my wedding dress and veil, visibly shaking in her stockinged feet.

"Harmony," Derek called out from further down the section where I was sitting.

"What is going on?" King Ferdinand stood up and pointed to the two Dorians. "Which one of you is my real son?"

I glared at Dorian. He had to go and ruin my perfectly laid-out revenge plan. Now I had to improvise on the fly. My fingers reached into my pocket and fumbled for a lock of my hair bound with ribbon—my backup plan in case this happened.

"I am," I yelled and stepped forward the same time Dorian did.

We came to the middle of the room and squared off. My glamour so perfect that he wouldn't be able to see any fault. "He is an imposter!" I pointed to Dorian and waved my hand in an elaborate wave.

He shook his head, and I rushed forward, tucking a lock of my hair into his pocket. "See!" I made a show of pulling out a button and waved my hand over him to glamour him into me. I heard Dorian's grunt of surprise. I whispered to him, "I'm sorry."

It was weird to see my own face react with Dorian's expressions. He was mad, very mad, but he held his tongue.

"What is going on?" King Ferdinand cried out. "I thought Evander was marrying that girl," he pointed to Harmony then to Dorian in an Eden glamour.

"Settle down, Ferdinand," Giselle spoke. "I'm sure there has been some kind of misunderstanding."

"It's the witch!" King Ferdinand hissed out. "She's come to fulfill the prophecy and kill my son. Guards! Arrest that woman!" The king pointed toward Dorian in my glamour and

I watched in awe as the guards rushed me—Dorian—and he quickly dispatched them all while wearing a sparkling wedding dress. It was mildly entertaining before I remembered I was supposed to kill Dorian. Or, actually, glamoured him was supposed to kill me.

I rushed into the fray, and he turned on me, his eyes wild with fury as his fist swung for my head. I jumped on him, knocking him to the ground. He was a better fighter than me, and he easily rolled me under him and had a knife to my throat.

Where did he get the knife? Then I remembered it was Dorian; he didn't go anywhere without a knife.

"Who are you?" he said, and I watched my golden blonde hair fall over his shoulder, and I quickly had to smother my laughter.

"You need to kill me," I murmured softly. I tried to open my mouth to explain, but my tongue began to burn. Giselle's spell was still as strong as before. The blade on my throat lessened, but not by much.

"Kill me," I said, my eyes blinking away the tears.

He pulled the knife away from my throat and moved away. He wasn't going to do it. I was desperate now. With a wave of power, I forced Dorian's dagger into my stomach, and he tried to pull it out, but it didn't work. I wasn't releasing him. He could fight my magic all he wanted, but as long as I could, I would hold him.

Oh snot. I felt my world start to fade in and out, even though it was a flesh wound. It still hurt a lot.

"Meri," I mumbled, grasping Dorian's shoulders. "Save Meri."

"Eden? Is that you?"

I nodded. "Save Meri," I whined and grabbed my side.

"I already did." Dorian frowned at me. "With the help of my fae spy network, we broke her out of the prison an hour ago. Now you don't have to marry Evander or kill me."

"W-What?" I sat there holding my bleeding side and looked around in confusion. "How did you know?"

"Well, Dinky found your enchanted bug flying around the palace and brought it to me. She showed me how to activate the spell, and well, I used it to spy on Giselle and Evander. I heard everything." He turned and glared up at Evander, who had taken a few steps up and now stood next to Queen Giselle. Both of their faces were pale.

"You mean I stabbed myself for nothing?" I cried out in distress.

"Yeah." He felt along his glamoured dress for my lock of hair and threw it on the floor. The glamour dissipated and Dorian stood over me, his hand pressing to my side to staunch the flow of blood.

"Which one is the murderer?" King Ferdinand called out in a confused voice. "Dorian, my son, is that really you?"

"Yes, Father. And the murderers are there." He pointed to Evander and Giselle. "He murdered Sisa. And Queen Giselle is the one who sent the men to burn down Mother's tavern. They were planning on murdering you and me today, using the prophecy as an excuse."

King Ferdinand turned on them. "Is this true?"

"No, my love." Giselle turned on the waterworks. "They are lying. That witch there is the one the prophecy spoke of. The one that will murder your son on his wedding day. I'm only trying to protect him."

King Ferdinand spun around, his face the color of a ripe tomato. "Somebody better start telling the truth, or I'm going to send everyone to the gallows."

As chaos called to chaos, the room began to fill with uninvited guests as the magical menagerie troupe members filed in. The guards were trying to hold back Bravado, the Ogress, Sorek, Humperstink, and others.

"You are not welcome here!" King Ferdinand screamed.

"Are you saying I can't come to my own daughter's wedding?" Bravado spotted me in glamour and waved proudly at me. "Hiya, honey."

I was even more surprised to see a beautiful blonde woman at his side. My father's face was beaming, and his arm was wrapped around her waist possessively. She waved at me, and I blinked in surprise.

"Mother?" She hadn't died but had escaped the band and must have apparated out of the room.

I meekly waved back and couldn't help but laugh. I watched as Humperstink the dwarf rolled in a cage of purple furred monkeys. He gave me a wink and opened the cage. They began to scamper through the guests, stealing items and necklaces. One ran right up to the queen's leg and onto her shoulder and stole the crown from her head.

My wedding was turning into a sideshow, and I was a spectator. "Someone, stop those monkeys," King Ferdinand ordered.

Bravado whistled between his two fingers, and the monkeys failed to respond. "Well, I tried." He shrugged.

"Try harder," Ferdinand yelled.

"They're not my monkeys," Bravado huffed indignantly. "But for the right price, say sixty gold coins, they can be your monkeys and your problem."

"Is that your father?" Dorian whispered to me.

"Uh, yeah," I said. "Don't judge me. I just met him."

"Same here, and you've met mine." Dorian squeezed my arm gently and I laughed.

During the commotion, Harmony had run over to Derek who had taken her in his arms. The guards still surrounded us with their swords drawn and pointed at both of us, but no one had moved, because we were both Dorian.

Evander and Queen Giselle had tried to escape out the back but were stopped by Bravado's strong man, Sorek.

"You have sinned, King Ferdinand, and must atone for those crimes," my mother, Amaryllis, said. "You tried to stop the prophecy and my child from being born and killed hundreds of girls and called it a plague."

King Ferdinand dropped to his knees, his head lowered to his chest. "I did it all for the sake of Dorian," he confessed. "I did very bad things to protect my firstborn. The prophecy could have been about either."

Queen Giselle had enough. "You did it all for the wrong son. You coward." She took a thin dagger from her perfectly coiffed hair and stabbed the king in the back. He gurgled and fell forward down the stairs and didn't move.

I grasped Dorian's arm and had him help me to a standing position, placing myself in front of him to protect him. Queen Giselle dropped the thin hair dagger on the ground and raised her hand toward me and Dorian. "I order you to kill them both," she hissed.

With her crown stolen, her hair twisted and hanging down her shoulders, she no longer looked like the poster child for the graceful queen. She looked crazed and demented.

Dinky stepped from the shadows and stood in front of the queen, followed by Pinky and the male house elf from the library. More house elves appeared from hidden alcoves and behind tapestries until they filled the room. The anger of hundreds of house elves was evident. They loved Dorian, for he was one of them. He loved them and treated them equally, and they now stood between the queen and their favorite son.

The head house elf, the one who still had her tongue, shook her head. "No more being abused by you. We are done."

Queen Giselle began to tremble, and her face turned white. "No, you don't understand. I only had your tongues removed so you would keep my secret."

"That you and your horrid son poisoned Prince Vincent's fiancée," the house elf said. "We would have kept your secret no matter what, for we are loyal to the house of Candor. But you are royal no more."

"What do you mean? I'm queen. You must listen to me."

Evander chuckled, "No, Mother, with father's passing, the crown is passed to me." He turned to the house elves. "Do what you want with her."

The house elves charged. Giselle ran but was swept up in a mass of brown as the elves grabbed her and took her out a secret door. Her high-pitched scream followed her out.

Evander grinned and walked over to his father's prone figure, picked up the gold crown, and placed it upon his head. "Now, I am king."

Evander turned back on the room and silence befell. "It seems that it is just us... brother."

I felt Dorian grab for me, but I used my waning magic to freeze him to the spot. "Yes, it is time to end this. You and me," I said.

Evander tilted his head and looked at me, judging me, trying to decide if I was the real Dorian or not. He reached for the ornamental dagger on his hip and drew it.

Amaryllis gasped, and out of the corner of my eye, I saw

my father pull her back, his hand over her mouth. I knew it would come down to this. It had to.

This was the prophecy. I had to kill the prince. My mother was right. It was about revenge.

I pulled Dorian's glamoured dagger from my belt and held it up the way I had seen Dorian do in a fight, but I wasn't like my sister Honor; I couldn't fight. I could barely do a spell right, but one thing I could do was put on a show.

As I walked, I shifted from Dorian, to Adelle, to the old woman version of me, to Derek, and back to me as Eden.

Evander drew close to me and stopped. "It's you."

I gripped the dagger tighter and watched him like a hawk.

"It's always been you." His eyes widened in realization. "That day in the barn, the first night of the ball, when I pushed Adelle down the stairs."

"Correction, when you tried to murder me," I said, anger coursing through my body. "And now I am here to fulfill the prophecy. To kill you. I would never have done it, Evander, if you hadn't betrayed me, your brother, and everyone. It is your actions that have brought this upon you."

Evander began to tremble, and he fell to his knees, his head bowed. "I owe you an apology," he murmured, the knife lowered to the ground. "For underestimating you."

There was something off about the whole affair. I paused and waited for him to continue. But when he raised his eyes to look at me, they were no longer amber but black, like Allemar's. "But you continue to underestimate me." Evander's lip curled up into an ugly smile, and his hand moved. I saw the flash of steel, but it was too late.

Dorian, unable to move from my spell, was the perfect target, the blade pierced his chest, and I watched as he tried to take a step, reached out for me, and tumbled to the ground. A red pool of blood flowed from around his body.

"Nooo!" I cried out at Dorian's murder. I summoned all the power within me, even that which resided in the corners of my mind that I had never dared touch. I let it build. My fingers tingled with power, and my hair flowed around my shoulders. I turned to Evander.

"*Incendium!*" I screamed, letting the dagger fly. Controlled by my magic, it flew true and found its target in Evander's chest. Where the knife touched his body lit up like a coal, and seconds later, only a pile of ash remained.

It was too much—too much power for my mind to summon or control. I needed to release the magic back into the world without destroying everything and everyone. I collapsed to my knees and released the magic into the air, refocusing it to the best of my ability.

Snow fell upon the room, coating everything in a fluffy white blanket, but it still couldn't hide what I had done.

I stared in horror at the pile of ash that was the remains of Evander as a dark, misty cloud rose up from those ashes, and I heard the whisper of joy.

"I'm free!" it hissed, and I wanted to throw up. I had done it. Done the unthinkable. I had unintentionally freed Allemar. He had gotten to Evander, taken possession of him, and through Evander's death, I had freed the evil sorcerer. He had warned me. He said death would free him.

I stumbled to my feet and rushed to Dorian's side, but he was gone. A pool of blood was all that remained. "Where did he go?" I yelled. "Where is he?" None of the guards would answer me. It seemed the house elves had already taken him away.

I keeled over, pressed my forehead to the stone floor, and

let out my grief. I had messed up. In trying to protect Dorian, I had insured his death and also killed the prince.

Pinky came over and hugged me. Her eyes glassy with tears.

"I'm sorry I couldn't protect him," I muttered. "I'm so sorry."

She gave me a reassuring pat and then pointed to someone who was being led into the chapel by Verik the faun.

It was Meri.

"Meri? You're okay?" I gasped.

"Of course, I'm okay. Been fine for hours. Eating the best food in a small room off of the kitchens with the house elves."

I pulled her into a hug and felt the guilt flow anew. She was fine. Dorian had taken care of everything. I didn't have to go through the whole charade. If I had just trusted him. Guilt continued to assail me and more tears came.

"Where am I?" a lost and confused voice spoke up. I looked up and saw Pinky the house elf standing in the chapel entrance. "What's going on? What happened to me, and why do I look like this?" She held up her hands and made a face at her brown skin. "One minute I was asleep and the next I was under a bed, and now I'm a house elf?"

"Adelle," Harmony gasped.

It was Adelle wearing Pinky's glamour. When I went to use Adelle's body, I tied Pinky's string bracelet on her wrist and glamoured Adelle to look like the house elf.

"Oh, Adelle." I ran to her and released the glamour, and the air about her shifted and she was once again Adelle, her long black hair gnarled from sleeping for hours and her makeup smeared.

"I had the weirdest dream." She stumbled over to Harmony. "You were in it and"—she pointed to me—"you were in it." She turned to Derek. "And I don't even know you."

Derek laughed and whispered to Harmony, who went to Adelle and took her aside. "Let's go get a cup of tea, and I will explain everything."

The palace guards were held in check by Bravado's men. Amaryllis used her glamour to make their small army seem ten times bigger.

"What should we do with them?" Bravado asked me.

I looked over at the scared guards and then to Derek who had come to my side. "I knew you looked familiar," he scoffed. "You were the flower girl and the old woman with the bad limp. I told you, I never forget a face."

"Yes." I smiled wanly. I was tired and slowly bleeding out still. "You were right. But I need you to take charge of this." I motioned to the chaos that I had caused. "I rid the kingdom of evil. Now it's time for a ruler to step up. And you have a pure heart. You and Harmony. I know you will do a wonderful job together."

Derek shook his head. "The throne should be yours."

"It is a heavy burden to bear alone, and I don't want it," I said truthfully. One of Humperstink's monkeys tossed the gold crown and it rolled to my feet. I could feel my heart breaking and knew that my soul was damaged from taking a life, even though it wasn't innocent. I knew the signs. "I'm broken, Derek. And nothing can fix my heart right now. If I took the throne, I'd make a great tyrant, but not a good ruler."

"As you wish," Derek said, bowing before me.

"Wishes are for the weak and those who still believe in fairy tales," I said as I looked down at my hand that was covered with blood and then at the destroyed wedding chapel. "And wishes *never* come true."

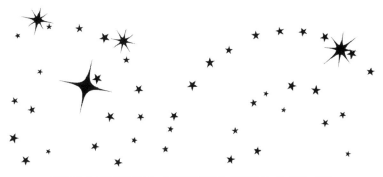

CHAPTER TWENTY-NINE

"Step right up, let your eyes be amazed at the wonder and glory of Miss Cinder De Ella," Bravado announced my new stage name, and I stepped onto the stage. De Ella after my parents. My hair was bound up in colorful knots, and I wore a flashy dress of purple and gold with my legs in stockings with gold slippers. It was flashier than anything I ever would have worn back in the drafty tower in the town of Nihill. But I wasn't in Nihill anymore. I was in the northern town of Legose and had my own act for part of the magical menagerie troupe.

My smile was fake as I paraded about, my arms beckoning to the audience members as I danced around a fire. Golden eyes followed my every move from within the flames, and with a wave of my hand, the fire elemental would rush out in a trail of fire and swirl up my legs and my outfit would disintegrate, leaving in its place a dress made of fire. And as my dress burned, I looked to be burning alive, but it was all an act—my glamour magic having grown in leaps and bounds over the last few weeks.

The audience *oohed* and *aahed*. The salamander dashed back down, and with a wave of my hand, the fire was doused and my body wrapped in black, like coal with a hidden fire deep within. My father called the trick a quick change, but there were no changes, only glamour magic.

I smiled at the young centaur who was squealing with glee as my dress became flowers, blooming in front of them.

With the salamander pretending to light me on fire between each bit, I changed my dress with every new spin. A dress of diamonds, gold, tree bark, and stars. "And now for the next bit, say goodbye to Miss Cinder De Ella as she travels to a faraway land."

I blew a fake kiss out to the crowd and waved at the young children. Looking down at the fire, I checked to make sure the traveling spell was still written in dark charcoal. It was orchestrated beautifully, except for one spot that was altered. The location wasn't correct. I hesitated on stepping into the blazing fire and turned to look over at my father.

He gave me a wink and pushed me from behind. I fell forward into the fiery blaze.

A trick that I had now performed dozens of times now terrified me. I had done the spell to have me appear out of the bonfire outside my parents' wagon, but it was altered.

The fire still burned as I traveled, but I became numb to the pain. A plume of smoke and ash billowed around me as I stepped into a familiar room. The room Dorian kept me imprisoned in beneath the palace.

"No!" I cried at seeing the familiar locked and warded door. Rushing to the door, I pulled on the handle and felt the tingle of magic. It was still warded. How? I didn't understand. I must have made a mistake on the spell. I chewed on my bottom lip and kneeled on the floor to look under the door.

The hall was empty and dark. I wondered if the house elves even lived below ground anymore after the king and queen of Candor were gone. I sighed in frustration and headed over to the bed. I took the quilt and wrapped it around my skimpy outfit and waited for the fire spell to wear off. It had to. It was only a couple of small logs, so maybe a few candle marks. I could wait it out, or my father would pour water on it and bring me back.

The room brought back sad memories, and I struggled to cope with the feelings.

I had made a new life for myself with my parents at the magical menagerie. The troupe fully accepted me as one of their own, and it felt like I had grown up there my whole life.

My mother, Amaryllis, explained what happened when I was a child. How there were two prophecies. Each prophecy set forth actions by all parties that would alter the fate of the country and put a bounty on my head. She also explained that I had released her from the spell, but in doing so, it sent her to the exact same spot where the curse was placed upon her—which happened to be in the field in the middle of Bravado's show. To hear Bravado tell the story, he thought he was having a heart attack when his beautiful wife appeared on stage next to him. Of course, they were so overjoyed, they didn't rush back to tell me. How could I be mad? They hadn't seen each other in twenty-one years.

Now, for Mother Eville, did I fault her for not telling me the whole truth? No. For she was right. If I knew what was to happen, I would have fought it tooth and nail.

Footsteps echoed on the stone, and I heard the key in the lock before the door swung open and Dorian stepped through.

"Dorian, you're alive? I can't belie—" He interrupted my joyful tirade.

His dark hair was cut short, revealing his scarred ears. A gold circlet was on his brow, and his face was cold and unreadable. He didn't smile, and I felt his burning anger toward me.

"You, Eden Eville, have been accused of high treason for murdering the prince of Candor."

"What?" I gasped and stood up, dropping the blanket from around my shoulders. My puffy entertainer skirt did little to hide my legs, and my knees trembled. "Surely, you don't mean that. I mean, based on the circumstances."

"You murdered my brother, Prince Evander," he hissed out between clenched teeth. He stormed over and grabbed my upper arms and shook me.

"I didn't have a choice. He was evil. He murdered Sisa. He tried to murder me. He wasn't going to stop until you were dead."

"And I told you, repeatedly, that I would handle it," Dorian growled. "I told you to not come to the palace. To not go to the ball. Did I not? If you hadn't, I would—"

"Be dead," I cried out, tears welling up in my eyes. "I couldn't let that happen."

"And yet, it was because of you that I almost died. You bespelled me." He dropped my arm in disgust, like he couldn't even stand to touch my skin.

I buried my face in my trembling hands. My performance makeup was probably running down my cheeks. "I didn't want you to get hurt," I muttered through my fingers. "I was trying to protect you."

"And yet you failed and left me for dead."

"You disappeared." I dropped my hands to my side. "I didn't know what to do."

"You left," he snapped. His blue eyes stared into mine, and I knew there would be no forgiveness. "You ran away."

"I thought you were dead. There was no reason to stay." My voice dropped to barely a whisper.

"So, the burden of the crown was too much for you?" he

said sarcastically. "You told me you wanted to be queen. You're a coward."

"I lied." I sniffed and turned to give him my back. "I was trying to hurt you, so that you would leave the palace and not come to the wedding. I had it all planned out. I was going to fake your death by using glamour and then rescue my sister."

"You could have told me," he accused.

"I couldn't. Your stepmother placed a spell on my lips. I was unable to tell anyone of the plot, or they would kill Meri."

"I told you I would take care of it," he growled.

"And I'm terrible at obeying. I don't trust a lot of people. And you wonder why? You put me in a prison." I looked around the room. "Twice."

"I was trying to protect you," Dorian repeated my own words, and I could almost laugh at the ridiculousness of our conversation. We were both stubborn, and it seemed we were debating each other in circles.

I was shivering, freezing in the costume, and the fire was almost out. I could see the flickering flames of the spell start to appear around my gold-colored slippers, and I knew I would only be with him for a few more minutes.

My heart began to thud loudly in my chest, and every part of me wanted to throw myself into his arms and kiss him wildly. But he had not declared his feelings toward me and had yet to say I was forgiven. I knew I had but a moment to declare how I felt.

"I'm sorry," I said, looking up into those unbelievable blue eyes. "I know you can't ever love anyone like you did Sisa."

Dorian blinked in surprise.

"Eden Eville, for the part you played in treason against the crown—" His voice was cold as his hand reached for his jeweled dagger. I clutched my trembling hands together and looked down. One silent tear fell to the floor. "—I order that you spend the rest of your life—"

I couldn't hear the rest of his words as my dress erupted in flames. I glanced up, seeing his eyes wide in surprise. He reached out toward me. His mouth moved, but no words came forth as I was pulled back to the camp.

≈

I appeared in a poof of sparkly smoke back on stage, thanks to my mother's glamour, and that helped hide the black ash and made it more show worthy. Bravado had a bucket and doused the flames to bring me back with a flair.

The crowd erupted into screams of delight and wild applause. I blinked, lost in confusion before I remembered I was still in a show.

My father leaned over to me and he said, "Eh? How was your trip?"

I turned to him with fear-filled eyes and murmured, "Not good. I'm wanted for treason."

Bravado's face paled, and he signaled to the giant at the back of the tent. They cut the show short, and everyone began to quickly pack up.

Despite it being a magical menagerie full of animals, there were enough magic users within the troupe that they could completely pack up and move locations in a few candle marks.

My father sauntered over to me, stroking his mustache. "Are you sure that you are wanted for treason? Maybe you misheard?"

"No, Papa." I waved my hands, and the rope began to wind up and float up to the wagon. My confidence and my magic had grown. I turned to him, my hands going to my hips. "Did you change the spell? Did you alter it to send me back there to him. You knew?"

His face turned red, and he held up his hands. "Aye, you got me, little one. But a bird found me this morning with a message from the prince. I had a request to grant him a few minutes of your time." He shrugged. "I figured what could it hurt."

"Bird, what bird?"

He waved over at my mother who was tending a small sparrow in the cage by their wagon.

"Isn't it the sweetest?" Amaryllis cooed at the brown bird inside and gave it some seed. "Who'd have thought the prince would switch to using sparrows?"

Even as she said it, a second messenger sparrow landed next to my mother, and she very carefully untied the messenger tube and read the note.

"It's an order of compliance. We are to remain here until the crown prince and his army arrive."

"Throw it away. Put it back. Pretend you never read it," I said.

"No, Eden, you need to reply," she said.

I grabbed a quill and, on the back of the parchment, wrote out my reply.

I am sorry that I had to leave on such short notice. But I have to decline your invitation to spend the rest of my life as your prisoner.

Cinder De Ella
Formerly known as Eden Eville

. . .

287

I tucked the note back into the sparrows tube and marveled at how small it was. It must have a lighter-than-air charm for the bird to be able to carry the message such a distance. I held my breath and watched the bird fly away.

My heart ached, knowing I would never again hear Dorian call me sparrow, for now I was on the run.

The wagons were packed up, and I loaded up my few belongings and grabbed my cast iron cauldron with hot coals and placed it on the floorboard next to my flatbed wagon. My fire elemental, the same one from the palace, snuggled up in the coals. I had heard my father explain the problem to the troupe. How, despite my attempts to help the crown and free the house elves from a tyrannical leader, I was now wanted for treason. We would have to cut our tour short and head to the next country a few months early. There were a few groans at the schedule, because we would be skipping a few cities. But for the most part, everyone wanted to protect their troupe leader's daughter.

I looked over my wagon, calculating my supplies, and then down at my sleeping fire salamander. It was dumb, but I didn't want to endanger anyone else, especially my parents who had just been reunited.

I climbed down from the bench seat and ran to my parents and gave them hugs.

"I'm sorry, Mama, Papa. But I'm not going with you," I whispered.

"What?" my mother exclaimed. "How can that be? We just got you back. Bravado, do something."

"Oh, let her go," the ogress cackled as she pulled her wagon up next to mine. She needed eight oxen to pull her hefty frame and supplies. "It's her destiny. I foresaw it. You can't stop her now."

I looked over at ogress, and she just shrugged and leaned over to whisper, "Who knows? I could have seen it. But I wasn't really looking."

I laughed and gave her a hug. She tossed a ring in the air, and I caught it. It was my silver ring. "It belongs with you."

"Thank you!" I slid the ring on my finger and watched as the troupe pulled away. When the last colored wagon disappeared over the hill, I pulled out a map and tried to figure out where to go.

I had already been to Florin and Baist; maybe I should head farther north to Rya? No, wait, the elves live farther north. I would go south. Turning my wagon around, I headed in the opposite direction, hoping that it would put Prince Dorian off my trail, especially if he went looking for my parents first.

I smiled at my plan. Yes, it was a great and well-thought-out plan.

It was a horrible plan. I swore as my canvas tent sprung a leak for the second time that evening. My salamander was running for cover and dodging all the water leaks for fear of being doused. I took a needle and thread and stood out in the rain, trying to sew up each of the holes. Holes, that I swore, kept appearing out of nowhere. Yesterday, my food rations had disappeared and one of my horses had run off.

"I think I'm cursed," I muttered as I tied the knot and then went back into my tent. I didn't want to use magic because magic could be tracked and I wasn't into Sion yet. I was still in Candor. So that meant I was surviving by not altering my surroundings or the weather. Or maybe it was my own turbulent emotions that were causing my personal rain storm. Because ever since I left my parents and went on the run, I had been miserable.

I had just adjusted my cot when I heard the rip and looked up as water poured in through the ceiling again.

"Oh, come on!" I growled but paused when I saw the shadow on the other side of the canvas. Someone was outside, and they were the ones splitting the seams of my tent. My salamander saw my hesitation; he growled and grew bigger to the size of a dog. "No." I waved him back to the fire. "It's not safe for you out there."

I pulled my hood back over my hair as I stepped out into the rain a third time. I pretended to sew up my tent, but instead I was scanning the tree line, looking for a shadow. No longer scared of being found, I used magic to seal the tent and walked around to the front and ducked back through the door.

I froze as a tall, lithe form was kneeling in front of my fire warming himself. The salamander was rolling in the coals like a dog in excitement at seeing him. I, on the other hand, was not as pleased.

"Hello, Dorian," I said.

Still kneeling, he turned. "Hello, sparrow." His hands were clasped on one knee, and he looked around my tent and nodded. "Being on the run doesn't suit you."

"Not if you keep ripping holes in my tent," I snapped, and then I took a deep breath. "It was you. You've been tormenting me for days, haven't you?"

Dorian moved over to the cot and sat on it, testing that it would hold his weight. "Of course. I wanted to see how you would fare out on your own. I do have to say you've been quite amusing."

"How did you find me?"

"I'm an elf. Tracking is in my blood," he said, crossing his arms.

"Half elf," I corrected, but kept my distance. I was surprised he had not immediately arrested me and dragged me back to prison. Instead, he had been tormenting me. "What do you want?" I asked wearily. I was cold, tired, hungry, mentally exhausted, and not in the mood to play his games.

Dorian stood up and moved right in front of me. I could smell the wool of his wet cloak. I closed my eyes and imagined his arms wrapped around me, imagined his heart beating as fast as mine. But I blinked away those dreams and waited for him to say the words that would break my heart.

"I've come for you," he said, his voice husky with emotion.

His hand brushed my arm. When I stiffened in fear, he stepped back, giving me space. I blinked back tears.

Dorian lifted my chin, and his eyes were filled with confusion. "Why do you run from me, sparrow?"

"Because a bird is not supposed to live in a cage," I whispered.

He frowned. "I hardly think being married to me is the same as a prison sentence. Though I wouldn't know. I would say the palace does sometimes feel like a gilded cage."

"What?" I blinked in surprise. "I think I missed something. I thought my punishment for treason was to spend the rest of my life in prison."

Dorian's face lit up in surprise. "You didn't hear it all, did you? I wondered if you did, because the spell took you back too soon. No wonder you ran away."

"I'm confused."

Dorian grabbed me and pulled me into a hug, and I felt myself melting. "No, my dear sparrow. I order you to spend the rest of your life... as my wife."

Oh, that was a relief that I was no longer going to be killed or imprisoned. But yet it was still a punishment.

"No." I pulled away. "I can't."

His eyes darkened. "Are you in love with someone else?"

I shook my head.

"Then I fail to see the problem."

"I don't want to be trapped in a loveless marriage, or one that only one person loves the other. It would be one-sided."

"Do you love me?"

"Yes," I breathed out. "More than anything."

Dorian cupped my face, his lips moving toward mine. "Then it won't be one-sided. For I love you as well, Eden."

"But what about Sisa?" I asked. "You gave up the throne for her."

"How can I so easily forget when you keep throwing it in my face." Dorian chuckled, his warm breath moving across my skin as he began to leave butterfly kisses up my neck.

I was left breathless and couldn't think. "Forget what?"

"I gave up the throne to protect myself and to keep anyone else I happen to fall in love with safe from Evander's jealousy." He nibbled my ear. "Sisa may have been my first love." He kissed my jaw and then my cheek. His breathing became ragged. "But you, Eden, are my last." His lips sought mine, and I began to drown.

My hands reached up to wrap around his neck, and he lifted me into the air as we drank each other in—seeking, tasting, and remembering as we discovered each other and our love.

He broke the kiss, his forehead touching mine. "I have spent the last few weeks coming back from the dead and explaining why I stepped down in the first place."

"Bet that threw a lot of people off." I chuckled.

He nodded, his lips brushing mine when he did, but he wasn't releasing me from his hold. "I want to be a good ruler someday. I want the fae and humans to be equal."

"Well, that's your first mistake," I scoffed.

His dark head turned to me, a confused look on his face. "Do you really think that is too much to ask?"

"I think your problem is that you only aspire to be a good ruler and not a great one," I teased.

Dorian let out a breath and chuckled. "And that is why I need you. To knock me off my pedestal sometimes." He sighed and became serious. "The crown is a heavy burden, and I can't carry it alone. I need you, Eden. Please, say you will marry me?"

"Say you love me," I whispered, "and I will be yours forever."

"I love you, sparrow." He grinned.

I bit my bottom lip and smiled back. "You're wrong," I said softly.

"About what?"

"A crown if shared isn't a burden at all but a gift," I whispered. "One that I will share with you. As long as you promise to stop calling me sparrow. I hate that nickname."

"Then I guess that's it. We can't get married," he mumbled, stepping away. He wrapped his cloak around his shoulders and prepared to step out into the night. The rain had mysteriously stopped once he kissed me.

"You're going to give up that easily?" I teased.

Dorian turned and gave me a long searching look. "I fell in love with you the first night I saw you at my mother's tavern. As soon as you walked in the room in that little brown traveling dress, your hair all askew, your blue eyes shining with determination and spirit. You looked like a little sparrow. I knew then, in that instance, that you were going to be mine. I didn't know your name, your history or past, and I didn't care. You were only sparrow to me. So, I will always call you my little sparrow."

My cheeks flushed in embarrassment. "Maybe you just call me sparrow when we're alone."

He turned to me, and his hands reached for my waist. "Can't promise that. I've already changed the royal birds to sparrows in your honor. And they've been in flight training for weeks."

"Stop!" I groaned out.

"Nope. There's more. I got you a horse. Guess what his name is."

"Sparrow." I began to laugh.

"And I've got two new royal hounds. Guess what their names are."

"No," I gasped, now laughing so hard, I couldn't catch my breath.

"Sparrow and Not Sparrow," Dorian teased.

"Okay, okay. You can call me sparrow."

He grinned. "Good, because I didn't really name the horse or the hounds that. That would be ridiculous."

The salamander came out of the firepit and rolled around on the floor. Dorian looked down at the fire elemental and said, "So you got yourself a new pet?"

"Yep." I struggled to keep the laughter down. "Guess what his name is."

"No?" Dorian choked on his own laughter.

"Sparrow," I wheezed out, and my salamander looked up at us and winked.

Dorian reached into his cloak and pulled out a pair of glass slippers. My breath caught in my throat. I'd thought they were lost forever, destroyed in the chapel during the skirmish.

He kneeled down and lifted my foot into the slipper. Sure enough, it slipped off my foot.

"Doesn't seem to fit," he teased. "No wonder you kept losing them."

"They never belonged to me."

"Don't worry." He tossed the glass slippers onto my bed. "For I belong to you."

Read Meri's tale in

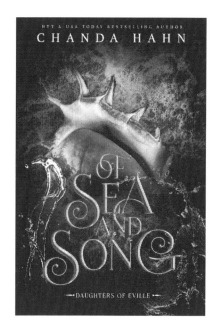

Of Sea and Song

www.chandahahn.com

Chanda Hahn is a NYT & USA Today Bestselling author of The Unfortunate Fairy Tale series. She uses her experience as a children's pastor, children's librarian and bookseller to write compelling and popular fiction for teens. She was born in Seattle, WA, grew up in Nebraska, and currently resides in Waukesha, WI, with her husband and their twin children; Aiden and Ashley.

Visit Chanda Hahn's website to learn more about her other forthcoming books.
www.chandahahn.com

Printed in Great Britain
by Amazon